Imagining Don Giovanni

Imagining Don Giovanni

Anthony Rudel

Atlantic Books
London

First published in the United States of America in 2001 by the Atlantic Monthly Press,
841 Broadway, New York, NY 10003
First published in Great Britain in 2001 by Atlantic Books,
an imprint of Grove Atlantic Ltd

10 9 8 7 6 5 4 3 2 1

A CIP catalogue record for this book is available from the British Library.

1 903809 20 7

Printed in Great Britain by Creative Print & Design (Wales), Ebbw Vale

Atlantic Books
An imprint of Grove Atlantic Ltd
29 Adam & Eve Mews
London W8 6UG

To My Daughters

Rebecca Katherine and Susannah Elizabeth

FOR LEARNING

To Wallace Gray

FOR TEACHING

Chapter One

∞

Finale

When the orchestra's final notes had sounded and the last reverberations had faded into the farthest corners of the opera house, an eerie silence remained. No one coughed; no one talked; it seemed as if no one even breathed. The silence lasted no more than a second or two, but at that moment, in that theater, it seemed longer. The liveried guards stood motionless in front of the curtained, arched stone exits.

Suddenly, from the back of the upper gallery, a lone voice pierced the stillness.

"Bravo!"

That cry opened the floodgates. In one swift motion, in unison, the audience rose, applauding in uncontrolled excitement. The opera house seemed to tremble in agreement. The sustained applause and cheering never decreased in volume or intensity as the singers moved to the foot of the stage, smiling and waving. When they had each had their moments of glory, one of the sopranos stepped forward to the edge of the stage and pointed her hand toward the small man standing at the harpsichord. His head was bent forward.

The musicians in the orchestra cheered, tapping their bows on the music stands and stomping their feet. Slowly, the man lifted his head, as if waking from a deep sleep, and looked around. A quirky, self-contented smile came to his lips. Taking a folded handkerchief from his cuff, he dabbed the perspiration from his forehead and stood, looking at the musicians around him and the singers onstage, who clapped louder than anyone else. When he turned to face the audience, the cheering became wilder. His body seemed to be pushed back from the noise's force, and he steadied himself by resting his right hand behind him on the harpsichord.

Those resounding cheers were not meant for the harpsichordist or the conductor. They were for him. The composer. He stood there, bowing slightly, exhausted and relieved. For half an hour the audience released the tension that had built up during the three hours of the world premiere of his newest opera.

They loved him—his music, his genius. In a box near the front of the first balcony his wife and friends watched him watch the audience as he slowly emerged from the haze that had seemed to envelop him during the performance.

"It was a good performance," he thought. "Despite the difficult rehearsals and the mistakes the singers made, it worked and they liked it."

But he had doubts. He wondered if the audience understood what they had heard. As they thought about the drama, did they shiver with fear, or did they simply laugh at the comedy? Riding home in their horse-drawn carriages, would they experience some new sense of freedom? When they walked past their servants, would they now realize the importance of human liberty? Did they even know they had been part of a revolution? Or would they go home to their small palaces, undress, and go to bed, anonymous mortals? Would *Don Giovanni* haunt their dreams?

"It's only entertainment to them," he thought, accepting it as he slowly looked around the full opera house, savoring instead the applause and the cheers, remembering . . .

Chapter Two

∽

A cold draft blew through the bedroom. Constanze, Wolfgang Mozart's wife, pulled the heavy blanket up to her nose, repositioned herself on the overstuffed pillow, and tried to go back to sleep. But in her semidreaming state, she gradually became aware that she was alone. She reached across with her right hand, hoping to find her husband asleep on the far edge of the bed. But all she felt was the cold, unwrinkled fabric of the unslept-on bedsheets. She sighed, sat up sleepily, and looked around the room. No one.

"Wolfgang."

No answer.

With a mixture of concern and frustration, she carefully climbed out of bed. The room was chilly, the bare wood floors cold. Tiptoeing, she made her way over to the floor-length mirror where she had hung her dressing gown the night before. As she put it on, she studied her profile in the mirror. The bulge in her abdomen was starting to show, distorting the tiny figure she had tried to maintain. With maternal care, she caressed her rounding stomach and thought of the child growing inside. Her happiness for her new pregnancy was tempered by thoughts of her two children who had died within months of their birth.

The dressing gown didn't conceal her stomach, so she wrapped herself in the woolen bedcover too, ran her fingers through her long black hair, and walked quietly into the outer chamber of the two-room suite that was their temporary home on the third floor of the Three Lions Inn on Kohlmarkt Street in Prague. A few dying embers glowed in the fireplace. Her husband's cloak and frock coat were tossed over the back of an armchair in one corner of the room. Two brass candlesticks, coated in fanciful drippings left by spent wax candles, sat next to a pen and opened inkwell at the edge of a small round table in the center of the room. Piled-up music manuscript paper—some written on, some still blank—served as a thin pillow for Mozart's head. He was sound asleep.

Constanze stood trying to decide what to do. Let him sleep, or wake him; look at what he had written on the music sheets, or ignore them; pity him or criticize him; love him or hate him. She had grown tired of hearing him talk about the wonderful times he'd had as a child, with his family, with his father. She felt sorry for her husband, but there was nothing she could say or do to heal the wounds, resolve the conflicts or fill the void left by Leopold Mozart's death. Before his father's death earlier that year in May, Wolfgang had regularly cursed the old man and his hometown of Salzburg. She had urged him to go back to Salzburg, hoping a visit would close that chapter of his life. He'd refused, choosing instead to remember his early years as some strangely enchanted time. When she reminded him that as a child he'd received the last rites of the church, not once but twice, he replied that that had been a way for him to learn about inspiration.

"But that's no way to treat a child, to let him be at death's door," she would say.

Mozart never responded, and didn't react when their own infants died. It wasn't until four months after their first baby succumbed that he wrote: "We are both very sad about our poor, fat, darling boy."

Staring at her husband, she recalled the day, just a week before, when they had left Vienna to come to Prague for the premiere of his new opera. Wolfgang was in a hurry, ordering the coachman to get the bags onto the *diligence* for the journey.

"Constanze, we have to go," he snapped repeatedly.

But she lingered, giving additional instructions to the nurse who'd been hired to care for their three-year-old son, Karl.

Wolfgang was already seated in the coach, impatiently waiting, when she came out of their house carrying their little son.

4

"Wolfgang, aren't you going to kiss your son good-bye?"

"Yes, yes. Of course."

He climbed out of the coach, took the little boy in his arms and hugged him. But when the boy started to cry, his father handed him to the nurse, took Constanze by the hand and led her away.

For the first few hours of the ride they said nothing, each gazing out a window at the passing countryside. Small farms dotted the landscape.

"I'm worried about Karl. Maybe I should return to Vienna while you're working in Prague," she said, breaking the silence.

"Don't be ridiculous. I need you with me."

"Why? Lorenzo will be there, and we have friends in Prague who'll keep you company."

"I want you with me. I need you to be with me. This opera's going to be very hard to produce, and I still have lots to compose. Besides, Karl will be fine. No. I want you with me."

But the whole scene was all too painfully familiar. She remembered a trip they'd taken to Salzburg a few years earlier. While visiting his father, they'd been awakened by a loud knock. Her husband and father-in-law answered the door. From the door of their room she watched as a messenger bowed to the two men and delivered his news. She saw Wolfgang's head sag. Leopold patted him consolingly on the back. The messenger left. Frightened, she ran back to bed. When Wolfgang returned, he held Constanze in his arms and told her that their first child, two-month-old Raimund, whom they had left in Vienna with a nurse, had died.

For the rest of the carriage ride to Prague, that memory plagued Constanze. She couldn't bring herself to speak to Wolfgang.

They had arrived in Prague on October first, and in the four days since, she'd barely seen her husband. She'd spent most of her time resting in bed, avoiding the rain that seemed to come every day during that autumn of 1787.

Now, asleep on the pile of music paper, the thirty-one-year-old Mozart looked to Constanze like a little boy, and sometimes she wanted to treat him that way. She imagined she saw the notes of music dripping directly from his brain through his ear and onto the music paper. It was a startling image, at once ugly and comical, and it scared her.

She had to wake him. He needed to act responsibly.

"Wolfgang." She shook him gently. "Wolfgang. It's time to get up."

"Let me sleep. Just a little longer."

"No. Get up. It's already ten o'clock. Get up."

Without moving his head from the pages, he slowly opened his large eyes. The spindly lines and black dots scrawled on the music sheets made sense to him.

"I was dreaming the most beautiful melody. Why did you wake me?"

"It's time to get up."

"But it was such a sweet melody . . . a serenade, tender, delicate . . ."

As was often the case, he didn't finish the thought, drifting off instead to some world only he knew.

"You'll remember it. You never forget a melody. Write it down. Then you'll have it. Now get dressed."

"I don't have to write it down."

"Are you going to use it in the new opera?"

"Probably . . . It might work as an aria for Giovanni . . . or for . . . Oh, what does it matter? The opera will never be finished anyway."

"You say that every time you write an opera. It's getting boring. I don't understand why you worry so. You and Lorenzo will fix whatever is wrong and it will be finished before you know it."

Mozart was less certain. His librettist, Lorenzo Da Ponte, court poet to Emperor Joseph II of Austria, had been invaluable during the rehearsals for their first opera, *The Marriage of Figaro*. But once the words had been written, his artistic assistance had turned political. Da Ponte, a master at manipulating the intrigues of the court, had no interest in making changes to a libretto he considered complete.

"Lorenzo? What do you think he is—some kind of miracle worker? He just claps his hands and voila we have an opera. Do you know what I found out last night? He's working on two other librettos right now, at the same time as the one for me. No wonder it hasn't come together yet. And further—"

Nothing Mozart said was new to Constanze. He complained of the struggles, but in the end he always completed the work. She returned to the other room and climbed back under the bedcovers. Wolfgang followed her, then shouted at her through the drawn-up bedsheets.

"What are the problems?" she asked, her voice muffled by the covers.

"It's a disaster. That's the problem."

"You're overreacting."

"The whole thing's ridiculous. The performers here can't sing, they can't act, they can't do—"

"It simply needs more rehearsal. You'll see, in a few days everything will be fine."

"You're such a . . . such a ninny. You have no idea what kind of disaster this could be"

"What do you think is so bad?"

"Everything!"

"Be reasonable. Be specific. Tell me. You'll feel better," Constanze said, sitting up and tapping the bed to indicate that Wolfgang should sit down next to her. "Come here, you silly boy. Tell me what's wrong."

"All right." Taking a deep breath, he composed himself. "Well, to begin with, the title character isn't believable, there's no time frame for the action and the scenes don't go together."

"That's all fixable. You and Lorenzo can work it out. You have to see the potential—isn't that what your father always said?"

"I can't see potential. I see disaster."

"I'm sure it will be dramatic."

"It will be booed. I should never have let Lorenzo talk me into writing an opera based on Don Juan. What a ridiculous subject! No one will like the main character. I should have turned down the commission."

"You said the same thing when you wrote *Figaro*."

"How can you compare the two? In *Figaro* I had real people to work with, not caricatures. You understand music, you understand opera, how it all has to go together, otherwise it's not believable. Remember the first time you heard *Figaro*? You said you cried during the last act when Figaro and Susanna reconcile, when he tells her he knew it was her, even through her disguise. You said it was so human . . . the way he recognized her by her voice. You cried because the words and music worked together."

"I cried because it reminded me of when we first met."

Mozart ignored her comment. "But it worked because those people were real . . . you understand their emotions. Don Giovanni is nothing more than a nobleman with common lusts and perversions . . . a common murderer, actually."

Constanze didn't know what to say. Music usually flowed easily from him. But in an opera house, the complexities and the large number of people and egos involved were hard to control. Mozart wasn't patient with performers who were less talented than he, and as his late father had often pointed out: "In all of Europe there are few, if any musicians with the talent of Wolfgang Amadeus Mozart."

"Can we spend the day together?" Constanze asked, changing the subject.

He turned toward her, calmed, and played with her flowing black hair. "Lorenzo and I have to meet with Signor Bondini—you know, the head of the opera company. We need to discuss delaying the opening."

"Delay the opening?" she asked, pulling away from him.

"Yes. We can't have everything ready by the fourteenth. We need more time."

"But that means we won't get back to Vienna soon. Maybe I should return now and be with Karl. I worry about him."

"No!" he shouted, starting from the bed. "How many times do I have to tell you I need you here? This is where you have to be. With me."

"But Wolfgang . . ."

Her protests were useless. Wolfgang got up and went over to the washbasin, which he filled from the blue and white pitcher left there by the serving girl. The water was cold, and it shocked the sleep from his eyes. Buttoning his collar and smoothing the front of his cream-colored chemise, he watched Constanze in the mirror. The sadness on her face brought him up short. He walked back to the bed and took her tiny hands in his.

"We'll have supper together tonight. I promise. Just let me survive this meeting."

He kissed her on the cheek.

"Let Lorenzo do the talking."

"You think I'm incapable of dealing with these people. You underestimate me."

"I know your talents, and they don't include ingratiating yourself with important people."

Pretending to be angry, he jumped onto the bed, landing next to her. "I know one talent I have," he laughed, pulling up her nightgown and kissing her stomach.

"Wolfgang, stop. Now go to your meeting."

"All right, all right, Madame Practical. You win, as usual. I'll tell the innkeeper to send the serving girl up. Have her arrange your hair; you always like that. And have some warm food. Indulge yourself. You'll feel better."

Mozart went over to the window, pulled the heavy curtain back and looked out.

"It's raining again."

"It's always raining. You should dress nicely anyway. You often look sloppy, and some of the important people in Prague have noticed. At least that's what I've heard from our friends."

"You know no matter what I wear it's going to get muddy on the walk to the opera house."

"Take a carriage."

"We can't afford to waste the money. I'll walk. It will help clear my head for the meeting with Bondini."

While they talked, he found a clean white shirt with a ruffled collar and clean white hose, which covered his legs up to where his black britches met them. He pulled on a dark green coat with black trim and gold buttons and smoothed his thick brown hair back into place. He turned toward Constanze.

"Much better."

He smiled, pleased to have pleased her. "I'll see you tonight, dearest, most beloved little wife. Be sure to rest. We'll have supper together."

Constanze jumped out of bed and ran over to him. Though he was short, when he wore shoes and she was in bare feet she had to reach up to hug him.

"It will work out. You'll see. Your music will make the difference. The opera will be a triumph. Be patient."

He kissed her gently on the forehead and left the room. Through the open door she saw him take his black cloak and tricornered hat from the chair. Then he quickly sorted through the sheets of music paper, taking some and leaving others.

"Make sure no one touches these pages," he called as he left the room.

Constanze went over to the window and watched. She saw him leave the inn and walk into the street, where a passing coach splashed him with muddy water. She couldn't see his reaction as he walked across the cobblestones, past the street vendors, toward the opera house.

Constanze went over to the pile of papers on the writing table and glanced at the pages of music, perfectly neat with no cross-outs or corrections. Off to one side she saw a piece of writing paper. Furtively glancing around the room in case someone else had entered, she carefully pulled the page out of the pile, making certain not to disturb any of the other papers. She recognized the writing; it was her husband's angular script.

Prague
October 5, 1787

My Dear Little Son,
How I wish I could tell you . . .

That's all there was. Constanze sat down at the table, pulled her dressing gown closed and turned over the letter. On the back, in Mozart's worst hand, was another hastily scribbled note:

"Good morning, dear little wife! I hope you've slept well, that you didn't wake too quickly, that you don't feel sick, that you aren't stretching or bending, that you're not angry and that you love me. I wish that nothing happens to you until I return this afternoon, for I shall always be your Stu! Knaller Praller

Schnip-Schnap-Schnur
Schnepeperl—
Snai!—

Chapter Three

Mozart walked along Prague's rainy streets. As he passed through the town square, he slowed down to admire the beautiful gold and blue astrological clock high atop the Gothic town hall. He waited in the rain to watch the procession of Christ and the twelve apostles appear in the clock's window as it struck eleven. Even though he was late, he waited for the end of the procession to see Death, the Turk, the miser, the fool and the cock make their brief appearance and to hear the chimes of the carillon. Only when the spectacle was complete did he resume his walk, hurrying toward the new opera house. It was an elegant, stone structure built just four years earlier. He loved its combination of sharp-angled walls and slightly curved windows and the imposing columns that held the roof aloft, allowing it to soar above the area's older buildings. His steps quickened as he neared the arched entryway. Inside was his escape, his world. Excitement and energy filled him every time he went into an opera house. He never tired of the feeling.

Lorenzo Da Ponte, dressed in a dark-blue, embroidered coat with shiny gold buttons, was standing just inside the stage entrance, his arms enveloping Teresa Saporiti, the soprano who was to create the role of Donna Anna. They whispered in Italian. Mozart paused at the doorway, hoping to overhear something of what they said. It was at times like this that he was grateful for all the journeys he'd made as a child, because it was during those trips he'd learned Italian, along with French and English.

He waited a few seconds, heard nothing of importance, then cleared his throat loudly. Surprised, Da Ponte moved his arms from behind Signorina Saporiti, pausing just long enough to enjoy the shape of the curve of her back. A mischievous smile came to her face as she nodded a greeting to Mozart.

"Maestro."

"Signorina Saporiti. Lorenzo. Is everything all right?"

"Quite. Bondini's in his office waiting for us. Teresa . . . uh . . . Signorina Saporiti and I were just going over some of Donna Anna's movements in the first scene."

"Before or after the Don tries to rape her?"

A barely noticeable blush showed through the young soprano's rouged cheeks.

"If you'll excuse me, gentlemen, I have to go for a costume fitting. Maestro Mozart, Abbé Da Ponte. Until later."

With a flourish the twenty-four-year-old soprano turned and walked toward the stage area, where a group of dressers was waiting patiently, holding different costumes and shoes. Mozart and Da Ponte watched.

"What a talent."

"Are you referring to her public or private performances, my dear Abbé? And when are you going to stop referring to yourself as an abbé? You only *studied* for the priesthood. As I remember the story, you had to flee Venice before you were actually ordained."

"It was a grand exit. Two women, one bed, and the master of the house came home at the critical moment. How tragic. I pulled on my trousers and jumped—"

"Yes, I know. You jumped from the window into a waiting gondola and never looked back. Very operatic."

"But fortunate for you because I ended up in Vienna, where we met, and that brings us to today. Listen, Wolfgang, let me handle Bondini."

"Because you're Italian?"

Da Ponte bristled. Though Italian by birth, he considered himself to be an indispensable part of Emperor Joseph II's court in Vienna.

"No. Because Bondini's a weasel, and he's afraid of conflict. I know how to make him do what we want. You agree with everything I say. We must be united."

Though only seven years older than Mozart, Da Ponte looked more worldly, and made the most it. Perhaps it was his balding head, or the severity of his hook nose, or the confident manner in which he carried himself, or the exquisite, jeweled walking sticks he carried. But whatever the reason, Da Ponte enjoyed the way people in the theater or at court bowed when he passed. He had succeeded because he was a fine poet, but also because he was a master manipulator who turned difficult situations to his advantage. Every composer in Vienna wanted a libretto from Lorenzo Da Ponte.

"Bondini will be reluctant to delay the opening," Da Ponte explained. "He's afraid to anger the Emperor and ruin the gala they've planned for the Emperor's niece and her new husband during their visit here."

Mozart was no stranger to royalty. As Lorenzo spoke, Wolfgang's thoughts drifted back to his childhood.

"Did I ever tell you, Lorenzo, about the time I met the Empress?" he interrupted.

"Your father told me several times," Da Ponte said.

Mozart looked crestfallen, so Da Ponte sighed and retold the story. "You were six, on tour with your family, and were invited to perform at Schönbrunn Palace, in Vienna. After you played the harpsichord, you impulsively jumped onto the Empress' lap and kissed her. Your father was embarrassed. He bowed and begged for forgiveness, but the Empress just laughed."

"Those were happy times," Mozart added, his voice trailing off.

"You miss your father."

Mozart stared at the black and white marble floor. People who knew Mozart whispered he'd never made peace with his father, but Da Ponte knew that Wolfgang would sort out his problems somehow. More important, he hoped they would resolve in some incredible musical outburst, and preferably soon, so they could finish their opera.

"It's good to have memories like that, Wolfgang. Savor them."

"And you, Lorenzo? You never talk about your childhood. Why?"

"There's not much to tell."

"Oh, you must have some secrets, some fond recollections."

"I do have secrets, but I keep them to myself. Sometimes it's safer if people know less."

"Why?"

"My life's busy now. I'm content, successful. Why think of harder times?"

"Because you'll forget them . . ."

"I *try* to forget." Da Ponte changed his tone of voice. "What do you want to do about the delay? I think we need a plan."

"*Figaro.*"

"What?"

"We'll play *Figaro* for the Archduchess. What's more appropriate for happily married newlyweds? That will give Bondini the performance he needs and will buy us some extra time to finish the opera."

"I'm not sure Bondini will agree."

"What choice does he have? I warned him we might need more time."

"But he's expecting a world premiere, and it should be an event."

"I'll conduct the *Figaro.* That will make it special, easier for Bondini to swallow. Besides, most of the cast we have for *Don Giovanni* sang *Figaro* when it was produced here last year. We won't need to rehearse."

"Maybe. Remember, we have to be united, in total agreement."

They had reached the large wooden doors leading to the impresario's office. Da Ponte knocked and a guard swung open the heavy doors to admit them. Pasquale Bondini, a mouselike man, sat behind a large leather-topped desk scattered with drawings of set designs for future productions. Da Ponte walked in quickly and embraced the impresario, who stood to greet him. Mozart lagged behind, watching with some discomfort.

"Gentlemen. Please, sit down. Can I offer you a coffee?"

"We're fine, thank you," said Mozart.

"I was just reading a fascinating letter from a friend of mine in Paris," Bondini began, excitedly pointing to a letter on his desk. "He writes about a rumor that Beaumarchais is writing a libretto for Salieri. Salieri's been staying at his house. Can you imagine the opera they would create; it would be superb if they collaborated. Don't you agree?"

In unison, Da Ponte and Mozart said: "Never!"

"And why not? Beaumarchais' *Figaro* was a wonderful play, and Salieri's last opera, *Tarare,* was based on another one of his plays. It seems natural."

"I adapted *Tarare* for Salieri. The Emperor ordered me to," Da Ponte explained testily.

Mozart shifted in his seat.

"Enough of such matters. Let's discuss the premiere," Bondini insisted.

"It can't be ready on time," Mozart began.

"What are you talking about? Are you insane? We must have an opera for the royal couple."

"We know that, Pasquale," said Da Ponte.

"Well then, perhaps we should mount *Tarare* for the gala on the fourteenth, as you proposed yesterday, Lorenzo. I'm sure the Archduchess would enjoy hearing the work," Bondini suggested, nervously rubbing his hands together.

Mozart's eyes opened wide. He stared at Da Ponte, and in a low voice said: "So that's your game. Get me out of the way to pay off Salieri."

"No. That's not it at all. I promise."

Mozart took a deep breath and waited for his librettist to continue.

"Pasquale, Maestro Mozart has come up with a wonderful idea, much better than doing *Tarare.* We should perform *Figaro* on the fourteenth and open the *Don Giovanni* opera a week later. *Figaro* was a success when you mounted it last year; it would be logical to do it now, in celebration of the royal newlyweds."

Bondini rose from his chair and paced behind the desk. His small eyes became nothing more than tiny slits in his forehead. "There are powerful people in Prague who will think *Figaro* is the wrong opera to celebrate the Archduchess' wedding. It's considered revolutionary, against the nobility."

"On the contrary. It's about love, pure love," Da Ponte defended.

"The play was banned in France. I can't risk having the Emperor take offense and close my theater."

"When will the powerful at court understand?"

Bondini and Da Ponte turned toward Mozart. "Understand what?" Bondini asked impatiently.

"That music is about people. It makes poor people feel noble, and makes the sick feel well. It can make you laugh or cry. When I was a child and my father took me to Italy, to your land, I saw people in the streets enjoying music, dancing, singing. Then when we went into the concert halls, the audience, mostly aristocrats, was more concerned with whether they were seen and acknowledged by the nobility. The music was incidental, unimportant entertainment. If they would only listen to the music and leave the politics out of it, we'd all be better off."

Bondini, pacing faster, looked at Da Ponte. "That's a lovely sentiment, Maestro. But I have a theater to run, and I've commissioned you to provide a new opera. So far you've failed and put me in a very uncomfortable position."

Bondini walked to the large window looking out over the side of the opera house. Mozart was about to say something, but Da Ponte silenced him with a quick movement of his hand. "Lorenzo, you can get the Emperor's permission for *Figaro*?" Bondini asked without turning away from the window.

"I can."

"I'm very unhappy about this, but you leave me no choice. We'll do *Figaro*. Mozart, you'll conduct. I'll tell the singers later today. Now, about *Don Giovanni*."

Bondini returned to his desk and looked across at Mozart.

"We need more rehearsal," said the composer. "The singers are not quick studies and they only work four days a week."

"That's the rule in this house."

"But we have a new opera to produce," Mozart argued.

"Is all the music composed?"

"Well . . . no . . . not yet . . . not really. I'm just waiting for a few scenes to come together."

"There's not much time, Maestro Mozart. Lorenzo, what seems to be the problem?"

"Maestro Mozart and I still have a few things to resolve."

"Perhaps I could be of assistance," Bondini offered. "Give me an example."

"The story's terrible," Mozart began without hesitation.

Da Ponte jumped up from his seat and glared at the composer. "It is not! You just can't seem to accept tragedy and comedy in the same work."

"What does that matter? That has nothing to do with how the action flows. I can't ignore the inconsistencies and I don't like the main character."

"You don't understand him."

"I don't like the whole thing."

"Give me specifics," Bondini pleaded in frustration.

"All right, since you asked. Don Giovanni constantly chases after women, every woman, regardless of the risks to him or his servant. He's childish; there's nothing likeable about him or the way he acts. He's supposed to be a nobleman."

"Nobleman is a rank, not a description of his character. It's one word, not two."

"Oh, you're good with words, Lorenzo. But his actions are not believable; what he does simply isn't done."

"Maybe *you* don't do it."

"That's not fair." Mozart lowered his voice. "I've had my share of . . . of relationships. But Don Giovanni chases after anyone, anytime. Day or night, rain or shine. I can't accept the character the way you've developed him."

"That's because you're not Italian."

"Never mind that. You must work faster to finish the opera. We need to open soon," Bondini pointed out curtly.

"Splendid! The music's incomplete, the story's disastrous and the singers aren't as good as the ones we have in Vienna; they don't even know the parts of the opera I have finished. Why don't we open tomorrow—everything seems ready to me."

"It's talk like that that gets you into trouble at court," Da Ponte cautioned. "You need to watch yourself. Your father was so good at—"

"Don't ever compare me to my father."

"God rest his soul."

The silence was thick and uncomfortable. Da Ponte walked to a wood table against the far wall and poured himself a cup of coffee from the silver carafe.

Bondini finally said, "Now listen to what I have to say before you disagree."

Mozart turned and looked directly at his collaborator. The fire in his eyes told Da Ponte he was not happy about Bondini's involvement in their creative process.

"We're listening," Da Ponte replied.

"I think the problem is that you, both of you, see the character of Don Giovanni in totally different ways. You come at him from different perspectives."

"Yes, that's true," Da Ponte said to Mozart. "To start with, you're married. You have agreed to make a commitment in the eyes of God. Don Giovanni would never do that. He would sooner spend eternity in hell."

"I'm married, not blind or dead. I still see women as women. I could have shown the soprano in the Vienna production of *Figaro*—you know, the young girl who sang Susanna—what the passion of a wedding night should be like. She was certainly willing and interested."

"But you didn't." Da Ponte continued, "I think what Pasquale is saying is that your idea of love is pure, sweet, tender, even beautiful. That's what made *Figaro* work. Those characters discover, lose, and recover true love. But, the kind of love Don Giovanni feels has to have fire, passion, lust. He needs danger to separate him from average men. He has to be supernatural."

"You mean he should be the kind of character Salieri would put in one of his operas. Some obese Greek god of love."

"No, Giovanni's not a god at all. More like the devil. Listen, we have to be daring. We're nearing the end of a century. We need to revolutionize opera, to challenge the conformities. With some help, we can make *Don Giovanni* the opera it should be. It will make a statement *and* be entertaining."

"What do you mean 'with some help'?"

Mozart stared directly at him with his large, innocent eyes; Da Ponte had to look away, unable to lie. Mozart's guileless, boyish stare made him uncomfortable. Untruths had never bothered him before, and he'd lied his way through more than one country, leaving a trail of abandoned women, angry husbands, cheated landlords and creditors in his wake. But he found it difficult, almost impossible, to lie to Mozart.

"I'll tell you . . . the truth. I swear."

"Let's have it."

"I've written to a friend," Da Ponte explained gingerly, "someone I've mentioned to you before, asking if he might come to Prague to help and work on the staging."

"Never. I don't want anyone else. I don't need anyone else."

"Hear us out, Maestro," Bondini pleaded.

"Who is this magician who'll save our opera?"

"It's funny you should say 'magician,'" said Da Ponte, "because this man once spent time in jail for being a magician—or was it for witchcraft, Pasquale? Never mind. He'll be a tremendous help, trust me."

Reluctantly, Mozart was intrigued.

"He's had a most unusual life," Bondini said, trying to lighten the mood. "He has a true understanding of the theater. His parents were actors. He's been a soldier, a spy, a musician, a dynamic character. He's traveled and lived all over Europe and has had more than his share of encounters with beautiful women. Thousands, he's told me. He's been arrested and imprisoned. He's made fortunes and lost fortunes. He's a gentleman in his sixties now and has accepted the position of personal secretary and librarian to a nobleman. The Count von Waldstein. He lives nearby in Dux . . . Bohemia."

"And this friend of yours—why should I accept him?"

"You'll like his spirit. But, more important, I think you'll like him because he believes in liberty and freedom."

"And does this free spirit have a name?"

"He likes to be called the Chevalier de Seingalt . . ."

"But that's not his name."

"No. He's better known as Giovanni Giacomo . . ."

"Another Italian."

"Casanova."

Mozart spun toward his librettist. After a moment of shocked silence that hung in the air, he burst out laughing. Da Ponte and Bondini were relieved. It was the first time they'd seen the strain lift from Mozart's face.

"What's so funny?" Da Ponte asked.

"You're joking!"

"No. Really. Casanova wants to meet you."

"You're mad. Casanova . . . what a ridiculous idea. Lorenzo, you once told me he was a thief, and now you expect me to work with him?"

"It will work. Trust me."

"Stop telling me to trust you."

"Meet with him. That's all we ask. He's here, in Prague. He's waiting to hear from you. He admires your music. I sent him some of the new libretto and he wrote back offering to help with the production."

"He likes my music?" Mozart asked with new interest.

"Very much," said Bondini quickly. "He thought the second act of *Figaro* was brilliant."

"He shows good taste."

"Yes, exceptional taste."

"And what is it you expect him to do?"

"He has experience. We thought his being here would help bring the characters to life. Casanova can show the singers what seduction is all about. It's a world he knows quite well—maybe too well," said Da Ponte.

"Da Ponte, Bondini, Casanova—all Italians. How very convenient."

"Casanova's Italian only by birth. He's a man of the world. Let him help. It will make a big difference. His experiences, my words, your music. Trust me, it will be fantastic. Casanova and I have arranged to meet later today, Pasquale. Everything will be finished. I promise. *Lo giuro.*"

"But we still need more rehearsal time," Mozart insisted.

"We'll see about the rehearsals," Bondini countered. "There's one question I have about the action, though. Were you serious when you told me we need to have a statue of the Commendatore burst into the Don's dining room and drag him off to hell?"

"Absolutely. It has to be dramatic, thrilling."

"If it has to be, I'll arrange for it. But Lorenzo, it does sound absurd."

"It will work, it will work. Meanwhile, I'll go to Vienna and get the Emperor's permission for *Figaro*. Leave everything to me."

"Make sure he gives a written order. There are people here in charge of the Archduchess' visit who won't want *Figaro* played. I'll need the Emperor's order to silence them."

Mozart gathered the music papers he'd placed next to his chair. Bondini walked around the desk, trying to get a good look at the sheets.

"Are those new sections of the opera, Mozart?"

"Two arias I wrote the other night. I have to give them to the copyist today."

"May I see?" Bondini asked cautiously.

Mozart spread the sheets out on the desk.

"They're two arias for Zerlina. She sings them to her fiancé, Masetto. He's a simple oaf. But she loves him anyway."

"My wife's singing Zerlina," Bondini reminded him.

"I know. She should have no problem with the part. She was a wonderful Susanna. Very believable, very loving," Mozart added.

"Thank you. I'll tell her you said so."

"I told her yesterday, privately, while we were rehearsing. In fact, her voice inspired me to write these arias."

Bondini gave a quizzical, sour look as Mozart put the sheets in order and picked them up. Then he bowed to Pasquale Bondini and followed Da Ponte out of the office. The guard swung the huge doors shut behind them.

When they were back downstairs, Mozart gave the sheets to the copyist. "When you've finished, bring me the soprano part. I'll deliver it to Madame Bondini myself."

"Very well, Maestro."

Da Ponte was standing outside waiting for Mozart. The rain had stopped.

"Have you lost your mind?" Da Ponte pounced.

"What?"

"Caterina Bondini, that's what. Pasquale is insanely jealous. He'll kill you if he thinks you have intentions . . ."

"And why would he worry about me? Didn't you just now tell him I didn't understand love because I'm not Italian and I'm married?"

"You're playing a dangerous game, Wolfgang. Please, let's get this opera produced without any more problems."

"I completely agree. Cancel the meeting with Casanova."

"No. I've arranged for you to meet him tonight at eight, at the Golden Lyre. He wants to be introduced to you. Please, give this a chance."

Impatiently, Mozart relented.

"I'll meet you at the restaurant."

"Excellent. You'll enjoy this, trust me."

Da Ponte climbed into a waiting chaise as Mozart returned to the opera house. He wandered around backstage, admiring the new machines which could change the scenes faster. He played with the trapdoors that had been designed when the theater was built, imagining the visual impact of having a character disappear from the stage, swallowed up by the floor. He was excited by the effects the large banks of candles could have on the stage, and how their light would make operas more dramatic, more realistic, more believable.

Now, alone on the stage, he imagined what the Archduchess and her entourage would see when the last act of *Figaro* was being played, the deceitful shadows cast through the onstage garden by flickering candles. With the music playing in his mind, he acted out the scene. Pretending to be Figaro, he held an imaginary Susanna in his arms, tenderly caressing her long hair in time with the music only he could hear. Every part in the orchestra, every nuance in the singing was as he wanted it to be; no one could ruin the moment. Slowly turning Susanna toward himself, he closed his eyes and imagined Caterina Bondini's beautiful face.

Chapter Four

⁀⧵⁀

*H*e's seated over there, sir. At the desk near the window."

"Thank you."

"Should I tell him you're here, sir?"

"You're very kind. Thank you, no. I'd give you a gold piece for your trouble, but I'm afraid I have none with me."

"Thank you, sir. It's quite all right."

The young student bowed respectfully and returned to his desk, pretending to study. But instead he watched over the rims of his tiny, oval eyeglasses at the elderly gentleman whose light-colored coat seemed out of place in the muted atmosphere of the library. The man moved confidently across the marble floor, heading directly for one of the wooden desks near the arched windows that stretched from just above the floor all the way up to the vaulted ceiling.

"Lorenzo, you look so studious."

Da Ponte looked up from the thick leather volume opened on the desk before him.

"Giacomo Casanova. It's wonderful to see you again. How was your journey from Dux?"

"Uneventful . . ."

"Which for you is an event itself."

Da Ponte stood up and embraced the older man, kissing him once on each cheek.

"I've never been in this monastery before," Casanova noted.

"I come here almost every day. It's quiet and I find this room inspires me to write."

25

Casanova looked around at the artfully carved ornate walls surrounding shelf after shelf of leather-bound books in the library of the Strahov Monastery. It was a long room known as Theological Hall, built a little over a century earlier. Light cascaded through the windows, reflecting off the well-polished floors and the brown and gold leather spines of the hundreds of volumes on the shelves.

"What a collection . . ." Casanova mused as he walked around admiring the literary riches. The only sound in the room was the even click of his shoes as he returned to Da Ponte's desk.

"What are you reading?"

"Shakespeare. I try to read a little every day. I enjoy his characters and the structure of his plays. It's very different from the way I have to develop librettos."

"Have you used any of his plays for an opera libretto?"

"I wouldn't dare. What poetry could I write to add luster to his words? Although I did once borrow an idea from one of his comedies—but nothing good came of it."

"Tell me more about our project," Casanova asked. "I was intrigued when I received your letter. I couldn't wait to leave Dux and the tedium."

Da Ponte pulled another upholstered chair over to the desk. Adjusting his waistcoat to make himself a little more comfortable, Casanova sat down, leaning forward to rest his elbow on the corner of the desk.

"Don Juan, Don Giovanni, the great rake . . . I convinced Mozart it— he would be an ideal subject for an opera. At first, Mozart agreed. Now, just weeks before we're to have the premiere, he's having difficulty finishing the score, and he's placing the blame on the characters I've given him, especially Don Giovanni."

Casanova rubbed his chin, but stopped when he felt the stubble of his beard.

"Tell me about Mozart. Is he an active man, with women?"

"He's married to a nice woman who's here with him. There are rumors that he has had mistresses, but I've never seen any evidence to prove it.

Mozart's cautious. I'd even say he's confused. It took some convincing to get him to meet with you. He's very reluctant. You'll have to convince him you can help with the opera."

"I'll do my best. Now, as I recall from memory and experience, the Don Juan legend is filled with adventures, seductions, escapades, exciting escapes—remarkably similar to my own memoirs."

"Yes, I've heard your stories. You should warn your readers about your habit of omitting the parts of stories that, shall we say, don't show you in the best light."

"How you wrong me. I write only what I remember."

Da Ponte removed his gold pocket watch from its pouch and looked at it.

"That's beautiful."

"It was a gift from the Emperor."

"Very impressive."

Da Ponte stood up.

"I want to go back to the inn to rest before we meet Mozart at the restaurant this evening. Would you walk with me?"

"Signor, it would be my honor."

Da Ponte picked up his walking stick, and together they walked out of the library. Da Ponte was struck by how Casanova's steps were less secure than they'd been the last time they met, just a few years earlier in Vienna. But, even though age was taking its toll, the older man still had an elegance and stature that made heads turn as they left the monastery grounds. They walked through the streets toward the Charles Bridge, which spanned the rapidly flowing Vltava River, dividing Prague in two. At the river's edge, under the stone base of the bridge, washerwomen scrubbed clothes. A small boat was tied up at a wood pier and cloaked men passed in and out of the shadows in a world separated from the shining elegance of the Prague that surrounded the river.

"I see you've exchanged your épée for a walking stick," Da Ponte remarked as they crossed the bridge leading to Prague's old town.

"There are certain things I wish I didn't have to give up just for the sake of being in style. A man should carry a sword. It's only proper, and safe. I'd wager Don Giovanni carries a sword."

It was late afternoon, and the weak remains of the day's clouded light cast shadows up and down Prague's narrow streets. Some of the small shops squeezed into the first floors of the buildings were already shut for the night, but others remained open, selling goods to the few people who were on their way home.

"Remember, Giacomo, you still have to convince Mozart of your usefulness. But I think he's interested. Just don't scare him off," Da Ponte counseled. But Casanova was distracted.

"Yes . . . yes . . . fine . . . very well . . . ah . . . but look at this, Lorenzo. Isn't this marvelous?"

Da Ponte stopped walking and watched Casanova stare into the window of the apothecary.

"What a fine collection. How wonderful . . ."

"What?"

"Lorenzo, come in with me," Casanova ordered as he opened the door of the shop.

Da Ponte, fatigued, followed him in. The shopkeeper was showing Casanova cut-glass vials filled with colognes and bath oils. With showy élan, Casanova waved each bottle beneath his nose, sniffing as if he were a connoisseur, guessing what fragrance was mixed into each bottle.

"I'll take the lilac; it's a wonderful scent—tender but not overwhelming," he said to the pleased shopkeeper.

"Very well, sir."

"Lorenzo, I have no money with me. Be a friend and lend me a few gold pieces? I'll be able to repay you in a day or two."

"You have no money? Why should I give you money for something so frivolous? As I recall you still haven't repaid the money I lent you in Vienna." Da Ponte shook his head, reached into a suede pouch and handed Casanova a few coins.

"I'll make it up to you. I'll save your opera," Casanova said.

Da Ponte had heard enough. As he walked out the door, he called back: "Just be there this evening, and please try not to make a fool of yourself."

Casanova completed his purchase, dabbed a bit of cologne behind his ears and followed Da Ponte out into the darkening street.

"Until later, my friend the poet," he yelled down the deserted street. Then, taking a deep breath through his nose, he walked toward the center of Prague's old town.

∞

"But why can't I come with you?"

"I told you: Lorenzo wants me to meet Casanova. We're having supper and talking about the opera. There's no place for you there. It wouldn't be right."

"But you promised we'd have supper together tonight," Constanze reminded him.

"I know, dearest, most beloved little wife of my heart, but I promised Lorenzo I'd give this a try. How would it look if I showed up to meet Casanova with my wife? It would be uncomfortable. Neither of them is married. You'd be out of place. Now, I must go, my little sweetness, or I'll be late."

Annoyed, Constanze sat on the bed watching Wolfgang dress. She wanted to be with him, but even more, deep down, she wanted to meet Casanova. Mozart kissed her on the forehead, bowed and left.

Constanze was alone, again.

∞

A wooden sign, hung high above a door, swung noisily in the breeze. When the wind stopped, the words carved into the sign could be read: the Golden Lyre.

Lorenzo Da Ponte sat at a round table facing the windows, talking and gesturing with Casanova. Every few minutes, leaning back in their chairs, they erupted into fits of loud laughter. Outside the laughs sounded muffled, but Mozart could see Da Ponte's broad smile, distorted though it was by the wavy lead glass of the windows.

Mozart watched for a few minutes, trying unsuccessfully to make out what they were saying. Frustrated, he ran his fingers through his hair, walked through the courtyard and went into the restaurant. Hanging his cloak and hat on a wooden hook near the door, he turned toward their table. Da Ponte was facing away, but his companion was fully visible. He looked to Mozart like an older man of indeterminate age, with a strange mixture of experience and youth etched into his face. He had chiseled cheekbones that set off his distinguished-looking forehead, and a full head of long, graying hair seemed to give his facial expressions excitement. And yet, there was a soft, elegant demeanor in his face that overrode all other impressions.

As Mozart approached, carefully winding his way through the tables and chairs, he could hear the conversation.

". . . and then she said: 'But Chevalier, I'm engaged to be married.' To which I replied, 'Give me your hand, my darling. Trust me, on your wedding night your fiancé will be singing my praises and thanking me,' and that's how I spent this evening before coming to meet you."

Da Ponte roared with laughter and tossed his head back. As he did, he noticed Mozart out of the corner of his eye.

"Ah, here he is. You're late. What took you so long?"

"I was with Const—I was working."

Da Ponte and his companion stood up. Casanova slowly rose to his full height. He was taller than both Da Ponte and Mozart, but he had a grace that made him seem almost delicate. He extended his hand.

"Maestro, this is a great honor for me."

Mozart beamed inwardly and took the man's hand in his. It was soft and warm, without any wrinkles, which surprised Mozart.

"Let me introduce you," Da Ponte said. "Giacomo Casanova, le Chevalier de Seingalt, meet Wolfgang Amadeus Mozart."

They held the handshake for a few seconds, as if concluding a deal. Mozart looked up at the older man. His face was indeed striking, with deep, dark eyes that danced against his light complexion, highlighted by the thin layer of white powder covering his beard. An elaborate silk shirt and scarf, a brocade coat and black shoes with gold buckles, and the way he wore his golden hair created a regal appearance.

"Should I call you Chevalier?" Mozart asked. Da Ponte laughed.

"No. Call me Giacomo or Casanova, whichever you like. And how do you like to be addressed, Maestro?"

"We call him Mozart, just Mozart," Da Ponte explained, shrugging his shoulders.

"Then I will too."

Da Ponte pulled another chair up to the table, and sat down. Mozart and Casanova bowed slightly toward each other and took the remaining seats. Mozart noticed the smell of lilac.

"This is thrilling," Da Ponte babbled excitedly. "I have dreamed of this moment. I can only imagine what will come of our working together—the ideas, the drama, the comedy, the liaisons, the women . . ."

"An opera," Casanova added quietly. "I believe it's the opera that interests Mozart most."

Mozart looked at the older man. Their eyes met, and he nodded a subtle agreement.

"Have you had much experience—I mean, with opera, Chevalier?"

"Certainly not as much as you or Lorenzo, but in my travels I've spent more than a few nights in the theater."

"And do you think that qualifies you to work on this new opera?"

"Mozart, there's no need to be rude. Casanova came here to—"

"No, Lorenzo. He has every right to ask. It's his opera . . ."

"Our opera," Da Ponte corrected.

"Well, yes, but the music is what people will remember. The words are there to accompany—"

"Oh, please don't start this argument," said Da Ponte. "The battle between poetry and music bores me, and it will never be resolved, so let's not revive it now."

"Well, then let me answer Mozart's question. As Lorenzo may have told you, during my travels and throughout my life, I've had experiences that may help with this opera. But I'm also familiar with the theater. My parents were actors in a troupe of comedians in Venice. They played in the Saint Samuel Theater. Perhaps you visited it when you were in Venice?"

"I was very young then."

"I've also studied the great playwrights, from the Greeks to Shakespeare to Molière and your friend Beaumarchais."

"But opera isn't the same. It's as different from drama as it is from a symphony or a concerto."

"I understand, and I have no intention of interfering with your music. God knows I would never do that, not after hearing your *Marriage of Figaro*."

"Our *Marriage of Figaro*," Da Ponte corrected, the annoyance in his voice becoming more evident. Casanova noticed a weak smile cross Mozart's mouth.

"Then what *are* you going to do?" Mozart asked.

"Perhaps nothing at all. Perhaps something none of us can anticipate now. Perhaps I can help with the singers. There may be something I could show them to help bring their characters to life. I've read Lorenzo's libretto, and can tell this is no ordinary opera. Actors standing at the edge of the stage singing at the audience and ignoring one another just won't work. No, the opera needs to be thrilling, and that means having emotions, action and reactions, based on real life, on experience."

"Exactly," Mozart interrupted excitedly.

The tension at the table eased a little. Casanova called a barmaid over. As she bent down to hear his whispered order, Mozart saw him take a long look at her round breasts. Casanova swallowed and closed his eyes, savoring the momentary pleasure. The barmaid smiled, curtsied and left to fill his order.

"What did you say to her?" Da Ponte asked.

"I merely whispered in her ear."

"You're lying," Da Ponte sputtered. "You propositioned her!"

Mozart relaxed and leaned back in his chair, trying to get a better perspective on Casanova.

"Lorenzo, you're crude. You think after a few words a woman will either accept or reject your advances. But it's far more complicated, and there are subtleties you miss, which is painfully apparent in your libretto."

Mozart had to laugh. Having someone around to put Da Ponte in his place was becoming enjoyable.

"If it doesn't bore you, I'll explain," Casanova said to Mozart.

"Please go ahead. I think I'll find it enlightening."

"You see, it's really quite simple: if, as you speak into a woman's ear, you blow very gently—almost like a soundless whistle—you can direct the air downward, like this, so it glances off the side of her neck. That gentle breath will make the hairs on her neck stand up. There are tiny secrets hidden all over a woman's body. But you have to be subtle."

Mozart raised his glass in tribute to the man's experience.

"Maybe your knowledge will be of use with the opera. But have you ever had to deal with singers? Do you know what problems they can be? I swear, after this opera is done, I'll never compose another."

"That would be a great loss for everyone."

Mozart had come to supper wanting to dislike Casanova, but somehow he couldn't. Instead he was filled with a mixture of admiration, respect and a desire to know him better.

The food arrived. Casanova took a pair of pince-nez glasses out of a pocket and carefully examined each plate. He seemed pleased by the offering.

"Food, wine, women—these are the joys of mankind," Casanova toasted.

The three men raised their glasses and drank.

"I've always enjoyed the food in Prague," he continued. "I was here first in 1753."

"I wasn't even born!" Mozart laughed.

Casanova looked at him wistfully.

"Youth—how it's wasted. You know, I should hate you," Casanova muttered, pointing at Mozart with his fork.

"Why were you in Prague?"

"I was en route from Dresden to Vienna. I was supposed to deliver a letter to the head of the opera here, a man named Locatelli. I was on my way to deliver the letter when I ran into an acquaintance, a Colonel Fabris. He insisted I dine with him, and I accepted. But after supper, the opera was closed and I couldn't find Locatelli. I had nowhere to go until I remembered a dear friend, a Madame Morelli, who lived nearby. I went to her home, where I received a very personal welcome."

"What happened then?" Mozart had stopped eating and was staring at Casanova, who was relishing being the center of attention.

"Well, I enjoyed Madame Morelli's company and she mine. For the next three days she took care of my every desire. We rarely left the bedroom, except to eat."

"Did you ever deliver the letter to Locatelli?"

"When Madame Morelli's husband returned, I thanked him for being away and walked to the opera house, where I delivered the letter. Locatelli was a character, more thief than opera impresario—"

"Aren't they all?" Mozart interrupted.

Casanova raised his glass toward Mozart in a silent toast.

"Locatelli did have one custom I found fascinating, though." Casanova filled the wineglasses, straightened the cuffs of his coat and leaned forward in an almost conspiratorial way. Mozart too leaned in, anticipating another good story.

"Every evening Locatelli ate his supper seated at the head of a long wooden table set for thirty people. He cast his dinners with actors, actresses, dancers, singers and a few friends. On my last night in Prague, the very evening I delivered the letter, he invited me to join his party. Perhaps it was accidental—I'll never know—but at supper Locatelli seated me next to his mistress, a beautiful young woman dressed in black, her chest covered by an enticing delicate lace which left little to my imagination. On my other side was seated a handsome young man, who I soon found out was the leading castrato of the opera company."

"I once wrote a part for castrato, in my opera *Lucio Silla,* but I was so upset by the idea of castration, I swore never to write for one again."

"Understood, but I must tell you, once I got over my initial disgust of the idea, I had a fabulous conversation with the young man. I spent the entire evening talking with him. I asked about his sexual appetite, what acts he liked to perform in bed, and many other things."

"And what did you learn?" Mozart asked.

"I learned I would never be castrated!"

This time Mozart laughed as loudly as the others.

"More important, at the end of the evening, I realized I'd paid no attention at all to the beautiful woman seated on my left. As I was about to leave, Locatelli came up to me and said: 'So, Chevalier, did you enjoy yourself?' 'Not as much as I should have,' I answered, looking directly into his mistress' deep blue eyes. He smiled, bid me farewell and, with his hand firmly around her derriere, led his mistress out the door, leaving me alone with thoughts of what might have been."

Despite his telling stories and illustrating them with frequent broad hand gestures, Casanova had managed to eat most of his food. Mozart was so intrigued by the stories that his plate was still half full. He quickly ate a few bites and drank some more wine.

"I should be getting home," said Mozart. "Constanze's waiting for me."

"Constanze?"

"His wife," Da Ponte whispered.

Dabbing the corners of his mouth with a napkin, Casanova asked Mozart: "Are you happily married?"

Mozart paused. "I am," he said, sounding almost as if he were trying to convince himself, or perhaps to place some doubt in the other men's minds. "Did you ever marry, Signor Casanova?"

Da Ponte laughed. Some of the chewed bread he had stuffed in his mouth spewed onto the table. Casanova grimaced and whisked the wet crumbs onto the floor.

"I had my chances, and often discussed marriage with the women I was in love with. But the charm of the idea always wore off shortly after we'd gone to bed. I suppose it was never meant to be. Maybe we could learn from each other, Maestro. But I'm curious, Mozart—the name Constanze. Isn't the heroine of your opera *The Abduction from the Seraglio* named Constanze?"

"Yes. You know the opera?"

"Not well. I've read the libretto."

"You know, Giacomo, Mozart has a good story about his wife and that opera. You see, the part of Constanze was originally sung by his wife's sister, and the rumor was that during the rehearsals our composer taught the young lady the part, note by note, showing her how to hit the highest notes without shrieking . . ."

"That's enough, Lorenzo. I don't think that's of any importance or interest to Signor Casanova."

Sensing Mozart's embarrassment, Casanova called over the restaurant's owner and ordered some coffee and chocolates, then explained that a meal without a sweet to finish it was like an incomplete sex act. "It starts with such promise, but ends with nothing but a stale taste in the mouth."

They were among the last people in the tavern. The clatter of plates and the noise from other conversations had subsided. The owner put another log on the fire, and the shadowy light danced on the vaulted ceiling. Mozart knew he should leave, but Casanova's voice was melodic, and his stories vivid. Besides, the barmaid had just brought a tray of cakes and chocolates and a third carafe of wine.

"So," Casanova said finally, "I've read the opera's libretto, but before we get into details about the characters or the singers, I must ask one important question: what is the opera's title?"

Mozart and Da Ponte looked at each other.

"We can't agree on that," the poet explained. "I think it should be called 'The Stone Guest' and he wants to call it 'The Punished Rake.'"

"It's more than that," Mozart added. "We can't seem to determine if Don Giovanni's tale is comedy or a serious subject that should be dealt with as such."

Casanova, wiping some chocolate and whipped cream from the edge of his mouth, took a deep breath. A thoughtful look crossed his face, as if he were about to make a crucial pronouncement.

"If I may . . ."

He paused. Mozart and Da Ponte urged him on, hoping his pronouncement would resolve the impasse.

"I think it is both. The opera has comedic moments, but it's also a drama. Maybe we should call it a dramatic comedy—no . . . actually it's more like a humorous drama. That's better; that captures it. There are funny moments, but Don Giovanni's life—his exploits, his passions, his character—are not funny. A life like that should be taken seriously."

Casanova sipped his wine, considering the question further. "I suppose, to some degree, I identify with Don Giovanni. All he wants is to enjoy his life; he's a true libertine. His undoing is the result of the way he leads his life and how that is viewed and judged by society."

Mozart was fascinated by this assessment, but his perception of the character was colored by the music he'd written for the part. To him Don Giovanni was a nobleman with passions, a lust for life and a sense of freedom.

"Now, about the title," Casanova continued. "We must get at the heart of the opera and think about why the events unfold, what sets the action in motion."

Mozart nodded. Da Ponte ate. Casanova went on.

"I think no matter what you title it, people will always call it *Don Giovanni*. He is the protagonist. All of the events are either caused by him or revolve around what he has done. That's what I think it should be called—*Don Giovanni*. Just that: *Don Giovanni*. Are we agreed?"

Casanova's diplomacy was a skill he had developed during his years as director of the state lotteries in Paris. Neither Mozart nor Da Ponte felt victorious; rather, they felt relieved that Casanova's logic had resolved the issue.

The restaurant was empty, and the owner stood near the front door waiting impatiently for them to leave. Casanova finished the last few sips of wine, stood up, tossed his napkin on the table and brushed a few crumbs from the front of his frock coat. With Mozart at his side and Da Ponte close behind, he walked to the door. Casanova slipped a gold coin into the hand of the tavern-keeper, who helped them with their cloaks and held the door open. The moment they were outside, he shut the heavy oak door and slid its bolt into place.

Outside the Golden Lyre, a light mist was falling. It was a raw night. A distant clock chimed eleven times. Mozart listened, thinking of what he would say to Constanze when he returned to their room at the inn.

"Maybe she'll be asleep, so I can work without telling her about this evening," Mozart hoped silently.

"Are there rehearsals tomorrow?" Casanova asked.

"Yes, in the afternoon. The singers refuse to work in the morning. Will you be able to attend?" Mozart asked.

"Absolutely. I'll watch and we'll meet afterward to see if there's anything I can add. I'll stay quiet during the music, I promise."

"That would be perfect," Mozart agreed.

Da Ponte was restless, furtively glancing up and down the street and around corners of buildings, as if expecting to discover someone hiding there.

"I'm hoping to get a letter from a dear friend of mine who may have some observations that could help us. It should be here any day," said

Casanova. "When I received the libretto from Lorenzo, I wrote to a friend who's imprisoned in the Bastille."

"Why is he in the Bastille?" Mozart asked.

"His mother-in-law had him arrested for 'deviant behavior.' I believe he's innocent and will someday be freed. But the experiences he's had and his perspectives might give us some excellent ideas for *Don Giovanni*. He's also a first-rate writer with a keen imagination. I hope it wasn't wrong of me to write to him."

"No, anything helpful is welcome. But I can't imagine there's anyone who's had more experience than you, Casanova. Who is he?"

"Donatien-Alphonse-François, the Marquis de Sade."

Da Ponte burst into hysterics and patted Casanova on the back. "You're not serious? I've read about him. He's insane."

"Perhaps, but I think his insights might be worth hearing. I'll let you know if he writes back. Mozart, I look forward to working with you. Now, if you'll excuse me, I think it's time I went to bed."

Casanova tipped his hat to Mozart and turned to face Da Ponte.

"Lorenzo, you must be getting old. You didn't look over at the church door. I used to admire your powers of observation."

Casanova raised his right arm, pointing across the courtyard to a small church barely visible through the mist. A figure concealed in a long black cloak and hood emerged from the shadows of the church's arched doorway and joined him.

"Gentlemen, I bid you good night," Casanova said, bowing to the other men. "Until tomorrow."

Mozart stared in silent awe as Casanova walked away, his hand resting comfortably on the barmaid's back.

Chapter Five

⌒

The bright mid-morning sun, filtered by the drawn damask curtains, woke Constanze from a deep sleep. She knew Wolfgang again wasn't in bed with her. The scratching sound of his pen as it filled the music paper drifted in from the next room. She smiled and waited until she heard a pause.

"Good morning."

"One moment, Stanzi. I'm just finishing a phrase for . . ."

He left the sentence unfinished, choosing instead to complete his musical thought. Constanze sat up, puffed up one of the pillows, placed it behind her back and took a letter from the bedside table. She was reading it when Wolfgang crept into the room.

"Boo!"

"I heard you coming. You can't sneak up on me anymore."

"You're no fun," he pouted. "What are you reading?"

"It's a note from Josefa Dušek."

"What does she want?"

"None of your business."

"Let me see it or I'll kiss you to death."

"No," she said, waving the note high above her head.

Wolfgang turned away, pretending not to care. Then with a sudden burst, he spun toward the bed, jumped onto the straw mattress and grabbed the note.

"So, the Dušeks are having a party this evening and we're invited. How exciting. '*I want you and Wolfgang to be there. Wear your nicest clothes,*'" he read in a falsetto voice. "I suppose we have to go," he whined, tossing the note back to Constanze.

"I don't understand you. The Dušeks were so generous when we visited here last year. Josefa adores your music. You've known her for more than ten years and she sings your arias in all of her concerts. Really, Wolfgang, sometimes I wonder about you."

"It's not Josefa I don't like, it's that music teacher husband of hers."

"Oh, František's not so bad. He's just a little . . . a little . . ."

"Old and stodgy. We should call him the *eminence grizzled.*"

"Try to be nice, Wolfgang. I like Josefa. In fact, she's coming here this afternoon. She wants to spend some time with me. I'm looking forward to it. I like having someone to talk to."

"That's nice," Mozart replied absentmindedly. He was looking at himself in the mirror, pulling his hair back as far as it could go.

"Wolfgang, what are you doing?"

"Oh . . . nothing, just looking. Constanze, what do you think I'll look like when I get old?"

"How am I supposed to know, and why are you asking?"

Wolfgang walked over to the bed and knelt at her side, taking her hand in his.

"Last night, I met Casanova. Constanze, there's something fascinating about him. He's the most intriguing man I've ever encountered. He knows about the world, about music, about theater, about wom—wonderful things and places. He's had a life filled with adventures that I can't even imagine. And he's handsome for a man of his age. *Très distingué.* You know what, now that I think about it, he's a little like my father, only less stuffy and more worldly. He's coming to today's rehearsal."

"He certainly put you in a good mood. You should invite him to the Dušeks' party. I'm sure they'd be delighted."

"I'll do that," he said as he gave her a quick kiss on the cheek. "Now, I must go rehearse. Give Josefa my warmest regards, and you be cheerful."

"Wolfgang, you never changed clothes last night."

"Oh, Stanzi . . . you're right. I was so excited when I got home I went straight to work on the opera. I guess I forgot. Oh well. I'll change before the party."

With a childish shrug of his shoulders, he left. Constanze shook her head in frustration and walked to the washstand. She knew she could call the serving girl to help, but she was uncomfortable dressing in front of a stranger. After washing herself, she chose a simple ankle-length dress of pale green and white stripes from among the clothes she had brought to Prague. The cheerful colors reminded her of spring.

She pinched her cheeks to add color, then brushed her hair, letting it fall naturally.

"I'll have to wear a wig tonight," she mused. Pausing in front of her open wardrobe, she contemplated the formal dresses that hung there, deciding which one to wear for the Dušeks' party. She worried that none of them would fit or look appropriate. Dismissing the thought, she picked up a small silver bell on Mozart's writing table and rang it.

A few moments later, a petite girl dressed in black came in and curtsied.

"You called, Madame Mozart?"

"Yes. Please bring some coffee."

"Immediately, Madame," replied the girl, who then quickly left the room.

Alone, Constanze glanced at the music pages Mozart had left on the table. A few lines were partly filled in. But most of the pages were blank. "He must have taken the new pages with him," she thought.

"Your coffee, Madame," the serving girl said when she returned.

"Put it on the little table," Constanze ordered without looking up.

"I'll do nothing of the sort," boomed a fuller, more confident voice.

"Josefa!" said Constanze with a start. "I didn't expect you so early. I'm not presentable."

"You look wonderful," Josefa Dušek said, gliding gracefully across the room to give Constanze a warm embrace. The serving girl put two coffees on the small round table in the corner of the anteroom, then asked, "Will there be anything else, Madame?"

"No, thank you."

Josefa removed her embroidered cloak and sat down in one of the two upholstered chairs next to the table, and Constanze took the other. Josefa Dušek was no beauty, but her face had a chubby, regal quality and the best tailors in Prague made her clothes from the finest fabrics to show her well-endowed body to its best advantage. Silently Constanze envied how well assembled Josefa's outfit was.

"Where's Wolfgang?"

"The opera house. He left a few minutes ago. He was excited."

"Why?"

"Well, apparently Signor Da Ponte invited Casanova . . . *the* Casanova to help with the staging. Wolfgang met him last night."

"I've heard of Casanova. He has quite a reputation."

"Wolfgang said that Casanova was worldly and interesting. I hope you don't mind, but I told Wolfgang to invite him to your party."

"Delightful! Of course he's welcome. But I see there's more exciting news. You're pregnant again. Congratulations."

"Yes, thank you. I'm so happy, but also nervous."

"Only natural. And little Karl . . . he's well?"

"He was fine when we left Vienna. We can only hope and pray . . ."

"He'll be fine. He's a robust little fellow. But, Constanze, you look pale."

"No . . . no, I'm fine . . . only, I've been in this room since we arrived in Prague. Wolfgang's been so busy and preoccupied he hasn't had any time for me."

"Well, what would you like to do? I'm at your disposal."

"Could we take a walk? I'd like to get out. It looks so nice outside."

"Absolutely," Josefa said, rising from her seat. "We can take my carriage and go to the Villa."

"If it's not a problem, could we walk around here, in town?"

"Of course, of course. That would be delightful. Come. Wear a cloak. There's a chill in the air."

Josefa put on her large cloak and wrapped a scarf around her neck. "Can't let the cold get to my throat."

But Constanze, having been around singers her entire life, already understood.

The two women—one large, the other petite and pregnant—left the inn arm in arm. As they neared the street Constanze paused, momentarily unnerved by the bustle and crowds. Josefa tightened her grip on the younger woman's arm to steady her. At first they walked in silence, carefully making their way through an open-air market where merchants had set up makeshift stalls to sell fresh fruits, flowers and bread. There was a large stone statue of a man on a horse in the center of the square; at the market's edge, a group of children were gathered in a semicircle. Laughter filled the air.

Constanze stopped and watched the children, who were gleefully enjoying the performance of an Italian street–puppet show. There was a small cart raised onto a rough wood platform. The cart was painted in bright blues, reds, greens and gold, with elaborate black lettering. The sides were opened wide, allowing the audience to see into the stage and its magical world of tiny characters who danced and jumped, acting out their miniature comedies and tragedies.

"Wolfgang loves these street shows. Every time he sees one he stops and watches. He laughs and gets lost . . ."

"Like a child."

"A little," Constanze agreed.

Constanze and Josefa watched as the marionettes entertained. The children laughed loudest when a lanky clown, dressed in red and white stripes, repeatedly stumbled and fell as he made his way across the uneven stage. Then they grew quiet when the young maiden, costumed in a frilly white dress and a veil, appeared in the cutout window of the stone castle. The voices coming from behind the cart's walls told the story of a fair maiden locked away in a castle waiting for her noble knight to set her free. The clown returned and tripped ungracefully a few more times. But then the children, in unison, let out an extended "Oooooh" as the knight, wearing armor painted in the official colors of Prague—black and gold—and brandishing a shiny sword, appeared and climbed the castle's wall. When he embraced his fair maiden, the clown sat down, put his head in his hands and cried pretend tears of joy.

The show over, the curtain was pulled closed and the marionettes disappeared beneath the stage. The children cheered. Josefa pulled a reluctant Constanze away, leading her down a narrow street to a nearby park. Even though it was autumn, the gardens were beautifully maintained. Constanze took a deep breath as they walked among the trees.

"So, how is our Wolfgang?"

Constanze paused before answering.

"He's been fine."

Josefa looked at Constanze. "Is there something you're not telling me?"

Constanze moved away from Josefa. Her legs were tired. She sat down on a wooden bench shaded by two large trees. Josefa sat next to her and waited as Constanze gathered her thoughts.

"Ever since his father died he's been . . . different. It's as if he's not sure how he should behave. He spends almost no time with Karl. He worries about his position at court and he does what people tell him. But the Emperor doesn't reward him. He composes most nights, but there are nights when he goes to the tavern to play billiards and doesn't come home until early morning."

"And how is he with you?"

"What do you mean?"

"Does he spend time with you?"

Constanze blushed. "Not since I became pregnant. He rarely comes to bed. He's often distracted and distant, but a moment later he can be giddy and childish."

"Do you think he has a mistress?"

"I don't know, Josefa. He's been so busy with the opera and with his father's affairs since his death, we haven't had any time together."

"What about his sister? Isn't she in Salzburg to handle the old man's affairs?"

"Wolfgang doesn't write to her. She wants him to move back to Salzburg, but he refuses. But I don't want to burden you . . ."

"Don't be ridiculous. I love Wolfgang . . . and you," Josefa added quickly.

"I know. And he cherishes you and František," Constanze fibbed. "How is František? You haven't mentioned him."

Josefa looked away and watched a bird fly onto a branch above her head. "Boring."

"What?"

"He's a bore—a sweet bore, but a bore."

"Josefa! How can you say that?"

"Oh, Constanze, you have no idea how dull he is. He gives his lessons and goes to the opera, but he's unexciting. He doesn't have fun. He allows me my soirées, but he'd rather spend his evenings reading or practicing the clavier. He has no idea of what the world is about. My only relief comes when I go on concert tours. At least he's stopped traveling with me. I can be alone; I can be free to play. You're lucky to be married to a man who's so talented and lively."

"And poor. Don't forget that."

"Are things bad?"

"You can't begin to imagine. One night last winter in Vienna, it was snowing, windy, bitterly cold. Wolfgang was composing. I was so cold I couldn't sleep. I asked him to relight the fire, but there was no wood left."

"What did you do?"

"Wolfgang came into the bedroom, pulled me out of bed, covers and all, wrapped us both up and we . . . oh, it's so silly . . ."

"What?" Josefa asked, moving to the edge of the bench.

"He sang a minuet and we danced to stay warm."

Josefa's sigh was a mixture of sadness and envy. Each woman looked off in the distance, lost in thought, enjoying the warm breezes and the sunshine.

"Come. We'd better get you back to the inn. You should rest before tonight. I'm hoping it will be an entertaining evening, and with Casanova there . . . well . . . who knows what may happen."

"Who knows," Constanze repeated softly.

"I'll send a carriage for you and Wolfgang. Wear your best clothes. Do you want me to have my maid come to your inn this afternoon to help you?"

"Oh no, thank you. I'll manage. Wolfgang will help."

Slowly they walked back through the market, avoiding the most crowded sections and the foul rivulets that flowed through the old streets. When they reached the inn, Josefa climbed into her waiting carriage as Constanze went inside alone.

Chapter Six

B y the time Casanova arrived at the opera house, the first scene of *Don Giovanni* had already been rehearsed. Noiselessly he eased into a seat in the front row next to Da Ponte, a few feet behind Mozart, who was conducting from the harpsichord.

"How are you this morning?" Casanova whispered to Da Ponte.

Da Ponte shrugged, pointed to the singers onstage and grimaced.

"Did you oversleep? Or did your barmaid keep you in bed all morning?"

"Are you jealous, Lorenzo? Or just spiteful, bitter and lonely?"

"Are you assuming I was alone last night?"

"It's intuition."

Raising his voice to a loud stage whisper, Da Ponte snapped back: "Your intuition is wrong."

Mozart, without missing a beat, turned around and glared, ending the argument. Casanova took a pinch of snuff from a small engraved silver box he kept in his waistcoat pocket and settled farther back into his chair. He watched as Mozart simultaneously conducted, played the harpsichord, corrected wrong notes in the orchestra and prompted the singers, silently mouthing the words for them. Occasionally he would stop the rehearsal to instruct a singer to phrase something differently. He seemed larger and more imposing than he had the night before; his control, his total dominance was impressive.

"He's remarkable," Casanova whispered.

Da Ponte ignored him, listening instead to Mozart's directions to the orchestra, which he gave during a brief pause while the scenery was changed. The new set was simple: a street leading from the back of the stage to the center, where it ended at what was meant to be a courtyard. Painted canvas stretched over large wood beams represented the buildings of Seville. An inn and an outdoor seating area filled the rear section of the stage.

"Did you get de Sade's letter?" Da Ponte whispered.

"No, and I'm worried about him. I've heard the trouble in Paris is getting worse. Some say there may be a revolution."

"Ridiculous. It could never happen. The King won't allow it."

"Don't count on it. There's a growing hatred of the rich and powerful. It's ironic, really—de Sade's neither rich nor powerful. He's had most of his property taken away and he's spent half his life in prison."

"Hatred doesn't discriminate. People should let others live as they please."

"Spoken like a true libertine. I'll let you know when the letter comes."

"Good. But whatever you do, don't give it to Mozart," Da Ponte cautioned. "He's impressionable, young, naïve and edgy, especially since his father's death. De Sade's advice, if that's what he gives, might upset or confuse him."

"I'll keep that in mind. What happens in the next scene, Lorenzo?"

"It's daybreak. Don Giovanni and his servant, Leporello, are on their way home. It's supposed to be just after Don Giovanni tried to seduce Donna Anna and had to kill her father, the Commendatore, who was protecting her honor."

"That part I remember. Then what?"

"Angry at his master, Leporello wants to quit, but Giovanni convinces him not to. Then—and this is a section I wrote particularly well—Don Giovanni thinks he smells a woman arriving. Giovanni and Leporello hide in the shadows. The woman, Donna Elvira, arrives in a chaise. She's dressed for travel, and a thick veil covers her face."

"Yes, yes. Now I remember—she's enraged about being abandoned by her lover. Don Giovanni, sensing a new conquest, goes to console her. They recognize each other—it's a very funny moment, Lorenzo—and we find out he's the very same lover who's gotten her so angry."

"If you two are finished chatting, I'd like to go on," Mozart interrupted. Not waiting for an answer, he turned back to the orchestra, sat down at the harpsichord and played the opening chords of the fourth scene.

Casanova sat up as Caterina Micelli, playing the part of the spurned Donna Elvira, emerged from the chaise and walked to the edge of the stage. Though a black lace veil covered her face, he could tell she was a petite beauty. She walked across the stage confidently, with a palpable strength that excited him. When the string instruments began the introduction to her aria, Casanova heard how Mozart's music and Da Ponte's words worked together to project her anger into the audience.

Casanova was enthralled by Micelli's piquant voice, with its Italianate passion, and he sat forward, trying to get as close to the stage as possible, silently yearning to act the part of Don Giovanni, wanting to ease her sorrow and pain. When the aria ended with Don Giovanni gallantly introducing himself to the upset traveler, Donna Elvira removed her veil, shocking her former lover. The few assistants standing around the opera house laughed at the surprise of the moment. Casanova gasped at her beauty, at her dark hair and fiery eyes.

"It's a fine aria," he whispered to Da Ponte. "But she doesn't convey what it is like to be loved and then abandoned. The anger doesn't really come through. Perhaps I could coach her."

But Da Ponte didn't hear him; he was busy helping the singers with the words to the recitatives so the pace wouldn't lag.

"No. No," he shouted. "Don Giovanni comes over to console her. Leporello tells him to leave. It's funny. Can't you get that across?"

Mozart went on, ignoring the librettist's corrections, conducting the orchestra through an aria he particularly liked: the Catalogue Aria, in which Don Giovanni enumerates his list of seductions—country girls, chambermaids, baronesses, countesses, females of every social class, size and figure. And every time he repeated that he had already seduced "one thousand

and three women in Spain alone," Mozart and many members of the orchestra laughed out loud. The music sparkled, and the musicians were enjoying themselves.

"No! No! That's ridiculous," Casanova's deep voice shattered the moment, stopping the Don Giovanni, Luigi Bassi, in mid-phrase.

Mozart's hands stopped conducting and fell to the harpsichord's keys, sounding a dissonant crash. "What is the matter?"

The singers froze in place and the orchestra sat silently staring at Mozart. Da Ponte leaned back, his grin hidden by the theater's darkness. Casanova got up and approached Mozart.

"Maestro, *perdon.* Excuse me. I'm sorry to interrupt. The music is sublime, the opera truly wonderful, but the aria, this beautiful, funny aria, should not be sung by Don Giovanni."

Da Ponte's cackle echoed through the silent theater.

"And why is that?"

"It's a question of class and station," Casanova explained. "Don Giovanni's a nobleman. He would never keep a written list of his conquests. He would remember each woman as a unique adventure, each with her own charms and attributes, even scents. This catalogue of conquests reduces women to a series of numbers, and that's far too crude for a man who loves women, who loves *all* women."

Mozart looked up from the harpsichord and slowly turned around.

"And so we should remove the aria?"

"No, no, no. It's too vital to take out; that's not what I'm suggesting."

"What *are* you suggesting?" Da Ponte asked angrily.

"Have Leporello sing it."

The singers onstage looked at each other, stunned. Mozart studied the handwritten score propped up on his harpsichord. Occasionally he'd play the melody with one hand, mouthing the words, considering Casanova's suggestion.

"It could work," he mused, rubbing his chin. "Yes, it might work nicely."

"You're not serious. Mozart, why are you listening to him?"

"Lorenzo, you're the one who asked Signor Casanova to help. Why shouldn't we listen to him?"

"He's here to help with the staging, not the words. This is preposterous. The Catalogue Aria belongs to Don Giovanni. It's a showpiece. The star has to sing it."

Casanova leaned over Mozart's shoulder and looked at the score. Having been a violinist, he understood the markings. He was astounded by the perfect manuscript.

"Your copyist has a wonderful hand," he told Mozart.

"There is no copyist."

"You recopied the score yourself?"

"No. This is the original, as I composed it."

For a moment the self-assured, almost cocky smile that had charmed and amazed the crowned heads of Europe when he was a child returned to Mozart's face. Casanova shook his head in disbelief.

"If I understand the music, the vocal range should be right for Leporello."

"That's right. He and Don Giovanni have the same vocal range," said Mozart, impressed.

"Not a note needs to be changed. Just Lorenzo's words and how the aria is introduced, but that's in the recitative."

"I'm not changing a thing. The aria belongs to the Don," Da Ponte said.

Luigi Bassi huffed loudly onstage, angry over the possibility of losing the aria. The other singers and the musicians in the orchestra were growing restless. The outburst they all expected from Mozart never came.

"Let's take a short break," Mozart suggested. "We'll rework the aria. Leporello . . . Signor Ponziani . . ."

"Yes, Maestro?"

"Come down here. I'll teach you the music while Casanova changes a few words. Lorenzo, are you going to help?"

"No." Da Ponte rose from his chair and marched angrily toward the curtained exit.

"Lorenzo, where are you going?" Mozart called.

"Vienna. I have to see the Emperor."

"For heaven's sake, why?"

"I have two other librettos to present. Salieri wants me there, so I have to go."

Before Da Ponte could exit, Mozart ran to catch him.

"Lorenzo, wait," he said, laying a hand on his shoulder. "Don't forget to get the Emperor's permission for the performance of *Figaro*. We still need it."

Da Ponte looked at Mozart. Those innocent eyes dissipated his anger.

"I'll do it for you. Be careful, Wolfgang. Don't be so eager to make changes."

"Come back soon, Lorenzo."

"I should be back within the week."

Casanova was busily changing the words on Mozart's score so it would make sense for Leporello to sing about his master's litany of conquests. With visible enjoyment, he hummed the melody, counting beats and finding words to fit the buoyant rhythm.

"Madamina, il catàlogo è questo . . ."

Felice Ponziani, the Leporello, was standing near the harpsichord listening to Casanova's advice on how to deliver the aria, how to blend a sense of grudging admiration for his master with the appropriate amount of humor.

"You're not making fun of him. You're explaining to Donna Elvira that, as one of the Don's former lovers, she's in good company. When you begin with '*Madamina*,' you must make her believe that what you have to say is of the greatest importance. It's your job to serve Don Giovanni, and you, Signor Ponziani, have an excellent comic sensibility. You look the part; your broad smile and round face shine. Relish the role; make it important; make *him* important. You know, it might be a nice touch to slowly unroll a scroll as you list the statistics of your master's conquests. It would heighten the comedy and show your appreciation of Don Giovanni's extraordinary accomplishments."

Ponziani nodded excitedly, trying to absorb all that Casanova was telling him. Mozart returned to the harpsichord and listened to Casanova's directions, then added, "It's not a very difficult aria, Felice; you'll learn the notes quickly. Remember, when you sing, keep it lively, and be sure to watch me. Make it important, as Signor Casanova said, but don't let it become heavy or plodding. Do you understand?"

"Yes . . . I think so."

"Good. Then let's try it. We need to move on."

The members of the small orchestra returned to their seats, retuned their instruments and waited for Mozart to continue. The singers went back to their positions onstage.

"We'll begin with the new words Signor Casanova has written. Don Giovanni tries to explain his behavior to Donna Elvira, but when she won't believe him he tells her to listen to this 'honest man.' Then he sneaks away, ordering Leporello to tell her everything. I'll sing the recitatives for now until you've had a chance to learn them. Then when the recit ends, Leporello sings the aria."

Mozart quickly improvised an accompaniment on the harpsichord for the new words. When he finished, he pointed to Ponziani, who launched into the Catalogue Aria, enumerating his master's every dalliance, all to Donna Elvira's dismay. Caterina Micelli's facial expressions showed a perfect blend of amazement and disgust.

The scene was better, and Mozart smiled broadly. He leaned back, away from the harpsichord, and stretched over the velvet-topped rail separating the orchestra from the audience.

"Ponziani's quite good, don't you think?" he whispered, and Casanova agreed. When the aria ended, the orchestra applauded and Ponziani bowed to them.

"Excellent, excellent," Mozart said. "There are a few spots we'll need to work on, but that was very good. We go on."

With renewed energy, he gave a downbeat and the orchestra played. But when he cued the chorus of peasant girls and men celebrating Zerlina and Masetto's wedding, the stage was empty except for Madame Bondini—Zerlina—wearing a peasant's wedding dress and a woven wreath of flowers in her hair.

"Where's the chorus?" Mozart shouted impatiently, halting the music. A timid old man emerged from the backstage area.

"There is no chorus today, Maestro."

"What?"

"There is no chorus—"

"I heard you. Why is there no chorus?"

"Signor Bondini told them they wouldn't be needed today, Maestro."

"What does he know about when the chorus won't be needed? How am I supposed to rehearse without the chorus? Does he want to ruin the opera?"

"Would you like me to find Signor Bondini?" Casanova offered.

"No, no, no. It would take too long," said Mozart, defeated. "I'll just have to skip the chorus and go on to the next part of the scene."

Mozart absentmindedly played a sweet melody on the harpsichord.

"What's that?" asked Casanova.

"Oh . . . it's a tune that's been in my head. I think I'll use it for a serenade or something," Mozart said, stopping the theme to once again concentrate on his score.

"It's beautiful, very cheerful."

Mozart never heard the compliment. Clapping his hands, he addressed the singers in a raised voice. "We'll move on to just after Leporello leads Masetto and his friends away. We need Don Giovanni and Zerlina onstage now."

While he waited for the singers to get into place, he turned to Casanova.

"This is the scene where Don Giovanni tries to seduce Zerlina. I wanted it to be tender. She resists as long as she can, but when she gives in to his advances, I gave her a musical sigh—she sings '*Andiamo*'—so we feel her reluctance vanish. Then they sing together, with the parts intertwining."

"Which of their parts are intertwining?" Casanova smirked, but Mozart gave only a short laugh and got back to work.

Casanova again sat back in his seat and listened to the duet. The music captured the act of seduction perfectly, each measure, each note sequenced to convince the vulnerable Zerlina to succumb to Don Giovanni. Despite her protests—or maybe because of them—Don Giovanni pushes on, his pleas gradually intensifying, until, helpless, she relents. Casanova loved that moment. When she sang *"Andiamo,"* the youthful resignation mixed with anticipation deeply excited him.

But despite being engrossed in the music, he did notice that Madame Bondini—the Zerlina—spent the entire scene looking directly at Mozart and that, when she gave in to the Don's advances, she sang her acceptance to the conductor, never once looking at the real seducer. Something had to be done.

"It's beautiful, Mozart, beautiful," Casanova whispered.

"I like it too, but I sense you have another idea."

"You're coming to know me well." Casanova stood up. "I think the singers need to make the scene more believable."

"What do you suggest?"

"Well . . . it's hard to explain. Perhaps I could demonstrate."

Without waiting for permission, Casanova walked over to the creaky steps that had been built to allow easy access to the stage during rehearsals. With confidence he climbed onto the stage and introduced himself to Madame Bondini and Luigi Bassi, who watched as Casanova elegantly kissed Madame Bondini's hand.

"Now, if you wouldn't mind, Signor Bassi, I will act out your role. You stand near me and sing the notes. Perhaps there's something you can learn from an old but experienced man like me."

Bassi, still unhappy because the Catalogue Aria had been given to Felice Ponziani, sighed loudly.

Mozart started the orchestra and Bassi sang. Casanova, without effort or large gestures, took Madame Bondini's hand in his, caressed it, played with it gently, rubbing each finger in time with the music. She sang her part with feeling, her eyes glued this time to her partner. As the music intensified, Casanova moved his caresses farther up her arm, drawing her closer to him. He could smell her perfume, and the sweetness of her breath encouraged him to squeeze her pale white arm. When the music reached the moment that she relents, her "*Andiamo*" was a breathless plea for him to take her. She fell into his arms and let him embrace her. She pressed her body against his, never losing her breath or the rhythm. The duet was perfect, their movements timed exquisitely to the music. Mozart watched with admiration and jealousy. Standing as close as he could get to the action, Bassi's singing became more passionate. He leaned in, wanting to be in Casanova's place. In the wings, just offstage, Caterina Micelli, still costumed as Donna Elvira, watched the scene.

When the music ended, Madame Bondini was wrapped around Casanova, who was kneeling on one knee. Bassi was leaning over them, and Mozart was wiping a bead of sweat from his forehead.

Pasquale Bondini's voice, booming from the back of the auditorium, broke the frozen tableau onstage.

"That's enough for today."

His wife quickly let go of Casanova, who held on to her fingers for one extra, lingering second.

"Yes," she said, trying to be professional. "That will work better. Much better. Good. Thank you, Maestro; Signor Casanova. You were very helpful."

Bassi stood near Casanova, who noticed a slight bulge in the young singer's pants.

"Did you find my acting believable, Signor Bassi?"

"It looked realistic to me."

Casanova gently patted the twenty-two-year-old singer on the cheek. The young man blushed. "Seduction is an art, like singing," Casanova said. "It can be learned, but it needs to be practiced, preferably every day. We'll work on it. Don Giovanni has to own this stage, this world and the women who—thankfully—populate it."

Bassi remained onstage, in costume, desperately trying to revisualize and remember every move and moment of the scene he had just witnessed.

The rehearsal over, the musicians packed up their instruments and dispersed. Mozart gathered up the pages of his score, stopping occasionally to play the insistent melody running through his head.

"I hope I didn't overstep my place," Casanova interrupted.

"No, not at all. I think they learned from what you showed them."

"Good. Are you free for dinner this evening, Mozart?"

"Oh, no. I'm afraid I'm not. My friends the Dušeks are having a party at their villa. Perhaps you'd like to come?"

"I wouldn't want to impose."

"Don't be silly. You'll come as my guest. You'll like the people, musicians mostly—not very good musicians, you understand, but musicians. Anyway, my wife will be thrilled to meet you," he said, picking up his music and walking to the exit with Casanova.

"And I will be equally excited."

Mozart wasn't sure how Casanova meant that. "She's pregnant," Mozart said hesitantly.

"How wonderful."

"The party's at eight. Any fiacre will know the house. Ask for the Villa Bertramka."

"I'll be there. Thank you. How should I dress?"

"The Dušeks are formal. They like to show the world they have more wealth than the average musician."

"Very well, formal it shall be."

Arm in arm, they left the opera house. The late afternoon remains of a sunny day cast long shadows on the cobblestone streets.

"I think I'll go home and write down this melody before it drives me mad."

"Is there music in your head all the time?"

Mozart nodded.

"How lucky. Is it always your music, or do you hear other composers as well?"

"Mostly mine, though sometimes I'll hear a melody of Handel's or Bach's. But I get rid of it by improvising variations around it."

"Incredible."

"No more than your ability with women."

"Your flattery is charming."

"As is yours."

They had walked less than a block from the stage entrance of the opera house when a sweet voice called out: "Signor Casanova. Signor Casanova."

It was Caterina Micelli.

"What do you want?" Casanova asked.

"It's a bit embarrassing, but I was hoping you might coach me in the scene where Elvira is with the disguised Leporello."

"I have to go somewhere this evening with the Maestro," he explained. "I only have a few hours."

"It shouldn't take long. It's a short scene," she implored.

"Well, perhaps we could go to your room."

"That would be helpful. Thank you, Signor."

"I'll see you at the Dušeks' this evening," Casanova whispered to Mozart.

Mozart shook Casanova's hand and headed up the street toward the Three Lions Inn, oblivious to the people around him, who were shopping, or talking, or selling goods from makeshift carts. Mozart's steps were timed to the catchy tune rattling around in his head. He didn't see Caterina Micelli and her "acting coach" turn the corner and climb into the carriage Casanova had hired to wait for them.

Chapter Seven

⌒

The only sounds were the clacking of the horses' hooves and the rolling of the carriage's wooden wheels as it made its way through the streets of Prague. Constanze eased the boredom by silently counting the beats. She wore her most beautiful blue floor-length gown. The wide skirt took up most of the coach's upholstered seat, so Wolfgang, who was sitting next to her, had far less than half the bench. Constanze had tied a white satin bow around her waist, but she couldn't pull it as tight as she would have liked and as the proper style called for. She had spent the afternoon adjusting her makeup and white wig until they looked just the way she wanted, and the way she knew Wolfgang liked most. The wig made her look much taller, so she wore her flattest shoes to avoid towering over her husband.

The carriage slowed as it crossed over the ancient stones of the Charles Bridge. The cramped, congested atmosphere of Prague's old town vanished. Open expanses and large, almost palatial houses appeared. Each villa was surrounded by magnificent gardens, small copies of the ones at the royal palaces of Vienna and Versailles. The expansive houses were positioned at the end of circuitous paths. This was the part of Prague where the estates of the wealthy stood, immune from the crowding of the city itself. It was here the Dušeks made their home, at the magnificent Villa Bertramka.

The carriage rolled on. The silence between Wolfgang and her made Constanze nervous.

"Do you like my dress?"

"What?"

"I asked if you like my dress?"

"Yes . . . it's, it's very pretty."

The noisy carriage wheels filled the long pauses between spoken phrases. Constanze counted silently until she couldn't stand the tension any longer.

"What's the matter with you?" she asked abruptly.

"I'm sorry. What did you say? I wasn't listening."

"I noticed."

"What do you want?"

"I wanted to know what was bothering you. You seem so distracted."

"I was thinking."

"About what?"

"Nothing really; some thoughts about this afternoon."

"Tell me. I'd like to hear. We haven't been together much the last few days," said Constanze, moving closer to him. "I've missed you."

He looked out the coach's small oval window. The gray stone walls and iron gates surrounding the estates rolled by, one after the other. Constanze rested her hand on his thigh and gently rubbed the black velvet of his britches.

"Tell me," she whispered.

"Stanzi, the strangest thing happened to me today."

Constanze shifted, adjusting her skirt, moving closer to him on the overstuffed pillow bench. She reached her right hand around his neck and played with his ear, tenderly stroking the lobe. She could feel him relax and lean farther back into the cushions, into her arm.

"Tell me," she whispered again.

"When I came home today I wasn't tired. The rehearsal had been incredibly exciting. Casanova made some suggestions that brought Don Giovanni's character more to life. For the first time I felt as if this character could really exist . . . that the drama could work. Anyway, you were busy getting ready. I didn't want to disturb you, but I had to do something, so I thought I'd complete some more of the opera. I took out my music paper, poured a cup of coffee and sat at my chair, ready to work. But all I kept thinking of was *Figaro*. No matter what I did, I couldn't get those melodies out of my head. At first I found it amusing, but after a few minutes it became annoying. I stared at the music paper, pen in hand . . . but nothing came to my mind except *Figaro*."

"That's not so bad," she teased. "Salieri would give anything to have *Figaro* running through *his* head."

"No, Constanze, really. I kept hearing those melodies, happy and carefree. It flowed so easily. But then I started worrying I'd never be able to compose anything that good again. What if that was all I have in me? You know I haven't even thought about the overture for *Don Giovanni*."

"You're ridiculous. You should have taken a nap or talked to me."

"I didn't know what to do."

Mozart sat forward, pulling away from Constanze's hand. She stroked his back. "So what did you do?"

"After about an hour, I put the music sheets away. That's when it happened."

"What?"

"I decided to write a letter, to put down my thoughts. I thought it might clear my mind. I was midway through the second page when I stopped writing."

"Why?"

Wolfgang looked away, craning his neck to see the stars in the sky high above. Constanze couldn't see his tears.

"I was writing to my father asking for advice and guidance."

Constanze said nothing.

∞

As the Mozarts' carriage rolled to a stop at the Villa Bertramka, Casanova was admiring himself in the full-length mirror in his room at the Vltava Inn. Turning to the side, he glanced at his perfectly straight nose and his sculpted, well-shaven cheeks. As he stared, he lifted his chin so the beginning of a jowl that had appeared during the last few years stretched out and disappeared.

Dressing to look handsome and desirable took longer than it used to. But he still wore his well-tailored clothes to perfection. He spent an extra minute adjusting the folded collar of his shirt, making sure the creases were entirely visible above the embroidered silk vest. He looked at his gold pocket watch.

"Too early. I don't want to arrive before Mozart. That wouldn't be proper."

Casanova removed his brocade coat and gently laid it on the bed, brushing off some white powder that had fallen from the bottom curls of his wig.

"I should work on my memoirs. Details, can't forget the details."

A small round table near the window would serve well as a desk. He found some paper in his traveling case and took out a bottle of ink and a quill pen.

"My eyes are tired. I'd better light an extra candle."

With two candles burning, he sat at the makeshift desk and stared at the wall. The memories of his exciting afternoon flowed onto the virgin paper before him.

Prague: a city I have cherished. She, this angel, came into my life unannounced, innocently, without fanfare or pomp; only the sweet sound of her voice calling my name, the words echoing through the narrow streets of this great city.

The moment we stepped into the carriage our passions, instant and intense, took hold. We did all we could, but that was almost nothing at all in the small space. Even though my lovely partner squirmed and maneuvered to help me, our attempts were fruitless, and the coachman, attracted by the rocking motion, kept turning around, forcing us to further moderate our desperate efforts. For the rest of the ride we amused ourselves with hand play.

When we arrived at her lodging, a charming young serving girl, whose glance caught my eye, curtsied and took our cloaks and hats.

"We're going to my chamber to rehearse." The young girl smiled knowingly at me, giving my legs the added spring they needed to bound up the rickety flight of steps, chasing my lovely carriage partner.

Once in her chamber, I was astonished by the display of dresses carefully hung in her traveling case. The tools of her toilette—brushes, combs, makeup, wigs, perfumes—were neatly spread across a table. Shoes and delicate embroidered slippers by the dozen lined her closet floor.

There was no waiting or subtlety. She removed her dress and untied the laces of the corset that had kept her beautiful form from achieving its divine fullness. I gallantly helped her remove the last stays from the corset. Once loosened, it dropped harmlessly to the floor. She stood before me wearing only the purest white linen I had ever seen. Her ebony hair fell to her alabaster shoulders.

"Pretend you're Don Giovanni," she whispered. "Take me as he would."

What a wonderful request!

My excitement was visible. Without waiting, I reenacted a scene I had demonstrated earlier in the day at a rehearsal, first taking her hand, then her arm, then her entire body, gently caressing every inch of soft, white skin, all while whispering the most tender phrases that formed in my imagination.

We spent the next three hours—all too short a time—enjoying one another and a wide variety of physical pleasures, never resting, except to talk, or for her to sing softly to me. The excitement of this blissful play was heightened by her sweet voice, a pure soprano that floated into my ears and filled my whole being, often resurrecting me when I was lying limp. There was one aria in particular—she said it was from one of Handel's Italian operas—that made the hairs on my body stand erect and sent shudders across my back. How I have often wished for a way to have music accompany love without the inconvenience of hiring musicians, whose presence disrupts the intimacy of the act.

My nightingale was happily asleep when I arose, dressed and made my way downstairs, where the serving girl was waiting with my cloak and hat.

"Sir," she said timidly, "If you have the time, perhaps we could . . ."

The notion was sweet and tempting, but the hour was late and I still needed to bathe and dress before going to a grand party being given that very evening. I offered no answer, preferring to leave this house knowing another adventure could still be found within its walls.

Casanova put down his pen and sprinkled sand to dry the ink. He admired his fine handwriting. Pleased with the memories, he rolled up the sheet and stored it carefully in his traveling case. Taking his coat from the bed, he put it on, then adjusted the shoulders so the whole outfit looked the way he wanted. He blew out the candles, felt his way across the dark room and left to join the Mozarts at the Villa Bertramka.

Chapter Eight

⚭

Carriages passed through the imposing gates and down the gravel drive leading to the Villa Bertramka. Torches burned brilliantly, lighting the outside of the grand building and the entryways to the maze of spectacular gardens and wooded areas ringing the property.

Josefa liked to give parties. They made her home a center of Prague's social activity. She cast her parties with a mix of people who were likely to ignite a few sparks and intrigues that would be talked about for days. František went along, a silent, reluctant partner. Josefa believed it was the combination of atmosphere, food and characters that made a party succeed. A Dušek party was an event, and this night would be no different. Even the weather, which previously had been wet and chilly, cooperated. Gentle breezes blew, rustling the nearly dead leaves. The clear sky was lit by a full moon, which cast its light like a million shimmering blue candles across the lawns and gardens of the Villa Bertramka.

When the Mozarts' carriage stopped in front of the house's main entrance, Wolfgang, still in a fog, swung the door open himself, ignoring the waiting uniformed servant who stood nearby. He jumped down from the coach and extended his hand to help Constanze, who carefully climbed down the single step. Hand in hand, they walked toward the imposing entrance. Mozart stepped slightly faster than his wife, almost dragging her along behind him.

Inside the arched doorway, a servant took their cloaks. The house was ablaze with light; hundreds of candles—in sconces on the walls and in elaborate chandeliers, hanging from the beautifully painted ceilings—lit every room. The well-polished parquet floors reflected their glow. It was splendidly cheerful, and Mozart's mood improved the moment he walked in.

"Maestro and Madame Wolfgang Mozart," the majordomo announced.

The few guests within earshot turned and applauded, the women gently tapping their folded fans against the backs of their hands. Wolfgang pulled away from Constanze and bowed low with a flourish of his right hand. He was elegant in his red frock coat with the polished mother-of-pearl buttons.

"Wolfgang, it's so wonderful having you back in Prague," Josefa said, kissing him gently on each cheek. Her thin nose brushed against his. Standing inches away, he looked into her large dark eyes.

"It's more wonderful to be back in your house."

"I need to rest for a few minutes," Constanze whispered.

"Are you feeling ill?" Wolfgang asked.

"I'm fine. Just a little tired."

"Why don't you go up to my antechamber. There's a daybed in there," Josefa offered.

Constanze thanked her and climbed slowly up the circular marble stairs to the second floor.

"Well, that leaves you to me," Josefa whispered to Mozart. "Come, let me show you some of tonight's delicacies." She took his hand, playfully caressing it, and pulled him toward the large doors on one side of the room.

"Mozart," a deep voice barked. "Mozart, where do you think you're going? How rude you are."

Mozart spun around, yanking his hand away from Josefa. František Dušek, looking older than ever in the black suit he always wore, stood a few feet away across the foyer. There was a large crooked-looking grin on his face, accentuating the wrinkles in his brow. Mozart never understood why Josefa had married a man seventeen years her senior, but he had come to accept their relationship as something strange and unique.

"You. Why should I answer to you?"

"Because I love your music, teach it to my students and play it at all the time."

"You call what you do to a pianoforte 'playing'? If I'd played that way when I was a child, I would've become a teacher too."

"Touché," František laughed as they embraced.

"Listen, František. I hope you don't mind, but I invited a new friend to join us this evening."

"That's fine. Anyone is welcome. Who is he?"

"He's a gentleman visiting from Dux who's come to help with the opera. His name is the Chevalier de Seingalt. But, he's better known as Casanova."

"I've heard of him," František exclaimed proudly. "Well, that should add to the entertainment this evening." He was used to his wife's soirées becoming somewhat wild, especially when actors, writers and musicians were mixed in with the more staid noble and bourgeois Praguers.

"How thrilling," Josefa said.

"And Casanova has some special appeal to you, my dear?" František mumbled to her.

"Don't start, František," she warned, softly but firmly. "I was just going to show Wolfgang where the desserts are. You take care of the servants, or something else."

"I'll see to the music," František said, adjusting the front of his plain black coat.

After František was out of sight, Josefa pulled Mozart into a private room hidden behind thick red velvet drapes. It was a cozy, dimly lit room filled with overstuffed furniture. Dark wood bookcases lined the walls, each one piled high with music, mostly harpsichord pieces. Mozart strained to see if any of the scores were of his compositions, but it was hard to make out the small lettering on the leather spines. He sat down on the off-white love seat while Josefa prepared a small plate of chocolates from a tray on the mahogany desk. Mozart gazed out the window into one of the gardens.

"Remember how much fun we had in that pavilion?" Josefa said, noticing he was looking at a small stone building in the corner of the garden.

"You're making more of that episode than it deserves."

"You're not being fair."

"I'm being honest."

"It wasn't as innocent as you'd like everyone to believe."

"What happened that evening wasn't what you've led everyone to believe either," he replied with as much anger as he could find.

"You're too hard on me." She sat down on the love seat, her wide forest-green skirt covering part of his leg. When she leaned toward him to slide a canapé into his mouth, he noticed the space between her ample breasts. Josefa's hair was curled, thoroughly powdered and piled high on her head.

"Is it good?" she whispered.

"Wonderful."

"Would you like more?"

He nodded slowly, closing his eyes as if awaiting his first kiss. "How can such a naïve child write the music he writes?" she wondered. On his previous visits to Prague there had been rumors about them, especially after they were seen leaving the garden pavilion late one night during a party. František suspected the rumors were true, but the musician in him had to forgive Mozart, although the talk had increased tensions between him and Josefa.

"I've missed you, Josefa. I've missed your friendship."

She leaned closer to him, grazing her breast against his right arm.

"What would Constanze say?"

"I don't know. It's been . . ." He stopped, seeming to lose his train of thought.

"It's been what? You can tell me, Wolfgang. I've come to know Constanze. Maybe I could help."

"It's been difficult."

"Why? She seems so happy. She's pregnant. Karl's doing well. What's difficult?"

"Ever since my father's last visit to Vienna, Constanze and I argue much more. You know my father never forgave me for marrying her. He hated her; he hated her family. They weren't good enough. He wanted me to marry someone who could help my career."

Josefa gently rubbed his leg. Mozart wanted to pull away but didn't want the pleasant sensation to stop.

"My father didn't hide his feelings, which made her try even harder to show him we belonged together. It's as if she had to prove she was responsible. When he visited Vienna, I tried to make it a good time. One night we had a little musicale. Haydn was there, and we played through the string quartets I'd composed in his honor. When we were done, Haydn turned to my father and told him I was the greatest composer he'd ever met. But when Constanze and my father started arguing it ruined the whole evening. They even argued about who was more responsible for my success."

"They're proud of you, Wolfgang."

She slid another sweet into his mouth. He swallowed.

"But why did they have to dislike each other?"

"What about you, Wolfgang? How do you feel about Constanze?"

The pause was longer than Josefa had expected.

"Do you love her?"

"Sometimes," he whispered. "When she holds me . . . at night . . . and I look into her eyes . . . then I remember why I married her. But the rest of the time, I can't forget the way she fought with my father and I wonder . . ."

"Would your father have been any more forgiving if you'd married anyone else?"

"What do you mean?"

"If you'd married me, for example. Would your father have been as critical?"

"My father envied you and František. He was a poor, provincial musician who wanted to be an aristocrat. That's all he ever wanted. He liked the way you live and the way you handle the politics of life. He was good at that, too. He would have enjoyed this party."

Wolfgang's anguish at once upset and pleased Josefa. In his anguish she saw opportunity, a chance to escape the boredom of her own marriage.

"Have you composed anything new for me to sing?"

"I didn't know you were still singing. Last time I was here you were talking about giving up the concerts and staying home."

"I changed my mind. František was teaching so much it was easier to continue singing and giving concerts. Sitting at home bores me. I missed the excitement of the stage. But, you haven't answered my question. Did you compose anything for me?"

"Well . . ."

Mozart escaped finishing the answer; for at that moment he heard František's deep voice booming in the next room.

"He has to be here somewhere. Josefa was going to get him something to eat. They couldn't have gone far."

Josefa bounced up as quickly as her full skirt allowed. Mozart reacted more slowly, watching her smooth the dress material. Before anyone could enter their hiding place, Josefa walked out between the curtains. Mozart stayed behind to eat a few more chocolates, then followed her into the large hall.

"Ah, František. I see you've met my friend Casanova," said Mozart. "And what a pleasant surprise it is to find you here as well, Signor Bondini. Well, this evening's showing more and more promise."

Bondini and Casanova greeted Mozart, who was enjoying the moment's awkwardness. Josefa Dušek stood next to her husband, with Bondini and Casanova on either side of them.

"Mozart, where's your wife?" Casanova asked. "I've been looking forward to meeting her."

"She's resting in my antechamber. Perhaps I could take you to her, Chevalier," Josefa offered.

"It would be my honor and pleasure to follow you anywhere, Madame," Casanova answered. František watched his wife walk across the room arm in arm with Casanova and left, red-faced, to help his musicians prepare.

Mozart was alone with Bondini. "How was the rehearsal today?" the impresario asked.

"Passable, although it would've been better if the chorus had been there."

"We can't have them standing around waiting. It's too costly."

"Then next time perhaps someone should ask the composer if they'll be needed. By the way, is Madame Bondini with you this evening?"

"Yes."

"Good. I have a few corrections I want to give her for the second aria. That way we won't have to waste time 'standing around' at the next rehearsal."

"Perhaps I could tell her for you."

"No. I'd rather do it. She responds best to me . . . when we're alone. Signor Bondini, if you'll excuse me, I should see how my wife is feeling."

On his way out of the room, Mozart could hear the wind octet tuning. Taking a glass of champagne from a waiter standing near the door, he gulped it down, then returned the empty, fluted crystal glass to the tray. Bowing to those guests—mostly barons, counts and countesses whose estates neighbored Bertramka—who recognized him, he walked across the room, pausing to take canapés from waiters who crossed his path.

In a room on the other side of the house, much like the one where he and Josefa had shared their few private moments, Mozart discovered Casanova seated snugly on a couch between his wife and Josefa.

"Mozart," Casanova said, "you didn't tell me we'd be surrounded by such beauty."

"At the moment only you are surrounded by such beauty, Monsieur le Chevalier."

"Wolfgang," Constanze interjected, "Signor Casanova was telling us about how the words and the music in the new opera are paired so beautifully. How did you put it, Chevalier?"

"Your music breathes life into Da Ponte's words, Mozart," Casanova said. "It's as if your notes can change the meanings of his words. Your music makes sadness sadder, joy more joyful, and love . . . and love . . . love becomes more passionate."

"And passion. What does his music do to passion?" Josefa asked.

Casanova looked toward a sparkling flame atop one of the candles in the chandelier, as if he knew that the shadows from shimmering light made his face look more handsome. Mozart noticed Constanze staring uncomfortably at her shoes, while Josefa was looking at Casanova's sparkling eyes.

"Passion, my dear lady. Passion is the combination of lust and intellect."

"Are you saying my music doesn't attain passion because it has no lust, only love?"

"Just the opposite," Casanova countered. "Your music is passionate because it combines the physical and the emotional. You give characters a way to reveal their passions, especially your women."

"For example . . ." Josefa pursued.

"Take Donna Elvira. Her aria in the first act is the result of passions: love, lust, even hatred. Women today are free to express themselves, to be emotional, lustful, excited. The truly passionate women we encounter are the ones we remember most."

"How observant," Josefa noted with delight. "Signor Casanova, you are welcome in my house anytime. I enjoy sharing ideas with men."

"Then we shall call you the Madame de Pompadour of Prague," Casanova said as he stood up from the love seat, sliding himself from beneath Josefa's skirt. "And having met that famous French courtesan, I can assure you, my dear Madame Dušek, you are far more beautiful and intelligent than she. Wolfgang, what do you think about all this?"

But Mozart was no longer listening to the conversation. "Do you hear that?" he asked softly.

"What?" the others said in unison.

"The music."

Josefa, Casanova and Constanze strained to hear, but all they could make out was the distant, muffled sounds of the woodwinds.

"What about it?" Constanze asked.

"It's my music. That's *Figaro*."

Without waiting, he walked out, drawn by the music, and retraced his steps back through the rooms.

The wind band—pairs of oboes, clarinets, horns and bassoons—was set up at the center of the Dušeks' music room, an airy room with a thick Oriental rug at its center and the walls trimmed in gold and blue. An exquisite pianoforte made of polished cherry with an ivory filigree inlay and a hand-painted harpsichord filled one corner of the room. Soft chairs, sofas and love seats were arranged in a semicircle, allowing listeners to be close to the music without distracting the musicians.

Mozart burst into the room, moving through the guests to the front of the band. Every head turned in his direction, and the wind band abruptly stopped playing. The thirty or so guests paused, looked at him, then applauded.

"No. Don't stop. Go on. I want to hear more." Mozart ordered.

The first oboist gave the downbeat and the music resumed. Mozart stood near them, eyes closed. Constanze and Josefa, who had just come in, escorted by Casanova, noticed that Mozart's right hand was moving in small circles, conducting, not for the musicians but for himself.

The wind octet played three arias from *The Marriage of Figaro*. Each one received warm applause. After the third, Mozart went over to the band and looked at the music propped up on the carved wood stands. Silence. All eyes were on him.

"Quite good. Very good. Who did this arrangement?"

"It's mine, Maestro," the first clarinetist said timidly.

"And you are?"

"Sedlak, Maestro."

"Well, Herr Sedlak, you're stealing from me. Out-and-out thievery!"

"Maestro, I meant no harm. It's just that it seemed a shame that these melodies are only heard when the whole opera is performed. This way at least they can be enjoyed more often and by more people."

"Bravo!" Casanova shouted. "Music for the masses."

Mozart looked to the rear of the room where Casanova now stood, then back at Sedlak.

"There's your verdict, Sedlak. Play on."

The guests applauded, and echoed Casanova's bravo.

The band started playing again. Casanova walked over to Mozart, and Bondini joined them.

"You know, Mozart, the melodies from *Figaro* are lovely played by the wind band. It's a pity there's no way to use the arrangement."

"Who says there isn't?"

"Why couldn't you use it in *Don Giovanni*?" Casanova suggested.

"Exactly what I was thinking!" Mozart said.

"Don Giovanni's a nobleman. He's a man who indulges his senses. Excess is his way. It would be natural for him to have a wind band play at supper."

"You mean the supper at the end of the opera, when he's dining alone?" Mozart asked.

"Yes."

"You don't think it would seem ridiculous for him to have a band playing just for himself?"

"No. It's the way any man with his style would live, if he could. He'd indulge himself. It would add to his larger-than-life appearance."

"But that will add to the cost of the production," Bondini protested. "It will mean extra musicians, extra costumes. I can't agree to this."

"Only a few costumes," Mozart explained. "We can use the wind players from the orchestra and put them on a corner of the stage."

"They should play the music from *Figaro*," Casanova added. "Don Giovanni would appreciate it. It would make his meal taste better. It would help to highlight the relationship between master and servant, especially since Figaro is a servant who outsmarts his master."

"Are you trying to close my theater?" Bondini asked. "I don't like this, not at all."

"Don't worry, Pasquale," Casanova advised. "It will work out."

"I'll write the wind band into the scene before our next rehearsal," Mozart said. Grumbling, Bondini left in search of a glass of champagne.

The Dušeks' wind band paused for a moment, then began to play a lively minuet. The stiff, liveried servants hastily moved some of the chairs out of the way to clear an area for dancing. The guests paired off as Mozart and Casanova watched from the side. The brightly colored dresses swirled over the elaborate patterns in the Oriental rug.

"Dance with me." Josefa grabbed Mozart and pulled him into the center of the floor. He bowed, she curtsied. She intertwined her slender fingertips with his as they executed the formal dance steps of the minuet.

"They look good together," František commented to Constanze.

He took another glass of champagne from a servant standing near the door and slowly walked out of the room. Constanze watched as Wolfgang and Josefa danced elegantly. Each time they moved toward each other in time to the music, Josefa pulled him a little closer. Soon there was no space at all between her chest and his. Ignoring the music, they slowly shuffled their feet in three-four time.

"Madame," Casanova said to Constanze, "I'm not as agile as your husband, but perhaps I could entertain you on the dance floor."

"Thank you. You're most gracious, Chevalier."

Casanova bowed his head, then removed a white linen handkerchief from the cuff on his right sleeve and handed it to Constanze. She dabbed the tears from her eyes and slipped it into her bosom.

"I will keep it here to remind me of a truly gentle, noble man."

"In a different place, at a different time, I assure you I would find a way to get my fine linen handkerchief back from its current resting place. For now I'll have to content myself with this dance."

Constanze blushed and let Casanova lead her to the dance area. At first they were back to back with Mozart and Josefa, but as the music's momentum picked up, the dancing became more animated, with a little bit of bumping, some accidental, some not. More than once Constanze felt Casanova's hand on her back. She enjoyed it. It made her feel alive, young and, most of all, not pregnant. As they danced, she noticed the other women sneaking looks at Casanova, who was a superb dancer.

Turning to the center of the room in time to the end of a cadence, the men bowed low to their partners. Constanze looked over the bent heads, searching for Wolfgang's bright red coat. Mozart and Josefa were gone. As the next minuet began, she kept glancing toward the doors, hoping Wolfgang would reappear. But he didn't. The music played on; the dancing continued. At the next pause, Constanze curtsied to Casanova and quickly walked off the dance floor. Unbending himself from a deep bow, he followed her out of the room.

"Are you all right?"

"Oh . . . Signor Casanova. I'm fine. Thank you."

"I hate to think my dancing made you leave so suddenly."

"No. You're a splendid dancer. In fact, every woman would like to be your partner."

"You flatter me. Is there anything I can do for you?"

"Did you notice where Wolfgang went? He seems to have disappeared."

"I didn't."

"Well, if you'll excuse me, I think I'll look for him. You know, with all the food the Dušeks have, he's probably gone into the kitchen to get a head start on supper."

"Your husband is a man of fine tastes. I envy him."

"Don't."

Casanova watched Constanze gather up her flowing skirt and walk into the center hall. Through the archway he could see her repeatedly poke her hand angrily into the thick velvet draperies, hoping—or fearing—she'd uncover her husband's hiding place.

"Giacomo!"

Casanova recognized Bondini's voice.

"Giacomo. I wanted to tell you how pleased I am you agreed to come help with this opera. I knew you'd be able to get to the heart of the problem and give me a show that will help my company make its mark."

"You're assuming too much, Pasquale. You give me the benefit because you know my parents were in the theater, and because I'm Italian. But you don't seem to value the treasure you have in Mozart. That's genius beyond anything I've ever encountered."

"Just another composer. Without a good libretto and good singers he'd be like all the others. I'd still rather have Salieri, but he's not interested in Prague, only Vienna and Paris."

Before Casanova could continue the discussion, a servant wearing a coat decorated with intertwined gold braids sewn onto the left shoulder announced that supper was being served. Casanova and Bondini joined the other guests making their way into the dining room. At its center a long table was covered from end to end with platters overflowing with mutton, pheasant, roasted vegetables, breads and desserts.

Casanova looked around the room, hoping to see Mozart's cherubic smile. As he surveyed the crowd his eyes locked with Constanze's, who was conducting the same search from the other side of the room. Before Casanova could make his way over to her, František Dušek snuck up behind her.

"What's the matter, Constanze? You look unhappy."

"Oh no. Everything's lovely."

"Have some food. I'm sure your husband is too busy to make certain you're well fed."

With a few subtle hand gestures, František ordered one of the servants to prepare two plates filled with samples of all the foods. The plates were placed on a small round table in the bay of a window that looked out onto the gardens. František helped Constanze into her chair, then sat down opposite her. A single candle burned between them.

While they ate, he told her in great detail about his students and the concerts he and Josefa were planning. But Constanze didn't hear him. Distracted, she played with her food, picking at the meat. Every time someone came into the room, she'd anxiously look toward the door. František droned on.

"František," she interrupted, "doesn't Josefa's behavior bother you?"

A fatigued expression crossed his face.

"It does . . . it does . . . But I've learned to accept. A man can't own a woman. Those days are over, I assure you."

"But she acts this way right in front of you, in your home."

"It's never as simple as it appears. Josefa and I have our music. You should hear her sing the concert aria Wolfgang wrote for her. Audiences cheer. I like accompanying her. I suppose that's our form of love. Our music-making is still good. Josefa's a strong woman. You know, Constanze, just the other day she mentioned how she can't understand how you cope with Wolfgang . . . I mean he's with those Italian singers all the time, and you know what they say about women like that. 'If I were Constanze,' she said, 'I'd keep a close eye on that man.'" He finished his wine. "Constanze, if you'll excuse me, I have some other guests I must greet."

František carefully folded his linen napkin and placed it on his empty plate. Constanze remained alone at the table, unable to eat.

On the other side of the room Bondini and Casanova found a small table and sat down to dine together. Casanova sat so he could see the door and Constanze at the same time.

"Where is Madame Bondini?" Casanova asked.

"She went for a walk in the gardens. She loves to explore gardens."

"To the gardens," Casanova toasted, raising his crystal goblet of red wine. "What a delightful claret."

Bondini, his mouth full of food, nodded in agreement. In the music room the woodwind band played a delicate serenade.

"Do you hear that, Pasquale?"

Bondini stopped chewing long enough to hear a phrase of the music. "What about it?"

"It proves Mozart's point."

"What point?"

"Music makes an excellent accompaniment to a meal. Were I still in the stage of life where I could settle down and have a household, I would find the money to have an orchestra play during evening meals. That's one of the joys of mankind."

"You'd grow tired of it, as you have of everything and everyone else in your life."

"I don't think so. For the last few months I've been working on my memoirs, and as I write, I realize how many chances I had to settle down, to marry. I wonder why I never did."

"You enjoy the hunt too much."

"It can be lonely."

"I'll never know," Bondini said with resignation.

"And I'll never know the feeling of growing old with someone whose only interest is my happiness."

"If you find a woman like that, let me know."

Casanova looked away from Constanze and put a piece of perfectly roasted mutton in his mouth.

"*Eccellènte!*" Bondini exclaimed as he washed the last morsel of food down with a gulp of red wine. "Giacomo, would you like some chocolate?"

"Nothing sweet for me, just yet."

Across the room Constanze stared out the window into the gardens. While Bondini was busy piling his plate with chocolates, berries and whipped cream, Casanova made his way around the serving table to her.

"We seem to keep meeting."

She didn't respond.

"It looks like a beautiful garden."

Constanze nodded slowly.

"I once visited a garden in Salerno. It had every flower imaginable, all with different colors and scents; and there were fountains gently spraying cool water, and mossy grottoes that allowed you to hide . . . from the sun. And the pathways in this Eden were made of vines, vines laden with grapes. I spent many happy hours in that garden."

"We had a garden at my home," she said. "It was small, but you could walk in it, and think. When we first met, Wolfgang would hide there. When

I'd near his hiding place, he'd jump out and hold me around the waist, swearing he'd never let go."

"Would you like to go for a walk in this garden?" Casanova asked.

"I shouldn't."

"Just a walk. It's a warm evening."

"Perhaps the night air will make me feel better."

"The garden air can be refreshing."

Chapter Nine

ome with me."

Without waiting for the minuet to end, Josefa Dušek pulled Mozart off the dance floor and out into the maze of gardens encircling the Villa Bertramka. He followed uncertainly, filled with misgivings. He tried to catch Constanze's eye to give her a signal, or to blow a kiss to her. But he couldn't see her through the dancers.

Josefa tugged at him impatiently, and he went with her. Teasingly she lifted her heavy skirts, backing carefully through the paths and flower beds, always facing him, keeping two steps between them.

"You love me," she taunted.

"Nothing of the sort."

"Of course you do. I'm everything Constanze will never be."

"That's unfair . . ."

"But not untrue."

"We shouldn't be out here."

His protest was weak, and he could feel himself drawn toward her. Josefa turned a corner on the well-groomed dirt path and backed up until she was leaning against a large tree.

"Embrace me."

"Not here. Not now."

Josefa played with the lace on her dress.

"You didn't answer my question before."

"Which question?"

"Did you compose anything for me to sing?"

"I've been trying to finish the opera, so I haven't composed—"

"That's no excuse. You always work on more than one piece at a time. Besides, I don't want an opera, just a song or an aria. Something I can sing at concerts so I'll think of you. I sing better when I think of you."

"We're both married. Why do you taunt me?"

"Because you're you and I want you to write something for me, now."

She laughed, trying to make her resonant voice sound lighter, younger and more girlish.

"What?"

"Compose an aria for me right now."

"Do you think arias magically materialize for me?"

"Yes, and you will write one for me."

Josefa skipped past him, pulling him with her down the path.

"We'll go into the pavilion in the corner of the garden. No one will bother us. I'll lock the door. You can compose, and then . . ."

Mozart watched her undo the silk purple lacing on her bodice, slowly pulling it through the eyelets. The top of her dress loosened, revealing her soft skin. The scent of sweet perfume was released into the night air. Mozart felt his knees wobble as she dropped the lace to the ground. He thought of picking it up, but instead followed her down the path.

A single lantern burned at the entrance to the white stone pavilion. Josefa opened the ornately carved wood door and went in. Mozart was right behind her. Three large standing candelabra with tall candles lit the small room. Two plain wood chairs and a writing table were at its center. On the table sat a stack of music paper, a quill and a bottle of ink. Josefa quickly pulled the door shut, locked it and slipped the key into her dress.

"You had this planned all along?"

Josefa nodded. "I'll be your inspiration."

Mozart took off his red coat, loosened the white collar of his shirt, unbuttoned his embroidered vest and sat down at the table. Josefa pulled the other chair closer and sat next to him. She caressed his back tenderly as he leaned forward to dip the quill in the ink. Carefully he drew a G clef on the music sheet's first line.

"What will you call it?"

"Shh."

Josefa leaned back and watched as his right hand flew over the page, scratching, dipping, then scratching again. The black dots and scrawny lines seemed to flow effortlessly onto the page as phrase after phrase materialized. Mozart was oblivious to everything around him.

∞

Not far away, in a small pine grove, Casanova and Constanze sat on a white wrought-iron bench.

"Are the stories about you true?" she asked.

"How do you know about me?"

"People talk."

"Some stories are true, and some aren't. My life's been filled with adventures, and truths often become larger than life when they're retold. I never correct the tales that are especially hard to believe. It would be unkind to those who want to believe in them."

"Have you ever been in love?"

"Always."

"That's impossible." Her girlish giggle charmed him.

"No. It's very possible—you simply have to know what you mean by 'in love.'"

"What do you mean?"

Casanova took her tiny hand in his and looked into her dark eyes.

"I love all women and am always in love with some woman, somewhere. But the love I have known is usually brief. Maybe I've never allowed it to develop into something more permanent, but I've often thought I wasn't the kind of man who could stay in love with one woman. And you, Madame Mozart . . . Constanze . . . are you in love?"

Constanze shifted uncomfortably on the bench. Until that moment she hadn't noticed Casanova's other hand resting on her skirt.

"It depends on what *you* mean by 'in love.'"

He smiled.

"Are you in love with your husband?"

"I love Wolfgang. He's like a sweet child."

"But?"

"But a woman sometimes needs maturity, and Wolfgang hates being an adult. He had no childhood, only performances to show off his talents, like a well-trained animal. He's still trying to live the childhood he never had."

"But his music is so mature, so complex. To my ear it's simply amazing."

"He becomes a different person when he composes."

"Do you love him at those times?"

"It's impossible to love him then. He goes to a private world, a place where ideas come to him out of thin air. No one can get near him then; even his father couldn't."

"You disliked his father?"

"He hated me."

"And now that he's dead your husband . . ."

"He's unsure . . . uncertain."

"What do you mean?"

"I don't think he knows if he wants to be a child or an adult."

"Does he love you?"

Constanze shifted on the bench. Her corset was tight and was digging into her pregnant belly.

"Signor Casanova, would you mind if we walked some more?"

"Whatever you wish, but you didn't answer my question?"

"I don't think he knows, and I certainly don't. But for now . . ."

She never finished the thought. Casanova saw her glance at her stomach. He stood up and gallantly extended a hand to her. Rising, she held his hand and let him lead her down the path. They walked in silence.

The light from flickering torches cast eerie shadows all around them. As they neared an intersection of two paths, Casanova noticed something lying near the base of a tree. As they approached, he deftly tried to kick it out of sight, but Constanze had already seen it, and she bent over to pick it up.

"What is it?"

"It's a lace from a woman's dress."

"Strange things happen in gardens," Casanova said, trying to sound lighthearted.

"It's from Madame Dušek's dress."

"How can you be certain? Let me see it."

Constanze handed the lace to Casanova, who held it up to the flickering light, pretending to examine it. He put it to his nose and sniffed.

"I don't believe this is Madame Dušek's perfume."

"You're a dear man, Signor Casanova, and a fine actor, but you don't have to protect me. I'm sure you're no stranger to such situations."

Casanova gave the lace back to Constanze. His eyes had lost their sparkle. Constanze rolled the lace into a ball, squeezed it into her fist and threw it to the ground. Casanova picked it up.

"Marriage, Chevalier, is itself a difficult situation. But it's worse when you're married to a man who can extricate himself from any situation by being charming or by spinning some melody. Wolfgang hasn't yet learned that life isn't like one of his operas; not every difficult situation can be made better with a happy ensemble set to a beautiful tune leading to a perfect resolution."

"Then maybe he needs to be taught," he whispered, leaning forward so their faces were almost touching.

He smiled and took Constanze's hand. Quickly they walked through the gardens, following paths that wound in seemingly random patterns. In the distance they could hear Josefa's soprano voice struggling to negotiate some difficult musical phrases. The music was punctuated by bursts of a man's muffled laughter.

Constanze and Casanova stopped and listened.

"This way," he beckoned, pointing down a dark path.

He hurried ahead, leaving Constanze, who had to lift her heavy skirt, to follow a few feet behind. The path ended at the white pavilion. The singing and the laughter grew louder. Casanova reached the pavilion and tried to see in, but the little round window was too high. He leaned against the door and listened.

"Mozart," he whispered, knocking softly on the door. "Mozart, it's me, Giacomo. Open up, hurry."

But by then Constanze had caught up with him. Forcefully she pounded on the door.

"Wolfgang. Wolfgang! Open this door right now."

The noise inside the pavilion stopped. Constanze banged again. After a moment of barely audible scurrying, a key was inserted in the lock, and the door opened. Mozart and Josefa poked their heads through the small crack.

"Constanze! What are you doing out in the garden, and with Signor Casanova?" Mozart said, stepping out of the pavilion and closing the door behind him.

"Your wife needed some fresh air," Casanova said.

"And what were you and Josefa doing locked in the pavilion?" Constanze demanded.

"I was composing."

"It's true," Josefa chimed in from behind the closed door. "He was composing an aria for me."

"Here's the proof," Mozart said, holding up four filled pages of music paper he'd been hiding behind his back. Wanting to believe him, Constanze took the pages and leaned closer to the lantern to examine them. He stood right behind her, looking over her shoulder at the new aria. The ink was still wet.

"It's quite good, I think," he said immodestly. "She locked me in the pavilion and wouldn't let me out until I'd written an aria for her. I agreed with only one condition: she has to sing it tonight for the guests."

Inside the pavilion Josefa couldn't believe her ears, although she was confident Mozart would never actually force her to sing the aria.

"But there's no accompaniment," Constanze pointed out.

"Yes there is, but it's still in my head." Mozart boasted.

While Constanze studied the manuscript, Mozart slipped back into the pavilion to retrieve his coat. When he came out, he put his arm around Constanze's waist and kissed her gently on the cheek.

"You see, nothing but an aria," he said as they walked away from the pavilion, matching steps while swaying from side to side. Josefa Dušek was still hidden behind the door. Casanova pushed it open and strode into the pavilion.

"I'm not properly clothed, Signor Casanova."

"Perhaps I could be of assistance."

"I don't see how, unless you'd be kind enough to return to the villa and ask one of my servants to meet me here."

"I think this is all you need." Casanova dangled the purple lace on his extended fingers.

"Thank you," she said, taking the lace from him.

Casanova turned away as Josefa adjusted her dress. "May I escort you back to the house?"

"I'd enjoy that. You're more of a gentleman than I'd imagined."

"One can be an adventurer *and* a gentleman."

"A perfect match."

"The Mozarts?" he questioned.

"No. An adventurer who's a gentleman. Signor Casanova, perhaps you'd be interested in completing what Mozart can never seem to complete?"

"With all respect, Madame, I think I'd rather hear the new aria. May I escort you?"

She took his arm as they strolled down the path to the villa. Inside, the other guests were milling around as the servants rearranged the music room so the clavier and a music stand were at one end of the room and the chairs and love seats arranged in a semicircle facing them. František stood near the French doors, urging the guests to take seats. When Josefa and Casanova came into the house, her husband clapped his hands to get everyone's attention. Mozart watched from the adjoining antechamber, anticipating the challenge awaiting him and the fun of the game he had set in motion.

"Ladies and gentlemen, dear friends," František announced, silencing the audience. "We're in for a delightful surprise. My good friend Maestro Mozart has honored us with a new aria which he has just written, and he has asked my wife to sing it for us."

Applause greeted this pronouncement. Josefa, standing nervously near her husband, smiled wanly. Casanova slipped unobtrusively into an empty seat in the second row.

"František, where's Mozart? What's this all about?" Josefa whispered.

"He's in the other room. When he came in he said you'd been rehearsing in the pavilion and you were going to sing his new aria. So I called everyone together to listen."

Josefa Dušek didn't wait to hear any more. Angry at Mozart for carrying the joke to this extent, she rushed into the antechamber to confront him.

"Have you gone mad? I never said I would sing the aria tonight."

"But you must have heard me tell Constanze and Casanova at the pavilion?"

"I thought it was one of your jokes. Oh, Wolfgang, how could you?"

"I had to make up a story or Constanze would have thought we were doing something in the pavilion. I couldn't let that happen. Besides, the aria's not hard. You can sing it."

He handed her the music. "I'll accompany you. The aria's expressive. Follow me. I'll play your line as well as the accompaniment to help you. Let's go. They're waiting."

Greeted by warm applause, Mozart walked confidently to the clavier, and paused to wait for Josefa to take her place at the music stand. They bowed to the audience. Nervously she looked at the music. It looked so much more complicated than it had a few minutes earlier in the pavilion.

"I'll play a short introduction, then I'll cue you when to start," he whispered. "Friends," he continued, speaking louder, "earlier this evening our hostess, Madame Dušek, asked me to compose an aria for her. At first I was uninspired. But then, an idea came to me and I wrote this. As you'll hear, it's in two parts. Don't be misled by the sad beginning; it's merely an introduction to the more ecstatic section. One other point: I haven't yet had time to compose the orchestra part, so I'll accompany on the clavier . . . I'll make it up as we go along."

Laughter and applause filled the room.

"What's it called?" František called out.

"*Bella mia fiamma, addio,*" Mozart answered.

A nameless baron seated next to Casanova asked him if he understood the title.

"It means, 'Farewell, my beautiful flame,'" he said, casting an eye toward Constanze, whose expression changed from smiling to frowning.

Mozart played the brief, sad introduction. Looking up from the keys, he nodded to Josefa, who sang the aria's first, plaintive notes. Mozart filled in the sections between her phrases with the music that would eventually become the orchestra part. With great difficulty, and more than a few wrong entrances and wobbly notes, she stumbled through the slow introduction. But when the introduction ended and the aria burst into its faster, more passionate section, the good feelings in the room vanished. František grimaced as his wife stumbled over the phrases, singing a series of wrong notes, creating dissonant clashes with the clavier.

"No, that's a C-sharp," Mozart corrected out loud, while continuing to play.

Her mistakes became more frequent and his corrections became nastier and more abrupt. It became clear she couldn't sight-read an aria as difficult as this. From his seat in the second row, Casanova could see the strain on Josefa's face. He was intrigued to see this self-possessed woman and experienced performer fall apart so quickly in the face of Mozart's harsh corrections.

"Don't slow down. Accent! Don't miss the accents! It's slurred, not staccato."

They stumbled to the end of the aria. Josefa was in tears. The moment she sang the last note, she ran out of the room. Mozart stood at the clavier looking at her. The audience sat still, silently watching the drama unfolding. It was not the performance anyone had anticipated.

"Maestro," a sweet voice called out from the back of the room. Mozart turned and saw Caterina Bondini standing in the last row near her husband. "Maestro," she repeated, "your aria is beautiful . . . inspired, and it would sit perfectly in my vocal range. If it wouldn't upset anyone, perhaps you'd let me try to sing it?"

Mozart smiled and extended his hands as if to lift her over the audience to the front of the room. He could see the grin on Casanova's face and the angry flashes bursting from Pasquale Bondini's eyes. Caterina Bondini walked around the seated audience and stood at the clavier next to Mozart. Polite applause welcomed her as she took a few moments to study the handwritten vocal line. Her shimmering red dress and striking white wig seemed to brighten the room.

"If you have any questions, Signora," Mozart offered, "I would be honored to coach you."

"No. I think I understand. If I need help I'll turn to you. Whenever you're ready, Maestro."

Mozart bowed and returned to the clavier. Before beginning the short introduction, he looked at Caterina Bondini and smiled. She closed her eyes and put one finger to her lips, as if to throw him a kiss. He guided her through the changes of tempo with subtle hand and eye movements. She was an excellent sight reader, and she negotiated the slow section without problem. As the fast second part began, Mozart used his right hand to conduct her while playing the accompaniment with his left. To Casanova the gestures looked strangely like caresses. To Pasquale Bondini, they seemed insulting and obvious.

Except for one or two spots where the notes rushed together, Caterina Bondini sang the demanding aria well. In her bedroom on the second floor, Josefa Dušek could hear Caterina Bondini's voice. Angry and humiliated, she sat at her dressing table staring into the mirror. Venomous thoughts of revenge repeatedly popped into her mind.

Anthony Rudel

František, who had followed her to the room, tried to hold her in his arms. "You have nothing to be upset about."

"What do you know? I hate him. I hate Wolfgang!"

"No you don't. You're upset. You love him, the way we all do. You'll forgive him in the morning."

"I hate him! Send them all home. I don't want anyone in my home."

In the music room, Caterina Bondini had completed the aria and was enjoying the rousing reception. Leaning against Mozart, she could feel him rubbing her back as they bowed. In the last row of the music room, Pasquale Bondini fumed. The applause continued until František returned.

"My friends," he announced. "Josefa and I would like to thank you all for coming this evening. We hope you've enjoyed the entertainment."

"To our hosts," Casanova shouted.

His cheer was repeated by the other guests, who then began filing out of the music room and into the center hall, where the servants were waiting with their cloaks. Mozart stood near the clavier accepting the congratulations of guests passing him as they left. Pasquale Bondini grabbed his wife's arm and pulled her away from the clavier, angrily muttering to her in Italian. She broke free long enough to throw one last kiss in Mozart's direction.

Casanova saw Constanze's anguished face. He yearned to console her. But before he could get through the crowd, she was whispering something to František, who immediately called over one of the servants and pointed to the second floor. The servant bowed crisply and led Constanze up the stairs. Mozart watched as she disappeared. The music room was almost empty.

"I'd call that an interesting evening," said Casanova, joining Mozart at the clavier. "You know a party's been successful when nobody's talking, the hostess is in tears and most of the guests are in shock."

Mozart laughed. The guests had left the house and were climbing into their carriages outside. František, looking more than a little weary, came into the music room.

"You're both welcome to stay as long as you like, but I have at least one and perhaps two very upset women to tend to upstairs."

"Is Constanze not feeling well?" Mozart asked innocently.

"I think she needs a good night's sleep, alone. She'll stay with us tonight. I'll bring her back to the inn tomorrow. Signor Casanova, I hope you'll excuse me for not remaining with you. Should you wish to stay, I've told the servants to bring whatever you may want. Well, good night."

Without waiting for a reply, František Dušek left the room and limped up the grand staircase to the bedrooms. Mozart quietly played a cheerful melody on the clavier.

"What is that?"

"A serenade I wrote called *A Little Night Music—Eine kleine Nachtmusik.*"

"How fitting for this evening," Casanova laughed. "Tell me, Mozart, did you really compose that aria tonight in the pavilion?"

"Tell me, Casanova, did you really sleep with a thousand women in Spain?"

"I don't see what one has to do with the other."

"We both have our talents and our secrets."

Chapter Ten

T hat's a beautiful watch chain, Maestro."

Mozart was absentmindedly twirling a delicate gold chain between his thumb and index finger while the friseur arranged his hair in the simple manner he liked to wear it during the day: pulled back and tied with a simple black bow.

"It goes nicely with your vest," the friseur prattled on. "Which coat will you wear today, Maestro?"

Mozart didn't answer, his gaze fixed on the tiny portrait of Constanze he had propped up on the washstand, his thoughts lost in the remains of the party and what had happened the night before.

The friseur he had hired to groom his naturally unruly hair had arrived at nine and woken him. It took well over an hour for the nervous man to wash, brush and style Mozart's thick hair. Now, after endless fussing, the friseur finished his work.

"Voila, Maestro."

"Fine . . . very nice . . . fine."

As Mozart admired himself in the mirror, the friseur brushed away the stray hairs that had landed on his brown vest. He helped Mozart into his green frock coat and slipped on a pair of black shoes with shiny gold buckles.

"That's a lovely ensemble, Maestro; very much à la mode."

"Yes, it is, isn't it?"

"Should I wait for Madame Mozart to wake, or would you like me to return later?"

"Madame Mozart's not here."

"Oh . . . then . . . perhaps . . ."

"That will be all for now," Mozart replied, relieving the little man of his discomfort.

"Very well, Maestro. I'll be on my way."

Silently the friseur packed up the lotions, powders, combs and brushes and dusted the washstand.

Mozart heard footsteps in the hallway outside, and quickly went to the door and pulled it open. František Dušek stood there, fist raised, ready to knock.

"Wolfgang."

"František. Good morning. Where's Constanze?"

"In my carriage, downstairs. She asked me to come up first."

"Why?"

"I'm not certain. She mentioned something about seeing you and Casanova leave the Villa together last night. I suppose she wanted to make certain you were . . . you were here, or . . ."

"Or what?" Mozart challenged.

"Alone," František whispered with evident embarrassment.

The friseur, loaded down with his leather cases, was standing nearby waiting for an opportunity to sneak by, but the two men blocked his exit. Sensing this, Mozart moved to one side and waved him past. The friseur hurried out the door.

František stepped into the room and looked around.

"There's no one here."

"Then I'll let Constanze know she should come in. But before I get her, let me just say I'm surprised at how you treat her. You know, Wolfgang, Constanze is a dear person and she loves you very much. I don't understand how you can be so cavalier about her. You upset her last night."

Wolfgang looked like a chastised child.

"I love her too, and she understands me and my music. Sometimes when I compose I imagine her face and new melodies come to me. But there are other times when I want to be free, without responsibilities, to do as I please without thinking of anyone else, without being judged."

"Like Casanova?"

Mozart paused, thinking. "No, not like Casanova, but freer than I am now."

František went over to the window, opened one section and carefully leaned out, giving a signal to his coachman. He watched Constanze, still clothed in the dress she had worn to the party, climb out of the carriage and hurry into the inn.

"You know, Wolfgang, I'm not one to give advice, especially when it comes to marriage, but . . ."

"But you will anyway."

"You should take better care of Constanze. She is your family now."

"I know. I'll try. But it's so hard, so difficult."

Constanze, pale and tired, appeared at the door.

"Good morning, my dear." Wolfgang hurried over and leaned forward to kiss her. She turned away.

"Don't, Wolfgang. Don't say anything." She paused. "František, thank you so much. I'm sorry Josefa was feeling ill this morning. Tell her I accept her apology."

"I'll let her know. Get some rest."

František tipped his hat, turned and limped out the door. Wolfgang closed the door behind him and leaned against it.

"I did nothing wrong," he said, looking at the door, his back to Constance.

"How can I be sure?"

"Because I . . . because I . . . because you have to."

"Poor Wolfgang. No one understands you, no one appreciates you. You're so wronged. Last night was outrageous. First I find you with Josefa, then you thumb your nose at Signor Bondini, the man who's paying you for an opera, then you make eyes and gestures at his wife as she sang. And what about me? Don't you think I was hurt by all that, that . . ."

"Music-making," he interjected hopefully.

"You don't understand the repercussions of your actions. Well, it's high time you learned." Constanze slammed the bedroom door, locking herself in.

Mozart shook his head. He poured a cup of coffee and sat down at his writing table. The incomplete score of the opera called to him, but no melodies came to his mind. Frustrated, he put the manuscript aside, took out some unused music paper and started writing down the orchestration for the concert aria he'd composed the night before. The sounds were clear in his head, and they translated easily to the page. Mozart tried hard not to think of the previous evening, but he couldn't keep the image of Caterina Bondini or the sound of her voice out of his head. She seemed closer than his wife, though *she* remained locked in the next room. The battle between devotion and temptation worsened each day.

By mid-afternoon Mozart couldn't write anymore, and without a word to Constanze he left the inn and walked to Leliborn's, where he sat by himself at a corner table and had some lunch. He then set off for the opera house, stopping to look in the shop windows, especially the ones displaying the newest coats and vests.

It took him nearly a half hour to reach the opera house. The stage was empty and there was no sign of activity. Unsure of what else to do, he walked up the stairs to Pasquale Bondini's office. An officious secretary greeted him with the news that Signor Bondini did not wish to see him.

"But I need to know why there are no rehearsals today."

"Signor Bondini has ordered there will be no rehearsals until the Abbé Da Ponte returns from Vienna."

"But that might not be for another few days. The opera will never be ready."

"Signor Bondini will send for you when the rehearsals resume."

"And what about the performance of *Figaro* on the fourteenth?"

"Signor Bondini will take care of that once the Abbé Da Ponte returns with the Emperor's permission. If you'll excuse me."

Mozart stared at the secretary. He hated the talentless officials who found pleasure in frustrating him. "Excuse me . . . but . . . would you know where Signor Casanova is staying?" Mozart asked.

"No."

"If he should come by would you tell him I was looking for him?"

"If I see him. Now, excuse me, but I do have work to do."

Mozart left the office and walked down the circular marble stairs, counting the steps as he descended. When he reached the main level he wandered around, hoping to see someone he knew. The stage area was dark and empty. Frustrated, he trudged back to the inn, stopping only to have a coffee at a small café.

Constanze was still locked in the bedroom. He could hear her moving around, but didn't have the nerve or desire to renew their discussion. He sat down and stared at the sheets of music paper, still spread out on the table. The score of the opera stayed incomplete.

Three days passed and there was no word from Bondini or Da Ponte. Constanze and Wolfgang coexisted in their rooms, sharing meals, but not the bed. She wrote letters to her son, her mother and her sister, filling them with fictionalized details of how well the rehearsals were going. Wolfgang paced and tried to compose, but he couldn't seem to focus. At night, when he knew she was asleep, he would quietly open the door to the bedroom, tiptoe in holding a single candle and stare at her face, looking for forgiveness or inspiration. A few times during meals, he'd cautiously begin a conversation with his wife, hoping it would thaw the personal chill in the room. But Constanze thwarted every attempt by simply ignoring him. Mozart stopped trying and stared out the window while Constanze returned to her letters.

When the sun shone through the window on the morning of October ninth, Mozart got up from the daybed and stretched. He somehow sensed that this abhorrent state of waiting was going to end.

He dressed quickly and went down to the lobby. A messenger wearing an imperial royal-blue uniform was standing near the front door of the inn.

"Are you Herr Mozart?"

"Yes."

"Wolfgang Mozart?"

He nodded. The messenger unrolled an official-looking document he'd been holding in his left hand.

"The Emperor has granted permission for a performance of the opera *The Marriage of Figaro* by Da Ponte and Mozart. It shall be performed on the fourteenth of October by Bondini's Italian opera company in Prague. Further, the Emperor has ordered that the new opera by Mozart and Da Ponte be produced as soon as possible thereafter."

Mozart felt like kissing the messenger, but he simply grabbed his hand, thanked him and turned to the innkeeper. "Please send the most wonderful breakfast up to my wife and tell her I've gone to the opera house to rehearse."

"Very well, Maestro. It will be done. May I tell Madame Mozart the good news?"

"Absolutely, tell her . . . tell her everything . . . tell her . . . tell her I love her," he yelled as he bounded out the door.

Skipping down the cobblestone streets, smiling and waving, his head bouncing from side to side, Mozart hurried to the opera house. When he got there, Pasquale Bondini was standing at the stage entrance.

"Mozart!"

Wolfgang snapped back to reality.

"Mozart! It seems the Emperor has obliged. I've worked out a schedule. We'll rehearse *Don Giovanni* for the next four days. Then there will be one rehearsal for *Figaro* on the thirteenth. We'll use the production from last season. There will be no rehearsals on the fourteenth. I hope you can manage it all."

"It won't be a problem. Thank you."

"Mozart. Don't disappoint me."

"I won't . . . ever."

The opera house was alive again. Mozart loved the energy coursing through the hallways, dressing rooms and backstage. Carpenters hammered the fairly simple sets; the odor of fresh paint filled his nostrils. He heard the singers going through excruciating vocal exercises to warm up their throats; the chorus rehearsed with their chorus master, who wore his pince-nez glasses on the tip of his nose; members of the orchestra tuned their instruments. It was a fabulous mosaic of sounds and activity.

With renewed enthusiasm, Mozart walked through the orchestra, greeting the musicians, and took his place at the harpsichord. Within a few minutes everyone was ready to begin. The cast was standing on the stage waiting for Mozart. He looked up from the score, smiled broadly, laughed and played the first bars of the wedding march from *Figaro* on the harpsichord.

"That always puts me in a good mood," he said loudly. "But today we're rehearsing *Don Giovanni*."

Laughter filled the opera house, breaking the nervous tension.

"We'll begin with the end of the first act. I'd like to work on the scenes leading up to Don Giovanni's party."

As he was speaking, some of the choristers moved to the back of the stage. Mozart flipped through the score. "We'll need Donna Anna, Donna Elvira and Don Ottavio in masks. We'll start with their entrance and continue through the party scene, including the minuet when Don Giovanni pulls Zerlina into another room."

The orchestra members turned their pages, looking for the scene Mozart had described. Leporello and Don Giovanni took their places on the stage as the singers portraying Anna, Elvira and Ottavio—Anna's fiancé—put on their masks. Mozart gave the downbeat, and the orchestra played.

In a box at the very back of the dark theater, Da Ponte and Casanova sat, listening, the poet to his words, the lover to the music. It was going well. The break in the rehearsals had given the singers a chance to study their roles. For the most part, Mozart gave his corrections while he conducted, but sometimes he stopped to change notes in the orchestra or to help a singer with phrasing.

"It's a good scene," Casanova whispered. "I've always liked masks and disguises. They add mystery and let you conceal or reveal as much or as little as you want."

"And you've used disguises?"

"Absolutely. Once I dressed as a valet just so I could take the boots off an incredibly beautiful woman. It was an experience I could never have had as myself, but disguised, it became possible. Haven't you ever wanted to be something you're not?"

"Often."

"At the Roman carnival people go around unmasked or masked, dressed as the devil, deadly sins, clowns, harlots . . . anything . . . anything they choose. You can't tell the nobles from the peasants, and when people are disguised it makes no difference who they are or what rank they hold."

"Very liberating," Da Ponte added with ennui in his voice.

"Yes! I do like masks."

Mozart had restarted the rehearsal, and Casanova appreciated the way the disguised trio of Don Ottavio, Donna Anna and Donna Elvira—all of whom were there to trap Don Giovanni and accuse him of murdering the Commendatore—accepted Leporello's invitation to join the party. The scene was playing beautifully, and Da Ponte settled into his chair, savoring the drama unfolding on the stage.

After about an hour, during which Mozart adjusted and corrected notes in passages that already sounded perfect, Pasquale Bondini walked onto the stage and suggested it was time for a break.

"Must we?" Mozart pleaded. "We have so much more to do."

But Bondini was in no mood to assuage Mozart. "The musicians need rest."

Bondini officiously ordered the singers off the stage. With apologetic looks in Mozart's direction, the orchestra players packed up their instruments. Mozart studied his score for a few minutes, mentally marking changes he felt would strengthen the scene.

"Mozart."

Instantly he recognized Da Ponte's voice echoing through the almost empty theater. A smile came to his face. "Lorenzo. I don't know how to thank you," he yelled from the orchestra. Jumping over the rows of chairs, he bounded to the parterre-level box at the back of the theater. He climbed in and took a seat, placing himself between Casanova and Da Ponte.

"Lorenzo, I'm so happy you were able to get the Emperor's permission."

"It wasn't easy, I can assure you. But I told his majesty that *Figaro* would be ideal for the Princess of Tuscany, and he accepted."

"How are things in Vienna?"

"Salieri's in charge; he's demanded another libretto from me."

"And the Emperor?"

"He accedes to what Salieri wants. Emperor Joseph's a conflicted man. He thinks of himself as an enlightened ruler, and actively revokes many of his mother's discriminations. But still he rules with an iron fist. He speaks of equality but . . ."

"But what?" Casanova asked.

"He's not credible. Nonetheless, I cherish my relationship with him. I worked hard to attain my position at court. It wasn't easy for an Italian poet with no noble sponsors to rise in the Court of Vienna. But I've succeeded, so damn them all!"

"Be careful what you say," Casanova cautioned. "Walls have ears connected to mouths that love to tell stories."

Da Ponte smoothed the front of his black frock coat. "So, while I've been in Vienna, nothing was accomplished here."

Mozart explained. "The singers here are slower and Bondini refuses to push anybody to work harder. He's afraid. If I were running this opera house people would—"

"You're not," Da Ponte interrupted. "The orchestra is playing better."

"The singers are beginning to act the way they should. What did you think?" Mozart asked.

"The end of the first act still looks a little rough," Casanova said. "But the music is . . . dramatic . . . exciting. I especially like the way Don Giovanni accuses Leporello of sneaking off with Zerlina when everyone knows he was the one who pulled her away from the party. What else is a servant for but to pay for the sins of his master?"

"I thought her scream, when she yells for help from offstage, was too weak. It has to be a real scream, a shriek. We must believe Don Giovanni is forcing himself on her, even though we don't see it happen."

"Yes, that's true, Mozart," Casanova said. "But would Giovanni force himself on her? Isn't he a nobleman?"

"Your view of him is too pure," Da Ponte argued. "Perhaps when she realizes what it is he wants to do she has a sudden change of heart."

"Either way, the scream needs to be more convincing."

"Let me work with her later, alone. You'll get the scream you want," Casanova said, adding: "It's a wonderful time we live in. Women are more sexually—"

"Available," Da Ponte tossed in.

"Yes! Exactly. They are freer, and therefore so are we."

Casanova paused, cleared his throat and continued in a more serious tone of voice.

"I received de Sade's letter yesterday. I've read it over and over, countless times, and all I can tell you is, right now, I'm grateful to be away from Paris."

"I never liked Paris." Mozart's thoughts returned to nine years earlier, to the summer of 1778. He was on tour. It was hot . . . the streets smelled . . . and he was staying in a tiny room with his mother. She became ill, and no matter what the French doctors tried she grew sicker and weaker. Mozart was alone with her when she died on July third. In his mind he could still see the letter he wrote to his father and sister. Unable to bring himself to write of his mother's death, he wrote only that she was sick. Then, a few days later, he wrote again and told the truth. He imagined his poor father reading his sad letters. The image haunted him for weeks, and now it was a painful memory.

"I have fond memories of Paris," Casanova said. "When I first arrived there I was struck by the magnificent roads Louis the Fifteenth had built. The hotels were clean, the food superb, the service friendly and quick, the serving girls friendly and willing. Paris was a home to foreigners. It suffered only from the unfair despotism of kings and laws which allowed a person to be thrown in prison for no apparent reason."

"And now?" Da Ponte asked.

"Well, it's been years since I've been there—after all, I was banished from that fair country—but de Sade's letter has made me sad . . . no . . . angry. Perhaps it would be best if I read what he has to say."

Mozart was returning from his thoughts of long ago. "I was wondering how you know the Marquis?"

"This should be good," Da Ponte mumbled.

"We've never met," Casanova explained. "But when we were younger, we had the same mistress—at different times, of course—in Italy, and so I feel a strange connection to him."

Casanova removed a small, folded piece of paper from the deep cuff on his coat sleeve. "Would you like to hear his letter?"

Mozart nodded.

"*My Dear Chevalier,*" Casanova read as he held a flickering candle to light the single page, which was crammed with de Sade's tiny black scrawl.

"*I was pleased to get your letter. Its words and ideas were welcome rays of light in this dark, wet, tiny cell they force me to call my home. The Bastille is an unimaginable horror. But it's made worse by the fact that I am kept in the tower called Liberté. That irony alone could drive me to insanity. Were it not for my books and my writing, and the comforting knowledge that Voltaire himself was once imprisoned here, I would have gone mad long ago."*

"I never liked Voltaire's writing," Da Ponte interrupted. "*Candide* was not a good book at all. Certainly unusable as an opera plot."
Casanova ignored him.

"What torture it is to know that, just outside these thick walls, there are people who are free to do as they please. They dance and sing and have feasts and parties, while here we suffer indignities that are inhuman. And how wrong is it for me to pay a penalty for the enjoyment of women? It is true I have thought of everything that could be done in the sexual realm. But I have not practiced everything I have thought, nor would I. I am a libertine, as I believe you are. But I am no thief, or murderer; only a freethinker. For my thoughts I am unfairly condemned by those who are in no position to accuse me. I am here because of a nasty lettre de cachet that gave the dishonest police the power to spy on me and to arrest me. The accusations against me are false. I have committed no crime. I am a libertine, that is all."

Casanova paused and looked up.
"Are you a libertine, Casanova?"
"Mozart, I believe in man's individual freedoms so long as they don't cause physical harm."
"And you, Lorenzo? Are you a libertine?"
"I've never given it much thought. But I suppose I agree with Casanova on this point. When you look at recent history, there are too many people who have been condemned solely because of their thoughts, their beliefs, even their heritage or religion."
"I'm surprised, Abbé," Casanova said. "You never struck me as someone who was concerned about injustices done to others, especially if you got what you wanted."

"There's a great deal you don't know about me, Chevalier."

"And you, Mozart; what are your thoughts on the subject?"

"I've come to believe in freedoms. But I've always been afraid to say it aloud. In Salzburg we were taught of the power of kings and the guidance of the church. Rank and religion protected you. When I was in the service of the Court of Salzburg, I was ordered to eat with the servants. I remember being angry; I was a musician, a composer—no one owned me. But when I thought about it, I realized the other servants were no less people than I. I didn't understand why we had to be ranked, and I swore that when I composed operas, I would fill them with good people, people of character."

"And that's what you did in *Figaro*," Casanova pointed out.

"Yes. And now we must remember that Don Giovanni is also a libertine."

"My libretto brings that out clearly enough," Da Ponte defended.

"Let me read the rest of the letter." Casanova refocused his eyes on the page.

"I was excited to get your request for ideas regarding the new Da Ponte– Mozart opera. As you may know, I consider myself to be a man of the theater, although none of my dramas has yet received a production or performance to do it justice. But locked up in this octagonal hell, I have time to think about the stage. Sometimes at night, when it's dark—a darkness so deep there are no shadows or images—I lie on my cot and try to visualize a stage and the actors on it. Your request for advice and ideas has given me a new set of fantasies, and I must tell you how jealous I am that you are working with the Don Juan legend. This is an opportunity which comes along but once in a lifetime."

"I'm glad he thinks this is an opportunity, but does he ever offer any insights, or is this simply a chance for him to share his philosophies with us?" Da Ponte groused.

"You've never been in prison, have you, Lorenzo?"

Da Ponte shook his head.

"Well, I have. The time you have to contemplate and think about your fate does strange things to you. De Sade is no different. Just listen."

Casanova again found his place.

"I can only imagine what great music will do for that story. I know there have been unsuccessful attempts by lesser composers. But you have the composer to make Don Juan breathe on the stage; to be the libertine we all wish to be. However, I suppose you have to be careful with the plot, given it has to be approved by the government censors. But with that said, let me give you my initial thoughts.

"First of all you cannot call the opera 'Il dissoluto punito.' By indicating that there is punishment for what Don Giovanni did, you're asserting his guilt. And what, I ask, is Don Giovanni really guilty of? Of seductions, of passion, of loving women . . ."

"He's a murderer," Da Ponte pointed out.

"I disagree," Mozart said. "He only kills Donna Anna's father after the old man attacks him. His crime was trying to seduce Donna Anna and being caught trying to leave her house."

"A crime we've all been guilty of at least once," Casanova added with a smile in his voice. "Let me read the rest of the letter."

". . . Of seductions, of passion, of loving women, of enjoying the good elements of being alive and free. Let me assure you, from where I sit, there is no doubt a man like Don Giovanni would do everything in his power to stay out of prison. This life, this hell, would kill him, so when he has to choose between repentance and damnation, I am certain he would choose damnation, because to repent would be admitting guilt, and in his mind—and mine—he committed no punishable offense.

"In the theater, I embrace characters and people who are true to their beliefs even in the face of horrible pain. If I didn't, would I still be housed in this hell? If I were willing to openly deny my beliefs, wouldn't I be released from this prison? Then I could be there with you, because nothing would give me greater pleasure than to watch you achieve the kind of drama Don Juan requires.

"Through sleep I escape these walls. In my dreams I will become Don Giovanni; I will see Donna Anna and Donna Elvira, take them in my arms, hold their warm bodies against mine and imagine how he, the legendary seducer, would treat these noble ladies. Then, I will imagine myself with Zerlina. There true pleasure lies, because it is the peasant girls who are most open to experiments of the kind a man with Don Giovanni's appetites would enjoy. There is no crime in the fullest enjoyment of physical contact. But it is a crime to starve a man, even when that starvation is the denial of his sexual freedoms.

"I will write to you again with the hope that some of my thoughts inspire your work. Then I can feel as if I have truly escaped these horrible walls.

"I leave you now, dearest friend. As you work with your colleagues, I ask you to keep one idea in mind: liberty—liberty must be saved.

"Until I write again, I am your true friend,

de Sade."

There was a profound silence, broken only by the soft sound of a few musicians who had returned to their seats and were practicing.

"I wish I could meet him," Mozart whispered. "He's suffered in ways I can't imagine, and yet he clings to the ideas and values of a libertine."

"Wouldn't you?" Da Ponte asked.

"I don't know. I never know how I'll react until I actually face a particular situation. I've never suffered like he does."

"But you have compassion, Mozart," Casanova said.

"How do you know that?"

"It's in your music. In every phrase."

"You're generous with your praise, Casanova." Turning to Da Ponte, Mozart added: "Lorenzo, we need to change the scene where the masked trio comes to Don Giovanni's party."

"Change it? Why? It was working so well before the break."

"When they arrive, and accept Leporello's invitation, Don Giovanni, not Leporello, should greet them."

"I don't know . . . ," Da Ponte said.

"I'll take care of it. Leave it to me."

And with that, Mozart leapt from his chair and hurried back to the harpsichord. Opening his score, he studied the page and played a few passages. Casanova and Da Ponte watched Mozart call the copyist over and instruct him to change the orchestra parts and give the changes to the singers.

Then Mozart sat down at the harpsichord. For a moment he stared at the keys. Then he started playing the second movement of his A Major Piano Concerto, a bittersweet piece he had written while finishing *The Marriage of Figaro*. One of the violinists sitting nearby stopped practicing and listened.

"Why are you playing that, Maestro?"

Mozart didn't stop. He was lost in the sad phrases spinning seamlessly one into the next.

"Maestro . . ." the violinist repeated timidly.

"It reminds me of a man—a sad, lonely man—a man I never really knew."

By the time he'd finished the movement, the rest of the musicians had taken their seats and the singers were standing silently in place onstage. The stagehands had stopped hammering. A hush filled the theater. Mozart wiped his eyes, stood up and addressed the cast.

"We're going to redo the beginning of the party scene with the changes you've been given."

And without waiting for any reaction or questions, he gave the down-beat. Da Ponte and Casanova saw the scene start just as it had before, but this time after Leporello invited the masked trio to join the party, Don Giovanni welcomed them with a toast, a short greeting they immediately echoed.

"*Viva la libertà!*"

As the new words and music resounded, the singers, the musicians and even Pasquale Bondini realized how Mozart's minor change made the scene shudder with excitement and meaning.

But Casanova, Da Ponte and Mozart didn't react to the change. At once their thoughts were with their missing, silent collaborator, who, locked away from society, was alone, sweeping the dirt from the cold stone floor of his cell in the Bastille's Liberty Tower.

Chapter Eleven

*L*orenzo Da Ponte lay in bed, pages of half-filled manuscript paper propped against Teresa Saporiti's curved back. Without her costume and makeup she looked more plain, but no less beautiful.

"Don't move so much," he ordered.

"But it tickles when you write. Your pen's digging into me."

"The Emperor demands new librettos. Without me all those composers he collects would have nothing to write. I have to finish this one for Salieri. *Don Giovanni*'s taken so much time I've fallen behind, and as much as I admire Mozart, Salieri's more important at court, so I can't disappoint him."

"That's not a good excuse."

She rolled over, crushing the manuscript paper on which he'd written the words for an aria. His annoyance was abated by the sight of her breasts, moving gently up and down as she breathed in and out. Da Ponte tossed his pen aside and climbed on top of her, his thirty-eight-year-old body anxious to exert itself.

"Be gentle. I have to sing tonight."

Da Ponte was less tender than the words of love he wrote. Most of his characters were elegant and compassionate, characteristics he demonstrated only when he was at court and needed to be politically astute. There he used his wit and talent to maneuver and manipulate situations so he was always in demand and at the center of Vienna's creative ferment.

Teresa Saporiti let out a long, deep breath as Da Ponte climbed off her. Gently moving her to one side of the bed, he gathered up his pages and went over to a writing desk in the corner of the room. Scraps of paper were spread across it. He pulled on a silk dressing gown and sat down at the desk, staring through the flame of a single candle.

"What are you working on now?"

"New librettos."

"Are there any parts for me?"

Da Ponte nodded.

"How many librettos are you working on?"

"Three, including *Don Giovanni*."

"How do you manage?"

"I separate them. In the morning I write for Martini and pretend I'm studying the sonnets of Petrarch. In the afternoons I write the words for Salieri; he is my Tasso."

"And Mozart?"

"I save my evenings for Mozart and imagine I'm rereading Dante's *Inferno*. There I find the passion his music calls for."

Teresa Saporiti had sung Mozart's operas and knew what his music could do, not only to the audience but to the singers as well. Whenever she sang the role of the Countess in *Figaro*, Mozart's music allowed her to display the full range of emotions, from sadness to joy, from loneliness to tender love.

"I have to get ready to sing." Da Ponte didn't hear her. He was reworking the words for one of Donna Anna's arias.

Slowly rising from the bed, she admired her naked form in the freestanding dressing mirror. Da Ponte continued to write as Teresa Saporiti slowly applied her stage makeup and put on her corset and undergarments so when she arrived at the opera house she would only have to slip into her costume for the performance of *The Marriage of Figaro*.

"Aren't you coming to the opera house?"

"Later. I have to finish writing."

He dipped his quill in the bottle of ink and returned to the aria.

∽

When Teresa Saporiti arrived at the opera house for the gala performance of *The Marriage of Figaro*, Mozart was acknowledging the applause of the audience as he took his place at the head of the orchestra. Peeking around the edge of the curtain from backstage, she could see the royal couple seated in their box at the center of the loge. She saw the Archduchess wave her gloved hand slowly, formally, toward Mozart. A large gold bracelet rattled on her wrist. On either side of the royal couple stood stiff, unmoving guards dressed in full military attire: crisp red coats trimmed with gold braiding, swords at their sides, off-white britches, polished black boots, white shirts and flowing neck-cloths.

In the adjacent box, Pasquale Bondini sat with Casanova and Constanze Mozart. From the safety of backstage, Teresa Saporiti stared at Casanova, wondering.

Flags and bunting in radiant colors were draped from virtually every sculpted surface in the opera house. Extra candles had been lit; the theater glowed with a festive air. Wearing the finest clothing they owned, Prague's most celebrated and important people filled every seat. The men's brocade coats were covered with medals commemorating their service to the Monarch. The women wore deep green or burgundy floor-length silk dresses adorned with sparkling jewels, gifts from husbands, or lovers. There was a constant swishing sound as the women adjusted their wide skirts trying to get comfortable in their seats. Their overdone wigs rose high above their heads, shifting from side to side.

When the whispered conversations quieted and the rustling of the heavy silk diminished, Mozart held his delicate hands in front of him. With the tiniest gesture he started the orchestra. The fleeting, quiet opening measures of the overture filled the silence, drawing everyone's attention to the conductor.

Casanova leaned back in his chair. He watched Constanze Mozart twisting a red silk handkerchief in her hands. The tension in her body distracted him. But when the curtain parted and the characters of Figaro and Susanna sang, his attention was instantly shifted to the stage. How loving they were, their actions and reactions so human and passionate, their impact immeasurable.

The first act sped by, introducing the love-struck teenage Cherubino, sung by Caterina Micelli, who, Casanova noticed, looked particularly alluring dressed in pants; the old maid Marcellina; pompous Doctor Bartolo; the music teacher Don Basilio; and Count Almaviva, a supposedly enlightened man whose greatest desire is to revive the droit du seigneur so he can sleep with Susanna as part of her wedding celebration.

"Oh, the inconsistencies of our enlightened rulers," Casanova thought.

The performance was energetic and belied the lack of rehearsal. During the short pause between the first and second acts, Casanova turned toward Constanze, who looked as nervous as she had during the overture.

"Are you all right?"

"Oh . . . yes . . ."

"You look pale."

"I am anxious when Wolfgang conducts."

"Why?"

"I don't know. I can't help it. No one in his family ever got nervous. His father was cold as stone; he expected everything to go perfectly. I expect performances to go badly, and I get nervous."

"Is that why you chose to stop singing?"

She nodded slowly. "That, and Wolfgang."

"Why?"

"He didn't want me to keep singing."

She untwisted the handkerchief. There was a sudden commotion at the rear of their box.

"But I am the poet Lorenzo Da Ponte. This is where I'm supposed to sit. Let me go! Let me in!"

Pasquale Bondini jumped up from his seat to intercede. The guards were holding Da Ponte between them. "He's harmless. Let him go," Bondini ordered.

The guards released the poet, who straightened his plain black coat and lightly powdered white wig. "The Emperor will hear about this," he threatened.

"Be quiet, Lorenzo. The second act's about to begin. Where have you been?"

"Working."

Bondini and Da Ponte reentered the box, bowing to the royal couple. The Emperor's niece quietly tapped her folded fan on her wrist in appreciation of Da Ponte's words. He bowed again, more deeply, with a flourish of his hand, and smiled. Taking an empty chair, he squeezed in next to Casanova.

"You're good at creating scenes, Lorenzo."

"Are you referring to the ones on the stage or the one in the theater?"

"You'll never know."

The second act began. Teresa Saporiti, now costumed as the Countess, in a simple cream-colored dressing gown, was seated alone at a dressing table, gazing at her reflection in a small hand mirror. Her long hair flowed naturally over her shoulders. The slow orchestral introduction set a poignant, contemplative mood.

"Watch her performance carefully," Da Ponte whispered to Casanova. "I made love to her less than two hours ago. When we were finished I left her in bed and started working at my desk. I wanted her to be angry, to feel spurned. It should make this scene work better than ever."

The grin on Da Ponte's face was short-lived.

"Don't be so certain. I've seen great actresses give their best performances in the bedroom simply to make the man feel important and powerful in ways he may not be. What they do on stage is entirely unrelated."

Annoyed, Da Ponte sat back in his seat. Whatever the reason, Teresa Saporiti's Countess had all the sadness and longing it needed, and when she finished her aria the audience erupted in extended applause and cheering. Despite the fact that all she could see of him was his back, Constanze could tell that Wolfgang was smiling at the soprano as she accepted the applause.

The act continued. Casanova studied the audience, but his attention was quickly pulled back to the stage when the Countess and Susanna cajole Cherubino into serenading them with his latest love song.

"*You have the answer, you hold the key,*" Micelli sang, accompanied by the soft pizzicati in the orchestra. Mozart's hands caressed the air.

Casanova slowly inched forward until he was perched at the edge of his seat. The adolescent flush of love at the heart of the serenade made him think of his younger years, when true, perfect love was something he yearned for and believed he could attain, but which always seemed to disappear as soon as the lady of his dreams was added to his catalogue of conquests.

When the aria ended he excitedly broke the spell that had fallen over the audience with a loud "Brava!" The suddenness and force of his yell snapped Constanze out of her own reverie, a sweet remembrance of a time when Mozart wrote melodies for her. Her head snapped around; her eyes locked with Casanova's.

"That may be the most perfect depiction of youthful love I've ever heard, seen or felt," he said.

Constanze smiled.

"Thank you. I'll tell Wolfgang you said so. It will mean a great deal to him. Your praise is based on experience, at least that's what he told me the other day."

Da Ponte, who had dozed off, was awakened by the applause and overheard part of their conversation. He waited for Casanova to lean back in his chair, then whispered:

"Will she be your next, or are you just playing around?"

"It astounds me. It just astounds me. How could a man as crude as you have written the words for this masterpiece?"

"High praise."

"The music reaffirms my faith in mankind, as you shatter it," Casanova countered.

"Quiet," Bondini ordered, frowning at both of them.

Da Ponte snarled inwardly, stretched his legs out in front of himself and closed his eyes. Casanova watched the opera, the royals in the next box and Constanze. He silently compared his own emotional responses with those suggested by her facial reactions, hoping to notice when they matched and when they diverged. But while he wanted to know more about this beautiful woman, deep down it bothered him that he was really trying to find out more about her husband, this man, this boy, this composer who could express love's tangled intricacies through perfectly placed notes and phrases.

The joyful second act ended with its wildly confused plot. The audience's polite applause woke Da Ponte from his nap. Liveried guards entered the auditorium and relit some of the candles as the intermission began.

"The singers were better in Vienna," Da Ponte said to no one in particular, although the criticism was not lost on Pasquale Bondini, who was nervously making certain the royal couple in the adjacent box were pleased with the performance.

"Make certain *Don Giovanni* is a triumph," he snapped at Da Ponte.

Da Ponte confidently waved the back of his hand toward Bondini as if to dismiss the director's concerns. Well-wishers entered the royal box, bowed or curtsied before the couple, exchanged a few words and were ushered out, each one requesting to be remembered to the Emperor. This pantomime was repeated countless times during the intermission.

Gallantly Casanova helped Constanze Mozart to her feet, gently sliding her chair back to make room for her large skirt.

"Thank you, Signor."

"Will you go backstage to see your husband?"

"Oh no. He doesn't like to be disturbed during the performance."

"What does he do during the intermissions?"

"Sometimes he composes, or visits with the singers, or . . ."

Her voice trailed off.

"I think I'll go talk to Mozart," Da Ponte interrupted.

He bowed slightly and left, disappearing between the red velvet curtains at the rear of the box. Casanova didn't know what to do or what to say to Constanze. All of the instincts and tricks that had served him so well during his exploits and adventures now seemed useless. Several times he cleared his throat as if to begin to talk, but words never followed. How he wished he could tell her his innermost thoughts, but at that moment only the purity of the love Cherubino had described in his serenade to Susanna and the Countess filled his mind. How could he possibly compete with perfection?

After what seemed to Casanova like an uncomfortable eternity, the third act was ready to begin. The elegantly dressed audience slowly took their seats, many of them lingering for one last conversation; Pasquale Bondini bowed to the royal couple and returned to his box; Casanova helped Constanze to her seat and sat down, maneuvering his chair closer to hers. The guards extinguished the extra candles and returned silently and efficiently to their posts. Da Ponte's seat remained empty.

Mozart made his way through the orchestra to his place at the harpsichord, then bowed low and slowly, savoring the applause and cheers. Quickly he turned around and sat down at the harpsichord to play the opening measures of the third act. Casanova forced himself to keep his attention on the amazing characters who populate this opera. He laughed with the audience at the funny plot twists, and melted into the seat cushion when the tender arias were sung. But as the plot thickened and unfolded and the work's revolutionary themes became more prominent, with Figaro standing up to his master, repeatedly thwarting the Count's attempts at lechery, Casanova couldn't resist watching the royal couple in the next box. He studied their faces, looking for any sign that they could see their images, or the Emperor's, projected by these fictional characters. But all he saw was their stone-cold, expressionless features as they watched unresponsively. He was particularly angered by the Archduchess, who was fidgeting with the large gold medal affixed to the royal-blue sash across her chest.

"They don't understand," he thought with sadness. "They're blind to what's happening. Enlightenment is a foreign concept, a distant concept, an ideal."

The wedding celebration at the end of the third act brought a big smile to Casanova's face. But it faded when he looked at the royal box and saw that the royal couple had fallen asleep. He wanted to go over, grab them by the shoulders and demand they appreciate the brilliance before them. He wanted to wake them from their dreamworld of castles and servants so they might see the world around them as it really was. He wanted them to understand that peasants feel the same emotions as aristocrats and royals. But he was stopped by the certainty that telling them would land him in jail. Besides, the final act was beginning.

Determined to enjoy the performance, Casanova tried to block everything else from his mind and savor the comical twists, revelations and denouements. Though it was just a set made of wood and canvas on a stage, he could almost feel the cool breezes of an evening in a Spanish garden. It took him back to an earlier time in his life, and the contented smile returned to his face. But when Susanna and the Countess exchanged cloaks so that, aided by the shadows of the evening's darkness, they could trap the Count in his attempt at infidelity, Casanova felt himself drawn toward the stage. How he yearned to be one of the male characters; to be snared by those charming feminine wiles; to hold Susanna in his arms and feel totally loved and in love.

And then it happened. It was at a pivotal moment in the opera when Figaro realizes the disguised person he is with is not the Countess but his new bride, Susanna.

"*How did you know?*" she asks.

"*I recognized your sweet little voice.*"

"*By my voice?*"

"*The voice I adore,*" he sang, holding her in his arms.

Casanova heard the truest love two people could experience, all expressed in those melodies. "Incredible. What unbelievable inspiration," he said out loud.

Constanze turned toward him. Tears streaked her face.

Casanova quietly pulled her chair back a few inches into the shadows nearer his seat. Then without anyone noticing he maneuvered his chair so he could put his arm around her shoulders. Without waiting, she buried her face in the breast of his coat. With each silent sob he moved his arm farther down, until he was rubbing the small of her back in a gentle circular motion.

The opera's final moments played out as the characters—the lovers—run out of the stone pavilion into the shadowy garden. The Countess and Susanna expose the Count's attempted infidelity, but weakened by his pleas for forgiveness, the Countess accedes to him. They embrace and all the couples happily celebrate the end of their crazy day, disappearing into the torch-lit garden as the final measures resound.

The audience applauded politely.

Casanova continued to hold Constanze in his arms. When the applause ended, she slowly sat up and wiped her face with a handkerchief.

"Thank you, Signor. You are a true gentleman. I feel safe with you."

"You may be the first woman to say that to me."

She smiled.

"That's better. Your face should always be all smiles."

"It used to be."

"How does your husband create these works? What is his inspiration? Is it divine or is it someone on earth?"

"Not now, Signor, please."

"But . . . Madame Mozart . . . Constanze . . . I must know," he pleaded.

"Not here. Someday. Some other time or place."

Mozart was taking his bow when the royal couple turned and in a rush left the theater, followed closely by the military guards. Once they were out of sight, most of the aristocrats who had waited impatiently for the opera to end hurried out after them. The smile on Mozart's face had become an angry glare, visible all the way to the last row of the parterre.

Lost in their own worlds, Casanova and Constanze didn't notice the hurt on Mozart's face. "May I escort you backstage? I'd like to congratulate your husband," Casanova said, extending his hand to Constanze. "It would be my honor to have you with me."

Constanze took a deep breath and stood up to her full height, calm and composed. Casanova saw a flash of passion burning in her dark eyes. How he wanted to take her, to have her, to love her. But there was something extremely unapproachable about her that he was powerless to overcome. Why? What was preventing him? Unhappy wives had always been a specialty of his. But now, here in Prague, he was unable to take advantage.

"Madame," he said, extending his arm.

Arm in arm, they walked in silence down the circular marble staircase, along a long corridor and through a small wooden door that led to the backstage area. A few stagehands were milling around. It was dark. Unsure of where to go, Casanova led Constanze onto the stage itself. The last act's garden set was nothing more than flimsy trees painted on canvas. When Casanova jokingly tried to hide behind one of them, Constanze laughed.

"I should find Wolfgang."

"Yes. Of course."

They saw Pasquale Bondini and Da Ponte talking on the other side of the stage.

"Good evening, Signor Da Ponte, Signor Bondini. Have you seen Wolfgang?"

Bondini took Constanze's hand and gently kissed it. "Signora Mozart. How wonderful to see you again."

"I saw him after the performance. He was talking to one of the singers," Da Ponte offered.

"I'll find him. He sometimes disappears for a few minutes after a performance."

"Allow me to help you," Da Ponte offered.

Casanova sensed insincerity in the offer.

"I'll come too."

The remnants of burning candles and torches in the backstage area lit their way. Carefully they walked through the dressing areas, but no one was there.

"What's over there?" Da Ponte asked, pointing to an area off to one side of the stage.

"That's where the new sets for *Don Giovanni* are being built," Bondini explained.

"Well, he wouldn't be there. Let's look on the other side of the stage," Casanova said, pointing across the stage.

"I'd like to see the sets," Da Ponte said, leading the others toward the half-built scenery.

Bondini removed a candle from a nearby stand and led the way.

"You see, here's the set for Giovanni's castle, and this will be the graveyard."

A noise from one of the other sets behind them caught their attention. They spun around as a door on the set slammed shut.

"That's Donna Anna's house," Bondini said as he walked the few feet over to the half-built structure.

Da Ponte went ahead and pushed open the door.

"New scenery . . . complete with composer. How delightful."

Mozart, seeming very flustered, stumbled out of the doorway.

"I was looking at the scenery. It will be perfect. Excellent, Signor Bondini."

With a nod toward Casanova and Bondini, Mozart walked over to Constanze and gently kissed her on the cheek. Casanova discreetly slid his arm away from her.

"Did you enjoy the performance?"

"It was magical . . . exquisite," Casanova gushed, trying to ease the discomfort.

Da Ponte silently slipped through the door of the set.

"Signora Bondini. What a surprise to find you here, and with Mozart. Are the sets to your liking as well?"

Da Ponte emerged from the shadows, leading Signora Bondini, still dressed as Susanna. Casanova looked at the soprano, wanting nothing more than to be her Figaro. Her costume alone was enough to arouse his desires.

"What were you doing in there with my wife? Writing another aria?"

"Looking at the new sets."

"I don't believe you."

"What a silly thing to be upset about. We have an opera to produce and we were simply examining the new scenery so . . ."

"Wolfgang! Stop lying! This isn't a game! This isn't some contrived opera plot that ends with everyone happily leaving with the person they love. This is real; this is our life."

Constanze's outburst took everyone by surprise. Even Da Ponte stopped grinning, and he stared uncomfortably at the ground.

"Constanze . . . Stanzi . . . please . . . it was innocent . . . nothing at all . . ."

"Nothing, you call it," Caterina Bondini shrieked. "To hell with you. Pasquale, let's go. I'm tired." Caterina Bondini was again the prima donna. She stormed past Mozart and grabbed her husband's arm, pulling him away with her. As they disappeared into the darkness of the stage Pasquale Bondini yelled back:

"We'll deal with this tomorrow, Mozart. I'm not through with you."

Da Ponte hid in the doorway of the set. Casanova moved into the shadows a few feet away as Mozart approached Constanze. He could see a boyish look on the composer's face; it reminded him of Cherubino.

"Constanze, please. It really was nothing. We just . . . Stanzi . . ."

"Stop. Those days are over. I don't believe you anymore," she yelled.

"But—"

"Stop. I don't want to hear it."

"But Stanzi. I wasn't doing anything . . . she was . . . we were talking about *Don Giovanni*. Giacomo, you believe me, don't you?"

Casanova stepped forward and cleared his throat, but before he could speak Constanze interrupted.

"Signor Casanova, would you mind taking me to the Dušeks' villa?"

"But Stanzi, don't be silly . . ."

"No. I'm leaving! Signor Casanova, please, I want to go now."

Casanova was drawn to Constanze's outstretched hand. With an uneasy, apologetic look toward Mozart, he took Constanze's hand and escorted her to the exit.

Mozart followed for a step or two, but quickly gave up and sat down on the stairs of the *Don Giovanni* set, his head cradled in his hands. A lone torch flickered nearby. Da Ponte emerged from the shadows and walked down the stairs, stopping dramatically on the step behind Mozart. He rested his right hand on Mozart's back.

"I thought you'd left."

"I wouldn't leave you, Wolfgang."

"Lorenzo, this whole thing's a disaster." His words seemed to echo hollowly around the empty theater.

"What about Constanze?"

"I don't know what to do. Maybe I should send her back to Vienna to be with Karl."

"Don't do that. She needs to be with you. It will all work out. You'll see. She'll calm down, you'll be reunited and *Don Giovanni* will be a success."

"I don't think *Don Giovanni* will ever be ready," Mozart whispered.

"You'll finish it, Wolfgang. I know you will."

"*Figaro* came easier. It was all so natural. This is much harder. I don't have a feeling for it. The melodies in my mind don't have the anger they need. I can write the sweet arias for Zerlina, even the tender one for the tenor, but every time I try to compose the music for the entrance of the dead Commendatore's statue, or the scene in the graveyard, I shudder, break into a sweat and am unable to write."

"Are you afraid?"

"No."

"Then what?"

"It's some kind of premonition, or maybe a memory . . . I don't know . . . It bothers me. I can't compose music for death . . ."

Da Ponte saw Mozart look toward the set of the graveyard. Extending his hand, he helped him to his feet.

"It will all work out. I know it will."

Side by side, they walked across the stage, which was still filled by the set for the last act of *Figaro*.

"It was a good performance of *Figaro*," Mozart said, stopping at mid-stage and looking into the dark, empty theater. "Did the royal couple enjoy the opera?"

"I heard Her Majesty say she would tell the Emperor how wonderful it was," Da Ponte invented.

"If only the Emperor would make me the court composer, then we could work together all the time, Lorenzo, without the struggles. I could be secure. He would be the happiest monarch in all of Europe . . . Has your life been happy, Lorenzo?"

"My mother died when I was very young and my father's only interest was finding a new wife. I suffered then. But now . . . now I have more than I probably should, and am happy at court."

"And what about your friend Casanova? How happy is he?" Mozart asked, with more concern than he wanted Da Ponte to notice.

Da Ponte paused. He leaned on the door of the garden pavilion near the corner of the set. "He's had his misfortunes. But he survives. He's getting old now. Most of his story's already been told. He lives in the past, remembering and retelling. I've heard all those stories before, some of them more than once."

"So why did you ask him to come to Prague?"

"Because of his past and because I find him irresistible. He remembers the world as it naturally was and he wishes it could be again. He abhors the formality and hypocrisy of our time. I've told him we spend our lives serving rulers who live unlike any of their subjects. How can we expect them to understand?"

Mozart nodded.

"I also thought you might find him helpful, instructive."

"Why?"

"He's older, wiser, freer."

"Somehow I don't think of him as a teacher my wife will approve of."

"We'll see," Da Ponte concluded. "Speaking of your wife, what do you plan to do?"

"I'll go see her tomorrow," Mozart said, attempting to sound confident.

"Give her time."

"Lorenzo, how did you know I was with Caterina Bondini before?"

"I recognized her sweet little voice," Da Ponte quoted from his own *Figaro* libretto.

"From her voice?" Mozart played along, singing the next line from the opera.

Their laughter reverberated eerily in the empty theater. Chilled by its sound, Mozart stopped laughing and looked for Lorenzo. But the poet had disappeared into the shadows of the stage.

"Lorenzo, where are you?" He waited. "Lorenzo, this isn't funny. Where are you?"

But there was no answer, because Da Ponte had already snuck away through the set's pavilion, offstage and out the back door of the theater.

Mozart was alone in the darkness of the pretend Spanish garden.

Chapter Twelve

⌒

No matter which way he turned, Mozart was lost. The sets for
Figaro and the unfinished ones for *Don Giovanni* were merged into a series
of indistinguishable buildings, gardens and graveyards. Rickety staircases
leading nowhere ended in dark precipices. Painted plants and trees grew
out of control, concealing passageways and exits. The graveyard's neat rows
of papier-mâché monuments had become a maze of imposing marble statues with gargoyle-like faces and chiseled epitaphs of doom.

A candle flickered in the garden pavilion of the *Figaro* set. The wood
door was open. Constanze was inside; a gauzy white veil covered her face,
through which Mozart could see her deep black eyes, glowing like coals.
He bounded up the three steps. Suddenly the candle went out and he was
in pitch darkness. Da Ponte's loud cackle pierced the silence.

Mozart spun around, searching for the poet. Through the eerie shadows,
he recognized the faces of people who hadn't even been at the performance.
Across the stage, through one of the glassless windows on the second floor
of the set for Donna Anna's house, he saw his mother and sister seated at the
harpsichord. It was a scene he'd witnessed countless times as a child. Standing on the stage below, he watched, enjoying the tranquil, familiar picture.

"Mama! Mama!"

His mother continued playing the harpsichord, deaf to his calls.

"Nannerl! Dearest sister. It's me, Wolfgang. Nannerl! Why won't you
answer? Look out the window, please."

But the figures played on, staring at the sheets of music, ignoring him.

He backed up to get a clearer look. Craning his neck, he could see his
sister move away from the harpsichord while his mother played one of

the minuets he'd composed as a child. Nannerl, dancing with a man whose back was to the window, moved gracefully, guided by the steady pulse of the music.

The music became faster and louder, obliterating the elegance of the minuet, its gentle rhythms replaced by a violent, unrhythmic series of motions, as if the harpsichordist had lost control. Desperately Mozart stamped his foot to reestablish the correct beat. But the music and dancing grew more frantic as Nannerl and the man spun wildly in a tight embrace.

"Nannerl, stop! Stop! Mama, make her stop! That's not how it goes! Listen to the beat! Stop! Stop!"

Pausing, the man looked up, grabbed Mozart's sister, pulled her to him and kissed her passionately, spinning her limp body to the floor. Mozart could no longer see her, but as the man removed his coat and shirt he looked out the window onto the stage below. A lecherous grin filled the window.

"Casanova! No! Nannerl, no. Don't let him. Mama, stop him! That's Casanova! *The* Casanova! Papa! Papa, where are you? Papa!"

Mozart desperately pulled at the door of the house, but it wouldn't budge. Then he backed up to take another look. The transformation in the window had evaporated as quickly as it had materialized.

Then the knocking started; soft at first, it grew steadily louder. It seemed to be coming from the direction of the cemetery set. Four even pulses, repeated, over and over: TA . . . TA . . . TA . . . TA. Mozart stumbled around, clutching in terror.

TA . . . TA . . . TA . . . TA . . . It grew closer and more insistent. He closed his eyes and prayed silently for mercy.

"Wolfgang," a deep voice intoned between knocks.

"NO!"

"Wolfgang!"

TA, TA, TA, TA . . . The knocking was loud, pounding, relentless.

"Leave me alone! Please, leave me alone."

"Wolfgang!"

TA, TA, TA, TA . . . The knocks were so loud Mozart had to cover his ears.

"Wolfgang! I want you now!"

"NOOOOOO!"

His scream was bloodcurdling. Suddenly the pounding stopped.

"Open the door," the deep voice ordered.

Keys turned in the old metal lock.

"Leave me! Stop. Go away! I'm afraid."

"Wolfgang! What's the matter with you? Let go of that bedcover."

Mozart slowly opened his eyes. He was drenched in sweat and was clutching the bedcovers. Gradually he loosened his grip, letting the blanket drop onto the bed.

"Wolfgang," a sweet voice asked. "Are you all right?"

Wiping his eyes, he looked around.

"Josefa . . . František . . . Where am I? What are you doing here?"

"You're in your room at the inn. What's the matter with you?" Josefa asked as she gently rubbed his forehead. "Are you drunk?"

"No. I must have been having a dream. But it was so real, I didn't know what to do."

Mozart sat on the edge of the bed, still fully clothed, his feet dangling, swinging gently from side to side in time to the meter of a proper minuet. Its steadiness calmed him, and he sighed to catch his breath.

"What are you doing here?"

"We came to collect some of Constanze's things. She's going to stay with us for a few days. She needs to rest."

"Is she all right? Is the baby all right?"

"They're fine. Constanze's a little upset. She wanted to return to Vienna, but I convinced her to stay with us. Being away from you will do her good. Besides, it will give you some time alone to finish the opera," František Dušek offered.

"Why is she upset?"

"Last night . . . ," Josefa began.

"What happened last night?"

"You don't remember?"

Mozart shook his head.

"Backstage . . ."

"After the *Figaro* . . ." they prompted.

"It was a good performance, wasn't it?"

"Yes, wonderful. I thought your conducting was particularly—" František began enthusiastically.

"Be quiet," Josefa interrupted, trying to get the conversation back on track. "Constanze was upset when you were found with Madame Bondini."

"Oh . . ."

Mozart sheepishly looked at the ground, then raised his big eyes toward Josefa.

"That was nothing . . . totally innocent. We were looking at the sets and we got stuck in one of the doorways, and before I could—"

"That's not what Signor Casanova told us," Josefa interrupted, using her most dramatic, reprimanding voice. "I'll gather Constanze's clothes. František, get the footman to carry the boxes. I'll have them ready in a few minutes."

"Yes, my dear," František obeyed, casting a cockeyed glance toward the bed as he left the room.

"Don't bother taking her clothes, Josefa. I'll come with you and talk to Stanzi. I'll explain to her and tell her I love her. Then she'll come home with me."

"No she won't. She needs time, Wolfgang. I talked with her this morning. I've come to know her, even understand her. She's such a child still. She misses her baby but is afraid to leave you in Prague alone. Let her rest at our house. It will be better for both of you."

"She should be here with me. Tell her to come back."

"No, you need to be apart . . ."

"She's my wife!"

"That's right, your wife, not your servant, Wolfgang."

"She should be here with me. My mother would have never—"

"Your mother died young because she was dragged along from country to country, staying in drafty inns and riding in uncomfortable coaches to look after you and your father. Do you think she enjoyed that?"

"I never thought about it."

As Josefa lectured she collected some of Constanze's dresses and shoes and tossed them into the leather traveling cases. "Wolfgang, you must think about your wife, your family, your responsibilities. You're not some wandering minstrel. I don't want her to end up like your mother, God rest her soul."

Josefa made the sign of the cross.

"Neither do I," Wolfgang whispered. "Why do you torment me, Josefa, one minute trying to seduce me, the next lecturing me about my responsibilities?"

"Because I love you, Wolfgang. Because I can only imagine what it would be like to be married to a man like you, and because I realize that, deep down, you love Constanze. You're just a little confused right now."

"You know me well."

"We'll take care of Constanze. She can rest at the Villa."

"But . . ."

"But what?"

"I need her, Josefa. I need her with me. Sometimes when I compose she holds my hand and strokes it, like this." He took her hand in his and gently rubbed the back of it. The tension and anger in Josefa waned. She looked into his innocent eyes. The simple green dress she was holding slipped out of her other hand and dropped in a heap on the cold wood floor.

"When she holds my hand I relax. The past and the problems of today vanish. Then my head is clear and melodies replace the problems."

"Oh, Wolfgang. You're such a child. And we're all to blame for letting you be the way you are. And don't think I've forgiven you for your stunt with the aria the other night at my party. I've never been so humiliated, and in my own house. And then you let that Italian harlot Bondini sing the aria you wrote for me. It's a miracle I'm able to look at you. You've no idea how angry you made me."

"I didn't mean for it to happen."

"You never do."

"Why did you call Madame Bondini a harlot? She's not a bad singer."

"I dislike all Italian sopranos. They think they know more than the rest of us. They're so unrefined."

"Josefa, are you ready? The footman's here. Where are the boxes?" František called from the outer room.

"Just a moment. I'm almost ready." She realized Mozart was still holding her hand. Pulling it away from his, she quickly gathered up the dress she had dropped. The footman entered, bowed to Mozart, who was still sitting on the edge of the bed, closed the straps on the leather case and carried it out of the room. Josefa stood in front of Wolfgang, looking down at his forlorn face. With the back of her hand, she tenderly stroked his unshaven face.

"I'll talk to her for you. Give her time, and think about what I said. She's not your servant. Now get to work. You have an opera to finish. Everyone's depending on you." In the most motherly way she could manage, she kissed him on the head.

"Wash up and get something to eat. You'll feel better. František will let you know when Constanze's ready to see you."

Josefa gathered up her skirts, blew him a kiss and glided out of the bedchamber. František followed, waving as he left. Mozart sat on the bed, his feet swaying from side to side, the minuet still playing in his head. When it finished he splashed cold water on his face. He desperately needed a shave, but first he needed some food.

In the outer room he found the silver bell on the mantel. He rang it, letting its sweet sound fill the room's silence. A young girl answered his call, entering the outer chamber and curtsying quickly.

"You're new."

"Yes sir. May I bring you something?"

"Yes! Breakfast."

"But, sir, it's late in the afternoon." Wolfgang was perplexed. He went over to the window and drew back the heavy curtains. Although it was cloudy, he could tell by the light it was indeed afternoon.

"My God! I've slept through the rehearsals."

"Excuse me, sir," the young girl said timidly.

"What?"

"The opera house was closed today."

"How do you know that?"

"I pass it on my way to work."

"And do you know why it was closed?"

"A man said the singers were recovering from last night's performance."

"You're a useful little thing, aren't you. How long have you worked here?"

"I don't work for the inn, sir."

"Then who hired you?"

"An older man hired me to wait on you."

Mozart studied her. "Do you recall his name?"

"He said he was a chevalier. He paid me in advance. I've been sitting outside your door since early this morning waiting for you to call."

"Did the people who were here just now see you?"

"No sir."

"How is that possible?"

"I hid when I saw them approaching. That's what the chevalier ordered me to do."

"Casanova . . ." Mozart mumbled. "Well, since you're here, get me some food."

"Yes sir," she said as she curtsied and hurried from the room.

Mozart sat at his writing table. Sheets of music were strewn haphazardly. He piled them up neatly, moved them to the far corner of the table and found some plain writing paper.

Dearest Friend! he wrote, addressing a letter to the Baron Gottfried von Jacquin and dating it Monday October 15, 1787.

You most likely believe that by now my opera is over. You would be mistaken. You see, here in Prague the singers especially are not as good as the ones in Vienna and so the preparations have taken far longer than they should. So, last night, despite the protests from the high and mighty ladies who didn't think the opera was an appropriate oeuvre to celebrate the royal wedding, we performed my Figaro. *How wrong they were. It was a splendid performance.*

In any event, Don Giovanni *is now scheduled for the twenty-fourth.*

"Your food, sir," the serving girl announced, carrying a small plate with a round silver cover.

"Bring it here," he ordered, pushing the letter aside. As the girl carefully placed the plate on his table, he admired her figure and wondered what Casanova had done with her. "These are the true joys of mankind," he said, pointing to a piece of roasted capon that the inn's chef had prepared.

"Yes, sir."

She backed up a pace or two and stood silently, her head bowed.

Mozart savored the meal, eating fast at first, then slowing down between bites. When the plate was about half empty, he leaned back in his chair, took a long drink of wine and looked at the girl. "You don't have to stand. I don't believe in that kind of ceremony. We're both God-fearing people."

She moved toward him. "I was told to stay with you, sir."

"Who told you?"

"The Chevalier, sir."

"What else did my good friend Casanova tell you?"

"I'm not allowed to say, Maestro."

"Maestro? So you know who I am?"

"Oh, yes sir, of course, sir."

"How?"

"Sir, the street musicians play your tunes all the time."

"What tunes?"

"From *Figaro*, sir."

"And do you like it?"

"Oh, very much, sir."

Mozart beamed inwardly. He took another sip of wine, surreptitiously ogling the girl. Though distorted by the rosy-colored base of the crystal glass, she looked quite pretty in a young, petite, innocent way.

"I told you, you don't have to stand. Come, sit down next to me."

Mozart pointed to the other chair. Timidly the young girl walked over to the chair and sat on its edge, perched as if ready to jump up in case someone should unexpectedly walk into the room. "What's your name?"

"Theresa, sir. But they call me Dorabella, sir."

"Stop calling me 'sir.' It makes me feel old."

"Very well, si—"

Mozart laughed. It was a warm laugh that relaxed her. "Who calls you Dorabella?"

"Many people."

"Does Signor Casanova call you Dorabella?"

"Yes, sir. He does, though I've only been with him once."

"And when Casanova asked you to come here, what exactly did he tell you?"

"I'm not allowed to say."

"But you must tell me. It will be our little secret," he said, using his most childish voice.

"I'll get in trouble."

"I won't let you, I promise."

Mozart noticed the blood rush into the girl's cheeks. Her discomfort was all too evident. "I'm new to this. That's why Signor Casanova chose me."

Suddenly her real purpose—her job—became clear to him. Mozart got up, tossed his white linen napkin onto the table and walked over to the door, which was still ajar. He pushed it closed and turned the key, locking it. "Now, my Dorabella, tell me what the good Signor Casanova instructed."

Without uttering a word, she stood up, then curtsied low, all the way down to the wood floor, her head bowed so that her soft, fragrant blonde hair flowed over her face. "I'm at your service, Maestro."

Then, still kneeling, she unlaced the top of her simple dress, revealing her young, full breasts. Mozart swallowed hard, stopped by the combination of innocence and sexuality kneeling in front of him. Her head was still bent down, but her eyes looked upward, longingly. Even though he knew it was an illusion, inspired by a still-to-be-made payment, the caring look in her eyes reminded him of the way Constanze used to look at him when they first met. His mind flooded with memories of the past, a time when he ached to see Constanze and she to see him. A time he yearned to recapture.

Without taking her eyes away from his, Dorabella moved her hands up the front of his britches, stroking the velvet, making it warm to the touch, inside and out. Her expertise surprised him, until he reminded himself it was Casanova himself who had selected her, probably after a lengthy, private audition. But, even as her actions became more intense, the innocence never left her eyes. Mozart had to stare into them. Again he was drawn back to another time, when he was planning to marry Constanze. Despite Dorabella's passionate embrace around his waist, he recalled the letters he had written to his father explaining why he needed to marry.

I can't live as most young men do. I have too much religion, am too honorable to seduce an innocent maiden and have too much fear of disease to be with whores . . .

But now, with Dorabella wrapped around him, he was faced with a choice: between what nature was urging and what he'd been taught by his father was morally correct. Standing up, Dorabella pulled him until they were touching. Slowly she backed up toward the bedchamber, her dress falling off a little bit with each step until—she wore no undergarments—she was standing naked in front of him.

"It's all right," she whispered, closing her eyes as if waiting for him to push her onto the bed.

But when she closed her eyes, the trance broke. Mozart pulled away from her and stumbled backward. Instead of seeing Dorabella, his mind was filled with images of Casanova and Constanze, laughing happily together.

"I can't let it happen," he yelled.

Frustrated yet still determined, Dorabella moved closer to him, rubbing his chest, kissing his neck. Then, when he least expected it, she started humming the music of Cherubino's aria from the *Marriage of Figaro*.

"No . . . don't . . . please . . . leave me . . . please," he moaned.

But Dorabella persisted, groping him faster and faster. His knees weakened and his breathing became labored. She was on her knees again, rubbing her chest against his pants, playfully laughing and singing at the same time. Mozart stood still, praying she would stop, and hoping she wouldn't.

It started to rain. The gentle pitter-patter tapping at the window caught Dorabella's attention, distracting her from her mission. In that split second Mozart was freed, and managed to pull himself away. It was a cleansing rain.

"Leave! Tell Casanova I was too tired to enjoy your services. You can tell them I said you should be paid for your efforts. But make sure they know nothing happened here. It's very important. Be sure you tell them. Do you understand?"

"But I was ordered to stay with you all night."

"No. I have to be alone tonight. Please, believe me . . . under different circumstances . . . I wouldn't be able to refuse. But not now."

Dorabella pulled her dress on, pausing before reenclosing her breasts.

"Are you sure you won't reconsider?"

Mozart, afraid the words would come out wrong or not at all, simply nodded and turned away to let her dress in privacy, which he realized later was probably not necessary. She finished dressing, straightened her hair and breezed past the table and the cold remains of his dinner.

Pausing at the door, she turned to look at him.

"I was looking forward to it. We could have done things you can't even imagine. Too bad."

As she left, Mozart saw that the innocent look in her eyes was replaced by the hard edge of experience. He wandered over to the window and pulled the curtain to one side, looking out onto the wet street below. A carriage with two beautiful white and light brown horses was stopped in front of the inn. It looked much like the carriage he and his sister Nannerl had traveled in when they were children on tour in Europe. They would pass the long hours drawing pictures of make-believe castles and palaces on the windows, pretending to be a king and queen, happy forever. How lonely he felt now.

As he emerged from this daydream, he saw a cloaked figure leave the inn. A footman holding a torch climbed down from the carriage and opened its door. The cloaked figure paused before getting in, turned and looked directly at his windows. Dorabella threw him a kiss and disappeared into the elegant coach. Mozart watched as the horses pulled the carriage through the streets, splashing anyone unfortunate enough to be near its path.

The rain fell steadily as evening turned to night. Mozart looked at the *Don Giovanni* score, and pushed it aside. He wandered around the darkened room for a few minutes, then removed a small leather box from his traveling trunk. Taking the lone candle from the writing table, he went into the bedchamber. He undressed and put on a plain white nightshirt. Climbing onto the bed, he pulled the bedcovers up to his neck and moved the leather box so it was next to him. Carefully he undid the pink silk ribbon holding it closed. With special care, he took out the fading letters he always kept with him. The handwriting, each one unique, brought the writers' voices back to him. He had his favorite letters: funny stories his sister had written; sad, lonely thoughts his mother had sent when he was in Italy with his father; and page after page of advice from his father.

Accompanied by the falling rain, Mozart reread letters he knew by heart until the bedside candle had burned out. He gently lowered the box of letters onto the floor. Yawning, he stretched out on his side, pulling Constanze's pillow to his chest and squeezing it tightly. He closed his eyes, hoping to dream of happier times.

Chapter Thirteen

y the time Mozart opened his eyes and peeked out from under the blankets, it was late morning. The rain fell steadily; the clouds were thick, a slate gray. Even when he drew the curtains all the way back, the room remained somber. Mozart stood at the window, watching the rainwater flowing down Prague's streets, pushing dirt and piles of soiled paper in its path. He liked the way little rivulets formed around the worn edges of the cobblestones, and he traced them back as far as he could see. But his line of sight was broken often by people hurrying across the streets, their cloaks pulled up around their necks to fend off the cold gusts whipping around.

Reacting involuntarily to the scene outside his window, Mozart shivered and tightened the belt on his dressing gown. "What I need is a fire and food," he said aloud. The sound of his voice echoing in the empty room surprised him. He wasn't used to being alone.

He picked up the tiny bell, to ring for one of the inn's servants, but paused to look at it.

"What if she came back?" he wondered. "What if she were here and came into the room, took me in her arms and kissed me? What would I do?"

But his daytime fantasy ended when he realized he was uncertain if his thoughts were about Dorabella or Constanze. Images of their two faces blended uncomfortably in his mind. He shook his head, trying to dislodge the picture. He rang the bell. Impulsively, he rang it again and again, making up a little dance rhythm. "I'll have to use that sometime," he thought, mindlessly continuing to ring the bell.

"I'm coming!" a deep voice called out from the outer hallway. "I'm coming, Maestro. Just a moment. I'll be right there. Be patient."

A loud knock interrupted his impromptu bell concert. Mozart grabbed the bell with his palm, silencing the final reverberations. He unlocked the door and swung it open. The servant bowed low. Mozart turned away and walked over to his writing table. But a deep, insolent voice stopped him in his tracks.

"Well, it's about time you woke up. I've been sitting out there all morning waiting for you. Who do you think you are? Some nobleman with nothing to do but sleep and eat?"

Mozart was about to reprimand the man for his impudence, but there was something familiar about the servant's muffled voice. "Casanova?"

"At your service, Maestro."

Casanova adjusted his collar, turned his cloak right side out, brushed the mud from his boots and tossed a folded newspaper onto the writing table.

"I'm surprised to see you here this morning. Didn't I send Dorabella back early enough for you last night? I assumed you'd be with her."

"I wasn't there when she returned. I was otherwise engaged. I saw her this morning when I went to have a bath and a shave at her house. What a sweet thing she is, much like her mother, who's also a friend of mine. Let me tell you, those women know how to pamper a man. Dorabella got right into the bath and gently washed me all over. Then, when I felt fully refreshed, she toweled me dry and arranged my hair."

"And that's all that happened?" Mozart questioned with a disbelieving tone in his voice.

"No more than that, I assure you. Only slightly more than happened here last night."

"She told you?"

"Everything, and in great detail.

"And?"

"I wasn't the least bit surprised that she failed, and that you refused."

"And why is that?"

"A theory about human nature and about you."

"And what, dear Chevalier, is your theory."

"It's quite simple and obvious really—you're in love with your wife."

"True."

"That controls your behavior."

"But, I'm not dead. I'm still a man . . . I still have desires . . . I still see women . . ."

"Yes. But you play out those fantasies—and they *are* nothing more than fantasies—in relatively safe places."

"You're insane!"

"On the contrary. I'm quite rational. It's you who's crazy, but that's what makes you creative."

"I'm never sure if you're insulting or complimenting me."

"Take what I say as a compliment. I wish I had your creative powers, just as you wish you had my experience with women."

"What do you mean about the 'relatively safe places'?"

"You know what I mean."

"Explain."

Casanova sighed and, with the gentlest, most fatherly voice he could find, explained his theory.

"You begin your little romantic scenes with women knowing full well you'll never play them out. For example, at the Dušeks', in the garden, you knew we would discover you and Madame Dušek in the pavilion. That's why you didn't pick up her lace. And the other night after the *Figaro*, you left signs all over the stage—like a trail—so you would be found with Signora Bondini. It's your way of proving to yourself that women want to be with you while always making certain the circumstances are such that the act will not—no, *cannot*—be consummated."

Casanova paced as he delivered his lecture, and Mozart had settled into the chair with his legs casually slung over the upholstered arm. "You don't know if I've always done that. Maybe I simply didn't want to consummate . . ." Mozart defended weakly.

"You're the one who claimed to be alive and have the desires all men have. I assure you, had I been with either of those women the outcomes would have been different; the acts would never have been left unfinished."

Casanova saw Mozart lower his eyes and furrow his brow, and was distracted by the nagging realization that this innocent man-child had found ways to expose and express all of mankind's emotions and frailties in his music. Even the stubble on Mozart's face seemed out of place to the older man. How he pitied and envied the composer, the creator.

Casanova cautiously knelt next to the chair so he was eye to eye with Mozart. He took the composer's face in his hands. Mozart tried to avert his eyes, but there was a magnetism to Casanova's stare pulling them together.

"Let me be your guide. Let me show you," Casanova whispered intensely.

"Show me what?"

"Show you that the life you have chosen to live is filled with rewards far greater than the momentary pleasures I experience. In the end, I will bring you and Constanze back together. Give me that pleasure; it's one unlike any I've ever had."

"And what do you get out of this?"

"It's not for me."

"Then, who?"

"For the world . . ."

"You're insane," Mozart repeated.

"No. Listen to me. I'm convinced you were placed on this earth to create, to raise us up and show what greatness we have within us, to rise above the wars and hatred filling our world."

Mozart guffawed. "You give me far more credit than I deserve." Mozart then waited until the silence felt too long. "Do you fear God, Giacomo?"

"Yes, but I don't believe in his uniform goodness the way you do. I've seen too much suffering to believe unquestioningly."

"I was taught to believe God has a reason for everything." Mozart paused and looked at Casanova. "It's God who grants me the opportunity to express through music what I cannot with words."

"Lorenzo told me the Masses you've composed for the church are gems."

"I composed as I was instructed."

"And why do you think God has given you your talent?"

Mozart considered the question. "I once believed God gave me my talent so I could improve my parents' position. That is what the gospel teaches."

"And now? What do you believe now that your parents are dead? Why do you compose now?"

Mozart closed his eyes. "It's all I know. If I couldn't compose I'd die."

"Let me help you. Let me make it my duty to assure you're able to compose."

"Why are you so intent on helping me? Composers come and go. We're merely entertainers; at best we're possessions the nobility collects and dangles before other courts as trophies."

Casanova rose, slowly pulling Mozart out of the chair. "Trust me!" he hissed with greater passion and intensity.

"Why should I?"

"Because we're as different as two men can be. And because you need Constanze and I know how to get her back."

Mozart wiggled free of the older man's tight grasp. The unfinished *Don Giovanni* score lay scattered on the writing table.

"Give me your hand," Casanova ordered. "We'll make a pact. I'll lead you to the love you need to compose."

"And what do I do for you?"

"You'll turn Don Giovanni into a legend; it will be your payment to me."

Mozart extended his arm. Casanova grabbed the outstretched hand and squeezed until Mozart pulled it away.

"How do we start?" Mozart asked, rubbing his fingers.

"First, we transform you."

Casanova bounded to the door and opened it, clapping loudly. A barber and an assistant marched in, bowed and swiftly set up a chair and a porcelain washbasin. The barber ushered Mozart over to the chair and removed his client's robe, replacing it with a plain white smock. Casanova sat down at the table and opened the newspaper he had tossed there.

"What are you reading?"

"The *Oberpostamtszeitung*."

Casanova scanned the thin pages of Prague's morning newspaper. "Anything interesting?" Mozart asked, his voice muffled by the shaving cream being applied to his cheeks.

"The usual news: petty crimes, the Emperor's latest reforms, a review of *Figaro*. Nothing special."

"A review of *Figaro*! Well, don't torture me; what does it say?"

Casanova scanned the page, reading silently. "It's not bad . . . very good actually."

"What does it say about me?" Mozart pleaded anxiously.

"Well, let's see . . . not bad . . . not bad at all . . ."

"Please, Maestro, you must sit still," the barber implored. "I can't shave your face while you're turning in every direction."

Mozart tried to sit still, but he kept fidgeting.

"Well, are you going to read it to me?" he asked exasperatedly.

"Oh, you want me to read it out loud? Are you certain you want these men to hear it?"

"Read!" Mozart shouted.

Casanova cleared his throat for dramatic effect. "'Prague's Italian opera presented a special performance of *The Marriage of Figaro* to celebrate the visit of the Archduchess and Prince of Saxony. The zeal of the musicians and the presence of Mozart, the Master, resulted in an event satisfying to Their Highnesses and the audience. Their Highnesses approved of the opera and the splendid performance."'

Mozart's face erupted in a wide grin, cracking the thick lather the barber had applied. "Well, that should silence a few people."

"*Figaro* has wonderful music, Maestro," the barber's assistant said timidly.

"Were you there, at the performance?" Mozart asked with surprise.

"No sir."

"Then how do you know the music?"

"There's a harpist at one of the taverns who plays the melodies from *Figaro*. I've heard him many times."

"Another thief with good taste!" Mozart laughed.

"Maestro, please. No more conversation," the barber insisted.

Casanova put the newspaper aside and began to read through the pages of the *Don Giovanni* score.

"You know," Mozart said after the lather had been shaved from near his mouth, "Figaro was a barber. In fact Beaumarchais wrote a play before his *Figaro* called *The Barber of Seville*."

"I saw the play in Paris," Casanova mentioned.

"And what did you think of it?"

"Not nearly as interesting or revolutionary as *Figaro*."

"Could it be an opera?"

"No. The story's too silly. Now be quiet and let this barber of Prague do what he needs to do. You know, Wolfgang, I have a shave three times a day. I like my skin to be smooth and clean. You should try it."

Mozart smiled and sat back to let the barber finish shaving his light beard. He enjoyed Casanova's company and wished he could see the older man's reactions to the *Don Giovanni* score he was perusing. But the barber kept Mozart's face looking away from the writing table, where Casanova's amazement increased as he turned the pages. Though he wasn't a great musician, his training as a violinist allowed him to recognize the brilliance of what Mozart had written. The work flowed from one scene to the next as characters were introduced and conflicts developed, all furthering the legend of Don Juan. How Casanova wanted to *be* Don Giovanni. Closing his eyes, he imagined himself onstage, elegantly dressed as the handsome Don, young, virile and demonic. The music he saw on the pages only made his desire to be Don Giovanni greater.

"Finished, Maestro," the barber announced dramatically, whisking some powder from Mozart's neck.

"Thank you," Mozart said, removing the smock and getting out of the chair. Wanting to pay the barber, he looked around for some money but couldn't find any. "Never mind. I've taken care of it," Casanova interceded.

The barber and his assistant packed up their towels and lotions, bowed toward Casanova and quickly left, closing the door behind them.

"I have to go to the opera house," Mozart said.

"I'll come with you."

Mozart dressed, admiring his newly coifed hair. He put on a brocade coat and slipped on the leather, knee-high boots that made him feel like a cavalier. He took his brown cloak and matching hat to ward off the rain. Casanova looked at his protégé, adjusted the collar of the composer's shirt, and bowed low with his hat in his hand, allowing Mozart to precede him through the door. "Your servant."

It took just a few minutes to reach the opera house, where they climbed the stairs to Pasquale Bondini's office. His officious assistant, who was usually seated just outside the large wooden doors, wasn't there. Mozart was about to knock, but the sound of raised voices within the office caught his attention.

"If we don't start rehearsing soon I'll have to return to Vienna. The Emperor doesn't like me to be away for long periods. He believes it stymies the creativity of his court composers."

"You take yourself far too seriously, Lorenzo."

"And you don't, Pasquale?"

"I run this theater. You don't."

"We need to rehearse. Mozart needs to finish the opera."

"I haven't forgiven him for the other evening," said Bondini.

"You didn't take that seriously, did you?"

"Of course. Why wouldn't I? He was with my wife. That's no minor offense."

"He's an innocent young man. You've nothing to fear."

Mozart was crestfallen, and he looked at Casanova, who returned the glance with a facial expression that said: "What did I tell you?"

"I don't know about that," Bondini mused, momentarily lifting Mozart's spirits. There was a long silence.

"Well, I suppose you're right, Lorenzo," Bondini decided. "He's an impetuous young man. He was probably just moved by Caterina's performance . . . nothing more . . . let's call it innocent, artistic behavior. I shouldn't forgive him, but we have an opera to produce."

Standing near the door, Mozart was about to barge in to defend himself. But Casanova put a firm hand on his shoulder, freezing him in place.

"Pasquale, you must order the singers to start rehearsing so we can get on with the opera," Da Ponte insisted.

"I'll send messages to them this evening. Rehearsals will resume tomorrow afternoon. Will you inform Maestro Mozart?"

"I will. Good-bye, Pasquale, and may I suggest you spend this evening with your wife."

There was no audible reply.

Mozart and Casanova scurried down a nearby corridor and watched as the office doors swung open and Da Ponte emerged. Sneaking on tiptoe, they followed him down the stairs and out into the street. The rain had stopped. Quietly they scampered around a puddle and grabbed Da Ponte's arms from behind.

"Stop!" he yelled, frightened by the surprise attack. "Oh, Giacomo, Mozart . . . thank God. I thought you were robbers."

"You're always so dramatic, Lorenzo. Are you going to turn this episode into a libretto for the Emperor? Perhaps it could be a plot for one of his stymied composers," Mozart teased.

"Listen, Wolfgang. If it weren't for me, Bondini would have canceled the opera entirely. I talked him into allowing you to complete the commission."

The three men walked a few blocks to the Unicorn Inn, passed under a stone archway and entered an adjacent café. When the owner realized who Mozart was, he greeted him loudly and, with exaggerated bustle, ordered the waiters to clear the finest table "for the Maestro and his guests." Making sure the few other people in the café were watching, he led them to the table. The three men removed their hats and cloaks and sat down. A young serving girl nervously took their order of coffees and tarts.

"Have you finished the score?" Da Ponte asked.

Mozart shook his head.

"He will," said Casanova.

"We're opening in a week."

Mozart's silence was uncomfortable.

"I've received another letter from de Sade," Casanova offered, filling the void.

"Oh, now that will make all the difference," said Da Ponte sarcastically.

"I've thought about him a lot since his first letter," Mozart said. "I can't imagine being stuck in a cell. I couldn't survive such torture."

Da Ponte sipped his coffee and sniffed at the plate of desserts the serving girl had brought. Casanova unfolded two sheets of yellowed paper stained with candle drippings, adjusted the pages of de Sade's letter, then read aloud:

"My Dear Friends, I address you this way for, although we have never met, I feel a kinship with you and with the creative effort in which we are engaged.

149

"Since I last wrote, only two days ago—although here in the Bastille two days can be longer than a lifetime—I have thought about nothing but your Don Juan. Just the idea of an opera about that grandest of legends has given me two nights of indescribable pleasure."

"I'm not certain I want to know what he considers to be 'indescribable pleasure,'" Da Ponte interjected.

Casanova continued.

"On the first night I dreamed of being with Donna Elvira. She must be played as a prostitute who has fallen in love with Giovanni. It would be an appropriate tribute to his sexual prowess to have a woman who charges for her services give him for free what others must pay for. It would wake this sleepy world to see Don Giovanni take this harlot into his castle, bind her hands and feet with thick rope and have her watch, totally unclothed, as he eats a grand supper. Be clear, though—he mustn't harm her.

"This connection between sex and food is undeniable; the Romans themselves included both as part of any orgy, and I can tell you from personal experience that a man's penis is never as stiff as when he has finished a sumptuous meal. And be certain Giovanni's meal includes a chocolate cake as dark as the devil's burnt ass. The chocolate must be dense and the cake's icing should encase the delicacy so that when Don Giovanni tears into it, the symbolism isn't lost on the silly aristocrats who fill the opera house."

Suddenly the custard oozing from the piece of cake Da Ponte had stuffed into his mouth lost its delicate flavor. Mozart took a sip of his coffee. His mind was a blur.

"Should I continue?" asked Casanova.

"Of course," Da Ponte shouted. "The Emperor's court poet can certainly learn about drama from the likes of the Marquis de Sade."

"Lorenzo, keep your voice down," said Mozart. Like a child experiencing something forbidden for the first time, he wanted to hear more.

"As to Zerlina, the charming peasant girl, be sure during the party at the end of the first act we see Giovanni with her. Don't leave the scene to the audience's imagination. Perhaps you could have a dungeon represented onstage, where he could do to her what he pleases. Alone with a nobleman, a girl like Zerlina would not only give in to his desires, but she would beg him to explore parts of her body her oaf husband would never see. That is the nature of the class system, and all the talk of revolution will never change human nature. Let the world see it, accompany the acts by pretty music, but be sure to shock, because through shock you gain social approval.

"(As an aside, this is a point I have made in my novel The 120 Days of Sodom. *Perhaps Maestro Mozart would consider this book as the basis for an opera. It would be an honor to rework it as a libretto, although its length may be an impediment.)"*

"Well, there you have it. Mozart, your next opera will be about Sodom. I'm sure His Majesty will be understanding. After all, he now allows the wedding dance in *Figaro* to be shown."

"Have you no pity, Lorenzo?" Mozart asked softly.

Casanova looked up from the scrawled, tiny words of de Sade's letter. Da Ponte squirmed in his chair. "It's not that I don't pity the man; only his arrogance bothers me. It's insanity to think we could put any of his perversions on a stage. These are dangerous times we live in. Consider the reaction to a work as simple and human as *Figaro*. The aristocrats called it 'revolutionary.' It was a struggle to get it produced, and it's about love. It's not that I have no pity. But I do have a healthy fear of prison, something the Marquis clearly doesn't share."

"He has no choice," said Casanova. "It's his mother-in-law who has him arrested, and every time he's released from prison, she petitions the authorities and they throw him right back into the Bastille. She is the monster in his tragic life."

"But you can't take his suggestions seriously."

"Of course not, but there were many times when my exploits with women bordered on the kind of behavior de Sade writes of," Casanova said.

"What stopped you?"

"Society, Mozart."

"Why?"

"Because to thrive we must live in a socially acceptable way. Without that we would be excommunicated and treated like animals."

"But de Sade believes that social acceptance can be gained by shocking. Perhaps there's something to that idea."

Da Ponte exploded, "If your father were alive he would take you by the scruff of the neck, drag you home and lock you in your room until you returned to your senses."

"He's dead! He's dead and doesn't control me anymore, Lorenzo. I'm alone—a father, a husband. I have my own thoughts now. My father lived his life looking for social acceptance. He dragged me from court to court like a trained monkey, showing what I could do on the harpsichord. The nobility applauded, tossed coins at me, fed me at their lavish tables, then dismissed me. My father spent his life in the service of the Archbishop of Salzburg. The man was deaf and my father played in his orchestra for decades, never asking for more than a salary. When my father died, what did he have to show for all those years? A drafty little house in Salzburg. No fortune, no vast collections, no marble statue in the town square, no memoirs . . . nothing. And when I die who will remember the symphonies, or the concertos, or the operas? At least de Sade may be remembered . . . not fondly, perhaps, but remembered."

The outburst brought all conversation in the café to a stop. The owner quietly walked over to their table and refilled Da Ponte's cup from a pewter coffeepot.

"Perhaps we've heard enough of the letter," Casanova whispered.

"No. I want to hear it. Please, read the rest, unless Lorenzo's innocent ears are too offended."

"Go on," Da Ponte mumbled.

Casanova swallowed the bite of chocolate cake he'd tasted during the silence.

"This next part deals with the scene when Donna Anna visits her father's grave.

"In the scene at the Commendatore's statue, Donna Anna should kneel to pray at his feet. When she sings of her love for her dead father, of the pain of his loss, there should be some implication that her love is more than that of a daughter for her father. Try to insinuate that the reason her father chased her attacker that night—of course the audience knows it was Don Giovanni—was to protect what was his. Make it clear that Donna Anna was more to her father than just a devoted daughter; that would make his attack on Don Giovanni more credible. Perhaps, to make it even more believable, you could have the Commendatore's ghost appear. He could then stand between Donna Anna and that simpering nobleman Don Ottavio who thinks someday she'll marry him."

"Well, there you have it. A little incest. The censors will be comfortable. Perhaps the statue of the dead Commendatore should be naked. That would give Donna Anna something to sing to. It would be a wonderful sight from the loge. I can see it now: a stone statue with an erection."

Mozart was silent as Casanova read on.

"I have given some thought to Don Giovanni's final scene. We must be sure the dinner he is enjoying is splendid, not some meager collection of stage props. There needs to be lots of meat: chicken, veal and mutton so he can tear into the flesh of each animal. But make certain there are no

messy sauces. One of the crimes for which the French should be punished is their insistence on sauces. All they do is hide the true flavor of food. Let the food be undressed, naked, splendid. Cakes, creams, apple fritters, cooked fruit should also be lavishly displayed so when Donna Elvira comes in to try to convince Giovanni to change his ways, it is clear to her that even when he dines alone he is a man of large appetites.

"I think the stage effect of having Don Giovanni dragged off to hell after his struggle with the Commendatore's statue will be hard to do without making the audience laugh. It should be a glorious moment. Urge the singer entrusted with this part to show the fine line that exists between pain and pleasure. The agonies leading to death must be slow and abominable if they are to quicken the pulse. The nobles in their finery must be made to squirm, to have their garments soiled by the delightful pain of release. When Don Giovanni grabs the statue's cold hand, his writhing and pain must be visible."

Casanova looked up from the letter. Mozart was staring at his hand, the one Casanova had squeezed so fiercely earlier that afternoon. Mozart used his napkin to wipe a bead of perspiration from his forehead while Da Ponte shifted in his chair, covertly adjusting himself under the tablecloth. "I'm not sure I've captured that particular emotion in the music for the final scene."

All three men laughed.

"Is there any more?" Da Ponte asked, draining his fourth cup of coffee and brushing some cake crumbs from his shirt.

Casanova turned the last page over, squinting to decipher the tiny, black scrawls. "A few lines."

"Well, let's hear them."

"A few other thoughts. As to the question of 'legend,' which has been obsessing me since you first wrote, allow me to tell you plainly how I see it.

154

"There is a characteristic of the ignorant to prefer the unknown, the preposterous, the outlandish, the far-fetched, the fantastic, yes even the terrible, to truth. Truth engages the imagination far less than fiction. The crudest among us want nothing more than to rehear stupendous fables filled with religious images and bizarre mysteries. The truly religious cater to the desires of the crowd and convince them there is indeed a God. But when we reason and think clearly, we must question, what is God but a myth . . . a legend passed down to us?

"To my way of thinking, the greatest mark one can make on this earth is to become a legend, to have the story of one's life so confused between fact and fiction that for generations to come, our exploits outlive us. And what are those exploits? Merely ignoring society's arbitrary laws. Someday we will realize that man is not controlled by laws, but by passions. It is the strongest of passions that led to mankind's finest artistic creations. Men who aren't motivated by strong passions are nothing more than mediocre creatures. Great passions yield great men. If there is no passion, there is decrepitude and stupidity.

"Don't for a moment think my incarceration has left me devoid of passion. I am filled with thirst for revenge, with disgust, with hate. But all of those passions are overwhelmed by my all-consuming desire for freedom, to break these chains and once again be part of the world. And so, isolated and desperate, I allow myself to dream. To dream of a world that acknowl-edges the necessity of personal freedom and expression. Late at night, after I have satisfied my physical needs, I fantasize about a new world led by men who are passionate about liberty. I wonder when my countrymen will rebel and break the chains binding us to a society unable to fly freely. When will you claim the freedoms—public and personal—you are due?

"Dearest Chevalier, I have rambled on far too long, but these words are the only way I can cast my spirit beyond these stone walls. Please tell Maestro Mozart how thoughts of his opera have helped me survive. Perhaps someday I will be able to take my place in the theater to hear the masterpiece Don Giovanni will be. On that day I will think of my friend *the Chevalier whose generous spirit allowed me to briefly feel like a free man.*

"Each night before I close my eyes, I say a prayer which I have written. I fervently ask our God for one favor."

Casanova glanced up from the page and saw Mozart cross himself.

"I ask Him to refrain from choosing as my correctors men more wicked than I. But in the end, just before I drift into my wonderful world of dreams, before I escape to the visions of your characters and the libertine world they inhabit, I beg Him to help my torturers concoct some other means to subjugate their fellow man.

"The time has again come for me to suffer. I will call down every curse upon my torturers. My pen drops from my hand. Farewell, until I write again. Don't forget your friend, de Sade. Vive la liberté!"

Casanova folded the pages and placed them on the table. During his reading the café had emptied. It was quiet now except for the distant sound of plates and cups being stored in the pantry area. The café's owner tended to the fire, keeping two small logs aglow in the raised hearth; their meager heat took little of the chill from the room.

Da Ponte reached across the table and gently touched the folded pages as if he were stroking a baby's cheek. Mozart stared at the far wall, afraid to look at either of his colleagues. "Well," Casanova broke the silence. "It has grown late. It's already dark."

"I hadn't noticed." Mozart replied wearily.

Casanova stood up, tossed some coins on the table, picked up the folded letter and put on his cloak. Da Ponte pushed his chair away from the table.

"I have to get to work on a libretto. Good night. I'll see you at tomorrow afternoon's rehearsal."

"Yes . . . good night . . . yes, I'll see you tomorrow, Lorenzo," Mozart replied.

"Are you going to sit here all night?"

"No. I'm coming."

Casanova walked with him out the door and into the street. It was dark. The damp chill of an autumnal Prague night ate through Mozart's thin cloak. Casanova saw him shivering. "Are you all right?"

Mozart nodded. "Fine, thank you. Would you join me for supper? I hate to dine alone. I'm afraid I don't share that trait with Don Giovanni."

Casanova smiled. "Normally it would be my honor and pleasure, but I'm afraid I have other plans."

"Some young girl . . . maybe a soprano . . . a mezzo . . . a married woman?"

"No. Nothing like that."

"Then what?" Mozart pleaded like a child whose parents won't tell him the whole story.

"An engagement."

"Dorabella? It's Dorabella. I knew she was yours."

"No. Nothing like that, either."

"Please tell me."

Casanova gave in reluctantly. "I've been invited to a supper party."

"Where?"

Casanova paused. "Can I give you this to keep?" he asked, handing de Sade's letter to Mozart.

"Yes . . . certainly. But please tell me where your party is."

Casanova walked up the block toward the inn's entrance. Mozart stood still and shouted: "Where? Damn it. I have to know!"

Casanova leaned back from the door and shouted: "The Villa Bertramka. Constanze invited me. See you tomorrow. Your servant," he added, tipping his hat as he disappeared into the Unicorn Inn. Casanova's laugh echoed into the street.

There was a sudden gust of wind. Mozart shivered, loosening his grip. He watched helplessly as de Sade's letter blew away, landing in a puddle left from the afternoon's rain. Mozart ran over to retrieve the fragile pages, but by the time he got there, the ink had run, smearing de Sade's words.

Mozart sat down on a nearby bench. By the illumination of the light blue fall moon that had broken through the clouds, he stared at the illegible pages. His tears blended with the inky rainwater.

Chapter Fourteen

František Dušek, wearing a plain black frock coat, white chemise, a white neck-cloth, white hose and black shoes, paced the hallway outside the bedrooms on the upper floor of the Villa Bertramka. When Constanze came out of her room, it looked to her as if he were talking to himself.

"František, are you all right?"

Startled, he looked at her. "I'm sorry. Did you ask me something?"

"Are you all right?"

"Oh . . . yes . . . yes. Fine. I get a little nervous before parties. Josefa gives me so much to do I have difficulty remembering."

"Can I help?"

"No. I'll be fine." He looked at her, a thankful expression crossing his face. "But you're not dressed for the party," he said, noticing the plain striped, ankle-length dress she was wearing.

"No. I thought it would be better if I stayed in my room this evening. I'm never comfortable at parties without Wolfgang."

"That's absurd! You'll be fine."

Suddenly he looked concerned, furrowing his brow.

"What's wrong?"

"I just remembered Josefa asked me to find you. She wants you to help her choose a gown for this evening."

"Where is she?"

"In her boudoir. I think she is having a bath. Please go now or she'll be angry with me."

Constanze went over to him and planted a kiss on his forehead. "You sweet man. Sometimes when I get frustrated with Wolfgang I think of you and how kind you are to Josefa despite her . . ."

"Her shortcomings," he completed. "Well, be that as it may, there's nothing I can do about it now, so I accept her as she is. Now, please go see her before she becomes angry."

Constanze walked down the hallway, past the large oil paintings of the Dušek family, each in its ornate, gold frame. She stopped at the arched doorway to Josefa's room and knocked softly.

"Enter," Josefa's rich voice sang out from inside.

Constanze opened the door and entered Josefa's large suite of rooms. Dresses of every color and style were spread across the settee.

"Josefa," Constanze called.

"In here."

Constanze walked into the inner chamber. Josefa was soaking in the large marble tub while one of her serving girls poured in pitchers of warm water.

"I'm sorry," Constanze stammered. "I didn't mean to disturb—"

"Don't be silly. Come. Sit near me. Show me what you're wearing this evening."

Constanze approached, trying not to look directly at Josefa, whose large body filled the tub. Vials of fragrances lined the marble shelf nearby. Josefa picked one, pulled the crystal stopper and sniffed. "Lavender," she explained, pouring the liquid into the tub.

Constanze stood a few feet away, nervously looking around the room.

"Why aren't you dressed for the party?"

"I thought I'd stay in my room this evening. I want to write a letter to baby Karl telling him I'm coming home soon."

"How do you know when you're returning to Vienna? You don't know when the opera will premiere."

"I've decided to return as soon as possible, maybe tomorrow."

Josefa rose gingerly from her sitting position and stood up. Constanze watched the water drip off her curvaceous body. The servant wrapped

Josefa in an oversized Turkish towel and helped her climb out of the tub. "Constanze, don't be ridiculous."

"I think it would be best for Karl and for me."

"And what about your husband? Is it wise to leave him here without you?"

"Wolfgang will do what he wants, whether I'm here or not. I have to accept his behavior. Perhaps he'll learn something while I'm away."

Josefa stood before the floor-length mirror admiring her form while the maid prepared her undergarments. With difficulty she struggled into her corset, which pulled her stomach in and exaggerated the curves of her full breasts. Even pregnant, Constanze felt small next to Josefa, who moved over to her dressing table and sat down so the serving girl could put on her stunning white wig, whose curls were teased to add height and glamour.

"You're wrong. If you leave now you'll never get Wolfgang back."

"If it's to be, then God has willed it."

Josefa spun around in her seat and glared at Constanze. The servant backed away. "Stop being a simple peasant girl. Do you think you're some poor maid who has to let events happen to her? That attitude will never help you. You're Madame Constanze Mozart. Remember that. Act like it; act the part."

Constanze stepped back, bumping into the settee.

"And what do you think I should do?"

"Do you know what you want?"

Constanze suddenly looked more hopeful. "I want a home and a family. I want a life without drama, without being subjected to the whims, tastes and politics of the court. I want to be happy again and to know he loves me."

"Oh, how different we are," Josefa said, shaking her head. She turned back toward the mirror on her dressing table and held a sapphire earring up to her ear, admiring the way it looked. "Well, if that's what you want," Josefa continued, with some ennui in her voice, "we need a plan to make it happen. I would suggest you speak to Signor Casanova and ask for his assistance, unless you . . ."

Josefa paused, letting the phrase hang in the air.

"Unless what?"

"Unless you have special feelings for him."

"Now you're the one being ridiculous."

"Does Signor Casanova interest you?" Josefa Dušek asked quietly.

Constanze looked at Josefa, who was being helped into a deep green silk gown.

"He's a gallant man."

"That's not what I asked."

"Oh, Josefa, you can't imagine how it feels when he touches you. When he holds your hand there's a power I can't describe."

Josefa saw Constanze's eyes blink rapidly. "Did he try to . . ."

"No! He's much too . . . sensitive. He can tell when a woman wants him and when he should . . . Oh, this is insane. We're married women."

"Then let Casanova help you," Josefa advised, trying to sound motherly. "Besides, that will leave the Chevalier to me," she laughed as she put on a gold choker.

"Are you sure Casanova's going to be here tonight?"

"Yes. I told him to come, but to be certain Wolfgang didn't find out about the party. Now get dressed and wear something that makes you look like the woman you are."

"But what do I say when people ask where Wolfgang is?"

Josefa Dušek looked at Constanze's worried face. "Tell them he's working on the opera."

"No one will believe me."

"I don't expect them to. It will add mystery. Now quickly, put on your finest dress and come downstairs. František is greeting the guests all by himself, and he's such a bad host."

"You're too hard on him. He's a dear man."

"He's a dear, *old* man." Josefa adjusted her outer skirt and primped her wig one more time so a few of the curls fell delicately over her shoulders.

She looked regal, and Constanze admired the transformation she had just witnessed. "I'll see you downstairs."

Constanze stood up and walked toward the door. "Thank you, Josefa."

"I envy you, Constanze. The thrill of being with a man like Wolfgang is something I have always wanted but never had. If I were a different person, I would have let you go back to Vienna."

Josefa swept out of the room and down the grand circular stairs leading to the foyer. She stopped on the fifth step above the landing, her view of the large front door unobstructed. She could see her servants, in burgundy velvet jackets and knee-length pants and stark white hose, moving efficiently through the room in an unchoreographed ballet, carrying silver trays laden with carefully prepared delicacies or crystal glasses filled with wine and champagne. The Villa Bertramka was alive, and she loved it.

Moving downstairs, Josefa inspected the trays of hors d'oeuvres waiting in the pantry. Then she proceeded to the main entryway, where she rearranged a vase filled with flowers so they would look larger. Finally, she paused before a huge, gold-framed mirror to adjust her jewelry and makeup one last time. She smiled and walked the few yards to a hallway near the entrance. There she waited. After a few minutes passed, she heard the muffled sound of horses' hooves stopping on the pebbled circular driveway. Another minute passed.

"Le Chevalier de Seingalt," the majordomo announced from his post at the front door.

František Dušek excused himself from a conversation and hurried to the door.

"Signor Casanova. I'm so delighted you could join us. You bring a great light into our home."

Casanova bowed his head.

"You honor me. But your home is already ablaze with candles and there is no shortage of light, especially when your delightful wife graces a room."

From her hiding place, Josefa could see Casanova glance around look-ing for her. Under the layers of clothing her knees quivered. Gathering up her skirts, she glided across the polished marble floor to where Casa-nova stood. František mumbled something about having to speak to the chef and walked away, leaving Josefa and Casanova staring into each other's eyes.

"I'm so glad you could come, Signor."

"It's my pleasure," he replied, gently kissing the back of her hand.

"Did you tell Mozart?"

"I confess, he beat it out of me. But I told him it was Constanze who invited me."

"You're so devious."

"Mozart is very naïve. That makes him an easy mark for my plans."

"And what plans do you have for me?" Josefa asked, trying to look as coquettish as she could.

"I never plan where a woman is concerned. Nature and circumstances usually solve those mysteries for me."

Constanze, wearing a lovely light blue gown trimmed with ecru lace, came down the staircase in time to see Casanova and Josefa disappear through the red velvet curtains into the small study. Taking a deep breath, she joined the party in the music room, where the other guests had gath-ered. František was in the middle of telling a story when she walked in.

". . . and when we were in Venice, Josefa sang one of Mozart's arias. It was perfect for her voice, as if he'd composed it especially for her. And then we went to Dresden, where she sang it again. Well, I can tell you the reac-tion was . . . Oh, Constanze," he said. "I thought you . . . I'm sorry, I didn't see you come in. I think you know everyone here."

The two other men, Count Thun, a nobleman with a passion for Italian opera, and Johann Josef Strobach, the director of Prague's church music, walked over to her. Each kissed her hand and bowed as she curtsied.

"Where is the Maestro?" Count Thun asked.

"I'm afraid he's not feeling well this evening."

"Nothing serious, I hope."

"Oh, no. He'll be better tomorrow."

"How disappointing," the Countess Thun lamented from the white sofa near the harpsichord. "I was hoping your husband would entertain us. He's so charming. Such a dear little man, and so funny. I enjoyed talking with him when he was in Prague last year."

Constanze glared at the Countess and the spectacular pearl and diamond choker and matching earrings reflecting every glint of a nearby candle's flame. She remembered Wolfgang's writing in a letter how the Countess Thun was the "dearest lady I have ever met," a memory which only aggravated her further.

"He'll be sorry he disappointed you," Constanze replied. "František, please go on. I didn't mean to interrupt your story."

"Oh . . . it was nothing important."

"Where is Madame Dušek?" Strobach asked.

František looked lost.

"She was showing another guest around the house," Constanze saved him.

"She loves to show people around the house," František played along. "You know, not only is she a singer—"

"A *great* singer," Strobach corrected.

"Thank you, Maestro. Not only is she a fine singer, but she runs this house like a great ruler. Everything is perfectly done, and it's no easy task. The cooks and the chambermaids and the stables are all run like clockwork. That's Josefa's doing."

"The dinner is served," the majordomo intoned as if on cue.

The guests turned toward him as he stood stiffly at the door, while the other servants stood at attention in the dining room, waiting. "Splendid! You see what I mean," František bellowed proudly, pleased to be relieved of the duty of having to entertain his guests.

Maestro Strobach escorted the Countess, leaving Count Thun to walk with Constanze into the dining room. František was standing at the side of the table trying to remember the seating arrangement his wife had explained to him earlier that afternoon. "I'm afraid we have an extra gentleman this evening," he mused, looking more confused than ever.

Suddenly a hidden door connected to a back hallway swung open. Laughing, Josefa pulled Casanova into the room, unaware anyone else was there. When she saw František's befuddled face and the bemused stares of her guests, she stifled her laughter. Casanova straightened his waistcoat, adjusted his cuffs and wiped a smudge from his cheek with a white linen handkerchief.

"Well," Josefa quickly took control. "Let's see. Constanze, why don't you sit between the Count and Maestro Strobach on this side of the table. Countess, won't you sit to my husband's right, and the Chevalier de Seingalt will sit on my left. There, that works nicely."

"I'm afraid your guests have me at a disadvantage," Casanova politely reminded Josefa as each person stood behind his assigned seat.

"Oh. I haven't introduced you. How silly. The Count and Countess Thun, Maestro Johann Josef Strobach, may I introduce the Chevalier de Seingalt, better known as Signor Giacomo Casanova."

"I'm pleased to know you," Casanova said, bowing politely. "And may I say this visit to your wonderful city has been one of the most interesting journeys of my long life."

Josefa beamed as she took her seat at the head of the table. The servants quickly moved to help the other guests with their chairs.

An uncomfortable quiet filled the room during the appetizer of chilled oysters and crayfish. Constanze saw Casanova delicately swallow an oyster. As he savored its flavor, she saw him lean toward Josefa and whisper. Josefa giggled and patted Casanova's hand. Constanze tried to stay interested in the conversation of the men on either side of her, but her gaze kept going across the table. Casanova had turned his attention to the low cut of the Countess' dress. Meanwhile Herr Strobach droned on endlessly about the recent rehearsals he'd conducted in St. Vitus Cathedral.

Already frustrated and upset, Constanze's patience with the mediocre musician quickly ran out. How, she wondered, could a musician be as boring as this? Whenever Wolfgang talked about music, his or someone else's, you could hear the melodies; he'd bring the music to life using animated gestures and funny faces. It breathed, it sang, it lived and brought life to others. Maestro Strobach's words sapped the life out of music, making it dull and dreary.

Across the table, Casanova was enchanting the Countess.

"Perhaps Signor Casanova would share his story with all of us. He certainly seems to have intrigued the Countess," Constanze said loudly.

Her outburst was a surprise even to her, and it brought the other conversations to a sudden halt.

"We were simply discussing our heritage. Countess Thun was telling me of her husband's noble family and I was about to reciprocate by telling her of my, more humble, beginnings."

"Well, I think *everyone* would be interested."

"Yes. Family histories are often filled with wonderful stories. You know my family was—"

"František, be quiet. Let Signor Casanova speak," Josefa cut him off.

"It really was nothing," Casanova continued. "I mentioned to the Countess I was working on my memoirs and it made me think of my parents and how they introduced me to the theater."

"So, you are well versed in the theater?" Strobach asked.

"I would say so. I've been a performer and a musician, and have studied the great dramas from the Greeks to Racine."

"František mentioned you've been to the rehearsals of Maestro Mozart's new opera."

"Yes, I have."

"Then perhaps you could tell us about the opera, and how it's going."

"Johann, are you asking as an interested music lover or as Prague's head of church music?" Josefa asked.

"A music lover, my dear. Simply a music lover."

Casanova dabbed his lips with his napkin and glanced across the table toward Constanze, seeking her silent approval. But she was staring at her plate, afraid to look at him, afraid to reveal her thoughts about him or her husband.

"Well," he began. "The rehearsals have been slow. It's a difficult piece. This opera is real drama, at once human and superhuman. But there are no mythological gods and goddesses holding forth through long arias. The characters in *Don Giovanni* are filled with emotion. There's action, pathos, humor, tragedy and love." On that word Casanova paused and looked at Constanze, whose eyes rose to meet his. "And the music Maestro Mozart has written captures and reflects all of those elements in a way I've never heard before."

Casanova's voice was soft, but intense, and the others stopped eating and leaned in to hear.

"What is most wonderful is that the music gives the singers the cues they need . . . real direction on how to act. They have to make the story believable."

"But what about the subject matter?" Count Thun interrupted. "How can the censors accept an opera that honors a man of such deviant, unnatural behavior?"

Through the burning candles placed on the table Casanova saw Herr Strobach nod in agreement.

"What is 'deviant behavior'? I would guess every person at this table has a different concept of what deviance is, or what they might admit to having done that could be considered deviant."

Casanova noticed Herr Strobach reach for his napkin.

"But, regardless of definitions, isn't Don Giovanni's behavior deviant?" Strobach persisted.

"The opera shows us a man living life as he chooses, but ultimately right—or right as society sees right—wins out. In the end Don Giovanni is punished, dragged off to hell by an avenging statue, and the moralists get to have the opera end with an acknowledgment that evil, as they define it, is always justly punished," Casanova explained.

"You seem uncomfortable with that. Why?" asked Strobach.

"Are you asking as an interested observer or as the head of Prague's church music, Maestro Strobach?"

Constanze laughed softly as the others shifted uncomfortably. Strobach took a sip of his wine, the red in his cheeks nearly matching its ruby color.

"Well, I preferred it when operas were about gods and muses," Strobach concluded.

"But those stories were myths," Casanova said.

"And *Don Giovanni* is also a myth."

"On the contrary. *Don Giovanni* is no myth. *Don Giovanni* is a legend. Please don't confuse the two."

"Signor Casanova, you talk as if you think a man like this Don Giovanni could have actually existed. I only know the basic plot of the story, but do you think it's possible for a man to have had that many, what shall we call them, adventures?"

"I'd like to think so." Casanova saw a mischievous smile cross Josefa's full mouth.

"Well, I've never met anyone like that. I'd still prefer if we kept our operas in the mythological worlds. It would be much less controversial," Strobach concluded.

"And I prefer works of dramatic importance. It makes better theater," Casanova added with annoyance.

"Signor Casanova, you do know your music. Are you a musician?" the Countess asked.

"In one of my previous existences I was a violinist, and during my travels I've spent some happy times with musicians in England, Italy, France, Spain and Austria. I once met a wonderful harpsichordist and organist named Peter Augustus. I believe he was the court organist in Dresden; a remarkable man from humble origins. His father was the valet to King Augustus the second. Do you know him, Maestro Strobach?"

"I never met him, but I'm familiar with his writings on music theory."

The servants cleared the dinner plates and marched out of the dining room. Constanze admired the calm efficiency with which they did their jobs.

Within moments the servants returned and placed a small, gold-edged dish filled with different chocolate delicacies at each place setting.

"I hope you like these," Josefa whispered to Casanova. "I had the chef make them especially for you."

Casanova reached across the table's corner and rested his hand on the back of Josefa's.

"They will be the second sweetest delicacy at this table."

Josefa took a deep breath. She enjoyed his sweet flatteries, his tender lies. The scent of Casanova's cologne filled her nose and pulled her closer to him. František noticed.

"You know," Strobach continued, as if the gap in the conversation hadn't occurred, "the world is filled with musicians and composers whose work remains obscure. Maestro Mozart is fortunate his music gets performed."

Constanze glared. "If he's so fortunate, why do we live the way we do, always traveling, looking for the next commission, for a post in a court, for the freedom and security he deserves? Isn't his music good enough?"

"Of course it is, my dear. But there are so many composers. How can one choose?"

"You know, Madame Mozart," Count Thun said. "Your husband would be most welcome here in Prague. It may not be Vienna, but Prague's a lovely place."

"Perhaps after *Don Giovanni* premieres he'll consider that."

"There's excellent music here," said Strobach. "In fact this Sunday we're performing a Requiem at St. Vitus. Perhaps you'd like to come, Signor Casanova. We've chosen a Requiem by one of your countrymen, Cavalli, Francesco Cavalli."

"I've never heard of him," Count Thun said.

"He's not well known. He wrote church music and operas. This Requiem is a powerful piece, and what's most interesting is he composed it for his own funeral."

"How eerie," Countess Thun said, wrinkling her nose in distaste.

"No," Strobach replied. "It's marvelous. Think about it. If you compose your own Requiem Mass you know before you die what will be performed at your funeral."

An uncomfortable chill went up Constanze's back.

"Thank you for the invitation," Casanova said. "I'll try to be there." Then, looking at Constanze he added: "Perhaps I'll ask Maestro Mozart to join me."

The dessert plates were nearly empty, and Josefa Dušek rang a tiny crystal bell. The servants marched into the dining room, opened all the doors simultaneously and stood at attention.

"Maestro Strobach. Perhaps you could entertain us with some music," Josefa suggested.

Strobach pushed his chair back and bounced up.

"I'd be delighted. Good food and delightful company always inspire me to play."

"I've shared that thought many times," Casanova grinned, looking directly at Josefa Dušek.

The other guests rose and followed Strobach into the music room. Casanova and Constanze were the last to leave the dining room. When they were alone in the passageway, she tugged on his sleeve. He stopped, held a finger up to his lips and led her into the little study off the foyer. "I'm sorry to keep you from Josefa."

"It's not a problem. Anything for you, Constanze."

"How is Wolfgang? I need to know."

"He's struggling," Casanova answered quietly.

"I should be with him. He knows what he did was wrong. I should go back to him."

"No. He needs to learn. If you go back now, he'll do it again."

"How can you say that? He's such a little boy."

"You underestimate him. Staying away will help him."

"I'm his wife. He needs me."

"He needs to struggle, to be uncertain."

"He struggles all the time. I'm pregnant. We're poor and he's often ill. Why should I make him suffer any more?"

"Because it will bring you what you want; it will bring you together. He needs to be less certain of your love."

"What do you know about love?"

A hurt look crossed Casanova's face. "I know about loss of love," he whispered, gently taking her hand in his.

"Why should I trust you?"

"Because I know what has to happen. I've seen it before. I've made all the mistakes he thinks he has to make. He needs to see, to learn. I understand what he can't. We're different men with different passions, but I know he'll understand. You must stay here. Let him find the answer. It will work out in the end. I promise." He paused. "Constanze, I know that your husband's a Freemason, as am I."

Constanze was surprised. Her husband's membership in the *Zur Wohltätigkeit* Lodge in Vienna had been a secret he guarded dearly.

"How do you know?"

"I was a spy once," he smiled innocently.

"Well what does his lodge membership have to do with me?"

"As Masons we're taught to believe in truth. True love is what Wolfgang has been taught to seek. But in order to know what true love is, he needs to be without it. Through trials he must earn your true love. Your absence and uncertainty will help him discover the true love he seeks."

Constanze was confused. But when Casanova took her in his arms in a fatherly embrace, she knew she had to believe him.

"Well there you are," Josefa's shrill voice pierced through the small room.

Casanova quickly pushed away from Constanze.

"I think I'll go to my room," she said. "I'm very tired. Good night. It was good to see you again, Signor Casanova. Will you be going to more of the rehearsals?"

"Yes. We rehearse tomorrow afternoon. Can I bring any message to your husband?"

"No. Not now, thank you. Good night, Josefa. Please make my excuses to the other guests and to František. It was a delightful evening, but I need to rest."

Constanze turned and left through the red velvet curtains.

"Poor dear," Josefa sighed. "It must be so difficult to be married to a man like Wolfgang. He's so young, a child really."

"And your husband?"

"He's certainly not young."

Josefa sat on the love seat and patted the place next to her. Casanova sat down, leaving a small space between them, which she instantly slid into. He relaxed, allowing her to rest her head on his chest. Her hair fell to one side; perfume floated upward. Casanova breathed deeply through his nose, savoring the lavender scent.

"Tell me a story," she whispered.

"What?"

"I want to know about you, about your experiences. Tell me about one of your adventures. Brighten my existence. That's why you're here."

"You think too much of me."

"Do I excite you?"

Casanova looked down at Josefa's round face and studied her features.

"You remind me of Clementine."

"Who's Clementine?"

"A wonderful young girl I knew long ago in St. Angelo."

"Tell me about her," she purred.

Casanova gently stroked her cheek, each pass timed to the melody Herr Strobach was playing on the harpsichord in the music room.

"She was beautiful, with a passion for books greater than any woman's I'd ever known. When I came to St. Angelo I brought her a sack filled with books. Like children with new toys, we spent an afternoon reading, page after page, chapter after chapter, book after book. 'You have come here to make me happy,' she said.

"Words like that from a beautiful woman turn a man into a god. There is a look that comes to the face of a loved one who is truly grateful. If you've never experienced this feeling, I pity you."

Josefa shifted her position so Casanova's hand could reach the front of her low-cut dress. At first he resisted, but her round, soft breast seemed to invite his caresses.

"Clementine and I spent several days enjoying the gifts of literature. I burned with passion, which was only increased by her intense love of learning. I could see her body, but I loved her mind. You see, Josefa, I enjoy a dish that is pleasing to the palate, but if it is unpleasant to the eye, I will never taste it. We see the surface first; the inner parts are experienced later. Clementine was more than pleasing to the eye."

With this last phrase, Casanova extended his arm and cupped Josefa's right breast in his hand.

"Finish your story. Strobach only knows a few pieces and those bores will be looking for us at any moment."

"That night in St. Angelo, I realized that in all the time I'd been with Clementine, I'd never experienced the slightest sensual arousal. I wondered why. It couldn't be virtue, because I've never carried virtue to such an extent. It wasn't fear or shyness, because those feelings are unknown to me. I contented myself with the knowledge that this platonic phase of our relationship would end; for when the intellect is part of the battle, the heart eventually yields; but the battle mustn't last long.

"Unable to sleep, I crept through the dark corridor to her room. She was asleep, with books spread across her bed. I moved them to one side and climbed in next to her. She was nearly naked save for a loose-fitting nightshirt, and I saw glimpses of her beauty that made me sigh and made my stomach tighten. She woke. We lit the candle on her bedside table. 'Have you come to read with me?'

"'If you wish,' I answered.

"'Then let's spend the night with *Dido and Aeneas*,' she suggested. And so, through the whole of that night we read of those mythological creations and how the gods toyed with them. Sweet Clementine found the story amusing and laughed when Aeneas is given the opportunity to prove his love for Dido while they hide in a cave during a rainstorm—far from comfortable accommodations. 'Have you ever been in a similarly uncomfortable position?' she asked.

"I told her there'd been episodes in my life where personal comforts were sacrificed for the sake of physical pleasure. And yet, even with that most personal of revelations we continued to read until daybreak."

"Don't ignore the other one," Josefa said, shifting her position so Casanova could easily caress her other breast.

"The next morning, Clementine exclaimed it had been the greatest night of her life. Unable to resolve the contradiction that was Clementine, I asked if she thought it possible to love the intellect without loving the body?

"'No,' she replied. 'Because without a body, the magical spirit would disappear. But we must resist those desires. We have duties to tend to, because if we leave them undone they will haunt us forever.'"

Josefa shifted so her head was resting squarely in Casanova's lap. He enjoyed the feeling, but was uncomfortable with the circumstances. He noticed that Strobach had stopped playing the harpsichord. František could be heard telling the other guests that Josefa must be around somewhere. Quickly she sat up and closed the front of her dress.

"How did your 'reading' end?"

"As the sun shone through her bedroom window, I watched Clementine dress. Before she left the room, she told me she had doubts as to how long we could resist the temptations of the physical. She threw me a kiss and vanished. Exhausted in a way I'd never been before, I turned over and fell into a sound sleep, filled with visions of Clementine."

František limped through the curtain as Casanova finished the story.

"There you are, my dear. Our guests are leaving."

"I'm coming," Josefa obliged grudgingly. "Signor Casanova, would you escort me?"

Graciously Casanova rose, and hooked his arm with Josefa's. The three other guests were standing near the front door.

"It was an honor to meet you, Signor Casanova," Count Thun said, extending his hand.

"The honor was mine," Casanova replied as he kissed the back of the Countess' hand.

"Please try to come to St. Vitus," Strobach reminded him. "It would grace our performance to have you there."

"I wouldn't miss your performance, Maestro. Your music this evening has already provided me the opportunity for pleasure." Josefa smiled as Casanova glanced conspiratorially in her direction.

"I hope we meet again," the Countess said to Casanova. "I'd like the chance to spend more time with you. You disappeared after dinner, before I had a chance to get to know you."

"Oh, we'll all be together again," Josefa said. "František and I will have another party on the night before the opera's premiere. To wish Mozart well."

After servants had helped them with their heavy cloaks, the guests left the house and climbed into the horse-drawn coaches waiting just outside the main door. Josefa held Casanova back, pulling him gently. Before he stepped into his small black carriage she whispered:

"Did you eventually get to enjoy Clementine's physical attributes as well as her intellectual ones?"

Casanova gently pulled his hand away from Josefa. He got into the carriage and sat back on the red velvet seat, then leaned forward to grasp the door's silver handle.

"That part of the legend hasn't been written yet."

He pulled the door shut as the driver yanked on the horse's reins. The coach disappeared into the darkness as it left the grounds of the Villa Bertramka. Josefa stared after it, then slowly, dreamily walked into the foyer. The majordomo closed the gate and door behind her and stood at attention. František was standing at the top of the stairs. He watched Josefa, a dark scowl crossing his face. Without saying a word, he limped to his room. The slamming door reverberated through the house.

Chapter Fifteen

o, no, no. You can't stand where everyone can see you. How many times do we have to go over this? When you exchange cloaks the audience mustn't be able to tell which of you is which, who is who. If the audience can tell which of you is Leporello and which is Don Giovanni, the whole effect is ruined."

The frustration of three days of tedious rehearsals could be heard in Mozart's voice, and it was etched into the lines of Pasquale Bondini's face as he stood on the side of the stage watching. The singers were tired, the orchestra bored and the composer angry. This rehearsal had reached an impasse. No matter what was tried, the scene looked and sounded ridiculous.

It should have been simple. Mozart had even written the vocal lines so Leporello would be able to sound like his master after they exchanged cloaks in order to deceive Donna Elvira. And yet, the two basses—Bassi playing Giovanni, and Ponziani as Leporello—couldn't make the scene believable.

"Signor Ponziani," Mozart yelled from the orchestra, "why are you suddenly so stiff? Just because you've put on the Don's cloak it doesn't mean you've become a corpse. Act like a nobleman who wants to seduce this woman, not one who's afraid to touch her. Grab her, hold her. Assert yourself. Do something! Let's try it again."

Mozart raised his arms and cued the orchestra. The music filled the empty theater as the singers took their places on the set of a Spanish street. But once again, the moment the men exchanged cloaks, the scene lost energy and ground to a halt.

"Lorenzo!" Mozart shouted as he slumped into his chair.

"Yes, Mozart. I'm here. I'm here."

"It's never going to work. Can we change the scene?"

With evident annoyance, Da Ponte walked toward the front of the theater, heading straight for Mozart. From the stage the singers could see Mozart and his librettist standing close together at the harpsichord having an animated discussion, punctuated by Da Ponte's repeated refrain: "Impossible!"

After a few minutes, a third figure emerged from the darkness and walked toward the harpsichord. He waited for an appropriate opening, then interrupted.

"Perhaps I could help."

"Giacomo," Mozart said, startled by Casanova's sudden appearance. "I didn't know you were here."

"I was in the loge."

"How can you help?" Da Ponte demanded.

"It's good to see you too, Lorenzo."

"What do you have in mind? You know we must finish the opera. The Emperor's annoyed with me. Salieri has complained about the length of my absence from Vienna. I need to guard my position at court. This delay isn't good for you either, Wolfgang."

Being reminded of the court made Mozart grimace. "Then what should we do?" he asked, frustrated by the entire situation.

"The problem as I see it," Casanova began boldly, "is the men have become quite good at their own parts. Bassi, although he still lacks the maturity and style I think Don Giovanni needs, has developed a distinct presence on stage. But when he has to pretend to be Leporello, he hunches over, as if being a servant means to appear smaller or beaten down. There's more to class distinction than simply hunching over. Further, Don Giovanni would never allow himself to appear beaten, even when in a disguise. On the other hand, Ponziani is believable when he plays the part of Leporello. His comedic timing is superb. But when he has to act like Don Giovanni, he freezes. His gestures become small and are lost on the stage.

"Ponziani plays the part of a nobleman by strutting around as if his every movement were being studied. There's nothing natural about him. He has to remember he's outside, on a street, in the middle of the night, and he's trying to seduce Donna Elvira. He needs to be passionate, to convince her of his love, even though we know it isn't genuine. Simply put, Ponziani doesn't know the difference between love and lust."

"And now that you've given us this brilliant critique, may I ask what you think we should do?" Da Ponte bristled.

"The singers need to see the action, to see the scene played by people who have experience."

"So we should hire other actors to show them?"

"Oh no. They need to see people who have real experience. Not actors at all."

"And where are we going to find these people?"

"Right here. With your permission, Maestro, I suggest, for now, that Bassi and Ponziani sing the parts from the side of the stage, while Lorenzo and I act out the scene."

"But I'm the court poet. I have to be aware of my position. What would people say?"

"That you're a true master of your craft," Casanova lied.

That comment had the desired effect, and Da Ponte nodded deliberately, agreeing. "Well, I'm willing to try."

Mozart cupped his hands around his mouth so the singers onstage could hear him more clearly. "Gentlemen. Please lend your cloaks to Signor Casanova and Maestro Da Ponte. They're going to demonstrate how this scene should be played. I'd like the two of you to stand on the side of the stage where you can see me and the action at the same time. You'll sing your parts and they'll do the acting."

Then, turning to Da Ponte and Casanova, he asked: "Which of you will be Don Giovanni?"

"We're not going to tell you," Casanova said with a grin. "If we're believable, you won't be able to tell who is who, just as it should be."

While Da Ponte and Casanova made their way onto the stage, Mozart took a moment to correct some notes in the orchestra, then waited until the cloaks had been turned over to the silent actors.

"Ready when you are, Maestro," a voice called from the back of the shadowy stage, lit to represent nighttime.

Bassi and Ponziani watched attentively as Mozart gave the downbeat. Some of the musicians in the orchestra craned their necks trying to see the stage as the two cloaked figures began to mime. Caterina Micelli, costumed in a black, floor-length gown, acted and sang the part of Donna Elvira, trying to determine if the man wooing her from the street below her window in the guise of Don Giovanni was Casanova or Da Ponte. Unable to tell, she tried to see the other cloaked figure lurking in the set's shadows, hoping that there she would find her answer. But the darkness kept his identity secret as well.

Mozart conducted with renewed energy, prodding the orchestra to capture the excitement of the scene. The musicians worked to achieve the effects he asked for. After a few seconds, the scene began playing exactly the way he'd intended: the melodic interplay matched the action; the humor and fun finally shone through. Inspired, the orchestra played better and better, with greater intensity. Mozart smiled broadly. Bassi and Ponziani sang their parts from the side of the stage. Now the scene made sense to them, too, and they laughed between phrases, understanding why it was so important for them to conceal their identities.

When the trio reached its resolution, with Donna Elvira happily agreeing to leave with the man she believes to be Don Giovanni, Caterina Micelli embraced the cloaked actor. As she did, he turned, pulling her so the audience couldn't see his face. In that split second, he bent his head forward and nuzzled it between her breasts. Mozart noticed her miss a beat in her last sung phrase but didn't correct her.

"Signor Casanova is seducing Donna Elvira," Mozart yelled from the orchestra. "I'm certain of it."

The singers and the orchestra stopped and stared. Caterina Micelli calmed herself as the still-disguised men walked to the foot of the stage. It was only then she realized that the man who'd held her in his arms wasn't Casanova.

"You're wrong, Maestro!" she sang out gleefully in surprise.

The men removed their disguises.

"I can't believe it. You completely fooled me, Lorenzo. Bravo! I didn't know you could act so convincingly, and with such passion and style. You seemed so noble."

"There are many things you don't know about me, Maestro Mozart," Da Ponte said as he climbed off the stage.

"Now," Casanova instructed, "let's see the scene again with Signor Bassi and Signor Ponziani acting their parts."

Everyone quickly took their places and Mozart restarted the music. This time it was even better, although for Caterina Micelli, the moment at the end of the trio would never have the same effect as it did when Lorenzo Da Ponte had held her in his arms.

From that point on, the rehearsal went beautifully. Mozart was confident, and he conducted the rest of the rehearsal with life and energy, happily making corrections and adjustments along the way.

Casanova watched, amazed at the way the performances were coming together. His only criticism was the nagging doubt he had that Luigi Bassi would look old enough or seem masculine enough to properly portray Don Giovanni.

"He's too young," Casanova whispered to Da Ponte. "Women don't react the same way to youth as they do to experience."

"It's interesting how you contrast youth with experience and not with age."

"That's because even as a youth, I was experienced."

Da Ponte slumped in his seat and watched the rest of the rehearsal in silence.

"Much better," Mozart congratulated.

The musicians packed up their instruments, only the clarinetist staying behind to practice a few passages while Mozart listened. The singers headed to the dressing rooms as a weary-looking old man in a long white apron swept the stage and blew out the rows of candles. "It's sounding better," Mozart said as the clarinetist finished practicing and cleaned his instrument.

"Thank you, Maestro. It will be even better next time. I promise. Good evening, Maestro."

Mozart stayed at the harpsichord, absentmindedly holding his frock coat, as he stared at the pages of manuscript spread out in front of him. He could hear and see the opera in his mind, scenes flowing from one into the next, as he'd imagined and intended when he was composing; comedy and tragedy were blended in his music. He closed his eyes, and his thoughts jumped to the scene in which Donna Anna passionately sings of her dead father. The tragedy and sense of personal loss had to be clear to the audience. He let the whole aria play in his mind's ear, making small gestures with his hands, conducting an imaginary soprano only he could hear.

"Bravo, Mozart. Bravo!"

The words broke his trance. Startled, he reflexively turned around to acknowledge his admirer.

"Really, Mozart, it's quite beautiful." Pasquale Bondini was standing right behind him, a proud grin filling his narrow face.

"Thank you, Signor Bondini. I'm glad you're pleased."

"More than pleased. Word of this opera will spread to Vienna. Mark my words. It will be a triumph for all of us."

"Let's hope."

As they spoke, Da Ponte and Casanova walked toward them from the back of the dark theater.

"Lorenzo," Mozart called. "Don't you think the second act moves well now?"

"Yes. It flows nicely. We need a few more rehearsals and we'll be ready to open on the twenty-fourth."

Pasquale Bondini shifted nervously and cleared his throat.

"Is something the matter?" Da Ponte asked.

"No . . . no . . . not really . . . well . . . you see . . ."

"Out with it!"

"Well . . . we may have to delay the opening."

"Not again. Impossible!" Da Ponte thundered.

Mozart rested his head in his hands.

"We have no choice."

"What's the reason?" Casanova asked in a calm voice.

"Madame Bondini's not well. She needs a few days to recover."

"Replace her!" Da Ponte yelled.

"I can't do that," Bondini replied, trying to sound forceful.

"And why not?"

"She's learned the role. I can't take it away from her. She's expecting to sing."

"You have to. There are plenty of sopranos around Prague who could learn Zerlina's arias in a day, two at the most. Mozart, maybe you could have Madame Dušek learn the part?"

"Her voice is too heavy for Zerlina."

"Then we'll find another soprano. Mozart will coach her, and Casanova and I will rehearse her in the stage business. There, it's settled. See, Pasquale, you have to try to solve problems, not create them."

Bondini tried to look stern and raised his voice.

"I won't stand for it. This is my opera house. I make the decisions. We'll delay the opening until Madame Bondini is well enough to sing, whenever that may be."

"I'll inform the Emperor of what you're doing," Da Ponte threatened.

"Lorenzo," Casanova said. "Lorenzo, think about the position you're putting Signor Bondini in. Be considerate. If he disagrees with you he may incur the wrath of the Emperor, although that's unlikely, since none of us believes the Emperor really cares when the opera premieres. On the other hand, if he gives in to you and replaces Zerlina he will incur the wrath of a soprano who happens to be his wife. Which do you think is worse?"

Da Ponte looked at Casanova with annoyance.

"How long a delay?" Mozart asked softly.

"A week at most," Bondini said, trying to find an ally in Mozart.

"Lorenzo, let's be reasonable. A small delay will give us time to fix the scenes that aren't fully staged."

"Yes, he's quite right," Bondini said optimistically. "And it will give you time to compose an overture."

Mozart glared at Bondini. "I'll compose the overture when I'm ready, whenever that may be."

"Arguing won't solve the problem," Casanova pointed out diplomatically.

"Less than a week," Da Ponte negotiated.

"Shall we set the premiere for Monday the twenty-ninth?" Bondini offered. "That's just nine days from now."

Da Ponte grumbled unintelligibly.

"Well, I'm glad we were able to settle that," Bondini said with relief.

"What ails your wife?" Casanova asked.

"She has a chest cold."

"In her case that's not a big problem," Da Ponte said.

"Gentlemen, if you'll excuse me. I have to return to my house. We'll rehearse again on Monday. Until then, I wish you well. I'll say a prayer for us, for the opera, in church tomorrow." Bondini bowed to the other men, then hurriedly left the auditorium.

"You do that," Da Ponte muttered. "Say a prayer for us. That's sure to help a great deal. Perhaps the good Lord will speak directly to the Emperor for me."

"Lorenzo," Mozart cautioned. "How can you speak that way?"

"I don't fear God the way you do."

"Enough, enough," Casanova said.

"I hate Bondini," Da Ponte added. "He's a weasel. He's dishonest. I'd like to seduce his wife just to teach him a lesson."

"That's already been done," Casanova whispered conspiratorially, looking at Mozart.

Da Ponte wanted to get the final word, but Casanova's comment and the questions it raised in his mind silenced him. Mozart packed up his pages of music and looked around the orchestra before putting on his frock coat and taking his cloak and hat from a nearby chair.

"You know, I was truly confused when you two were disguised onstage. I was certain it was Casanova seducing Donna Elvira and not you, Lorenzo."

"Why? Don't you think I can be elegant and make women love me?" he asked testily.

"I was only pointing out that your demeanor was so confident. I've never seen you like that before. And I must say, the way you held Elvira in your arms, covering her with the cloak . . . remarkable."

"I too can be a lover, even though that may not be what I'm remembered for," Da Ponte said.

"You were convincing. I thought you'd become Don Giovanni, and I must tell you, I think Signora Micelli was also convinced."

Casanova remained silent, hiding a broad smile behind his white handkerchief.

"I did enjoy the moment. It's a good scene."

"Mozart, have you visited Constanze?" Casanova asked, abruptly changing the subject. The three men had reached the stage door of the opera house.

"No. I was thinking of going to Bertramka tomorrow and talking to her."

"No. Don't do that," Casanova advised. "I have a better idea. A man named Strobach invited me to a Requiem he's conducting at St. Vitus tomorrow. I believe Constanze and the Dušeks will be there too. You'll come with me. It will give you a chance to see her. Trust me, it's a better plan."

"Strobach's conducting a Requiem?" Mozart asked, more interested in the music than in Casanova's plan.

"Yes. Why?"

"Whose Requiem is he planning to ruin?"

Da Ponte laughed. He knew Mozart was as intolerant of average musicians as he was respectful of the great composers who'd come before him.

"I believe his name was Cavalli."

"I'd like to hear that," Mozart smirked.

"Excellent. Then you'll come with me. And you, Lorenzo?"

"I've nothing better to do, although the thought of going to church on Sunday is less than thrilling."

"And to think you were trained for the priesthood!"

"Only prepared and, one might say, never consummated."

Casanova and Da Ponte howled. Mozart smiled wanly, the religious boy in him unable to ridicule the church.

"Then we'll see each other tomorrow morning."

"No supper tonight, Mozart?" Da Ponte asked.

"No. I'll have something in my room. I need to write."

"The overture?"

"No. A letter."

And with that, Mozart left the theater and walked toward the inn. The taverns were full. As he passed each one, he thought of going inside but chose instead to return directly to the inn.

"Good evening, Maestro," greeted the innkeeper. "May I bring something for you? We have roast mutton tonight."

"Just some soup would be nice. It's quite cold out."

"Very good, Maestro." He turned toward the kitchen, but paused, remembering the envelope he'd stuffed into his coat pocket. "This arrived by post this afternoon."

Mozart took the envelope from him and slowly walked up the stairs to his room. He could tell from the handwriting it was from his sister in Salzburg. He held the wax-sealed, cream-colored envelope to his nose, hoping the smell would bring back memories of their happy childhood in Salzburg. But the paper only held the musty odor of an aged, leather mail pouch.

A servant opened the door to the room and walked in ahead of him to light the candles and draw the curtains shut. Mozart thanked the man, threw his cloak on the bed and sat down at the writing table. He opened the letter. Holding the single sheet near the candle, he read.

My Dearest Brother,

"How I long for news of you. It is so lonely here in Salzburg since
father died. The days are long and cold. The streets seem sad. Even
though some of the musicians we know invite me, I no longer go to
concerts. It's too painful. If you were to return, then I would go. But I find
no solace in the music when I'm alone. The memories flood my mind and
my eyes fill with tears. How I miss the days when we were all together.

*Every afternoon I visit Papa's grave. It's a simple, square stone, but I
tend to the few flowers planted near it. You won't believe me, but when
I'm there, it's almost as if I can hear his voice rising from the ground. It's
at once horrifying and comforting. One moment I hear him scolding you
and the next I hear him singing your praises. I so want to talk to him
again. I have to keep myself from calling out: 'My father! Dearest
Father! Beloved Father!'*

As Mozart read his sister's words, he couldn't avoid comparing her
strong, sad emotions with those of Donna Anna; the parallel of devoted
daughters grief-stricken by the deaths of their fathers intrigued him.

"Your soup, sir."

The servant set the bowl and a basket of dark bread on the table. Glad
to have the interruption, Mozart put his sister's letter aside, adding it to the
pile of unanswered correspondence and unpaid bills. He sipped the broth
and remembered Salzburg, all the while mentally drafting the letter he
would write to his sister. He'd explain that returning to Salzburg would be
impossible; the musical world he needed was in Vienna. There his talent
could be seen by important, worldly people, not the small-minded burghers
of Salz.

He finished the soup with a wedge of bread, then picked through the
messy pile of papers. He was looking for the letter he'd started writing to
Baron von Jacquin the day after the *Figaro* performance. But instead he kept
coming across the beginnings of letters he'd tried to write to the Marquis
de Sade.

Dear Marquis, they all began. But after the salutation, there was nothing but cross-outs. Again he picked through the pile of papers.

"There's the letter to Jacquin," he announced to no one.

He reread the beginning of the letter he'd started several days earlier, picked up his quill, dipped it into the silver bottle of ink and continued from where he'd stopped.

More delays with the opera, this time caused by one of the singers, who claims to be ill. As the company is quite small, the impresario is overly cautious because he is afraid the 'disease' may spread to the other women in the cast.

I noticed in my mail a letter from you. I would toss my cap in the air to celebrate, only it is cold here and I am in frequent need of it! So I will tell you in plain words I was pleased to hear from you.

The servant knocked gently on the door.

"Come in."

"Maestro, I'm sorry to disturb you, but this letter was delivered for you."

"Who delivered it?"

"A footman, sir."

"Did he say who sent him?"

"No sir."

The servant silently removed the empty soup bowl and backed out of the room. Mozart studied the envelope. The writing wasn't familiar. He couldn't tell if it was from a man or a woman. He held the envelope up to the flickering candle, not certain of what he was looking for. Finally he tore open the seal. The black ink was smudged.

"Tears or water?" he wondered.

Come to the Villa Bertramka the night before the opera's premiere. The gardens will be open; the air refreshing; the mystery intriguing.

Your truest friend.

Nothing else. Mozart studied the invitation, but there were no clues to be found. Annoyed, he threw it onto the pile of papers and tried to get it out of his mind. Taking a fresh sheet of music paper, he dipped his pen in the bottle of black ink and in his best hand wrote:

DON GIOVANNI
DRAMMA GIOCOSO

Then with a flourish he added:

Wolfgang Amadeus Mozart.
OVERTURE

Suddenly distracted, his eyes fell on his sister's letter. He imagined he could hear her voice, her tender cry, her lonely sobs. He opened the opera's score to Donna Anna's first-act aria and penned some new words. The sad melody capturing Donna Anna's impassioned cries of grief mingled with his thoughts and memories of his sister. He composed the music to accompany the text he'd just added: "My father. Dearest Father. Beloved Father!"

Chapter Sixteen

ozart slept soundly, peacefully, without dreaming of his wife, his sister or his father. Climbing out of bed, he went over to the windows and pulled back the curtains. The sun sparkled through the cool, crisp autumn air. Mozart pushed the window open and breathed deeply. The breeze ruffled his flimsy white nightshirt.

Remembering his agreement to meet Casanova and Da Ponte at the cathedral, he rang the tiny bell to call the valet.

"Yes, Maestro."

"Ask the friseur to come in. I need to look my best."

"Immediately, Maestro." The young valet hurried out. Mozart put on his green dressing gown and sat down at the writing table. Ignoring the spread-out sheets of music paper, he took a piece of stationery and his pen.

My Dearest Little Wife,

 How I have longed for a letter from you. The days have seemed endless; my nights lonely.

 Since we are apart, I have a number of requests to make.

 1) I beg you not to be melancholy,

 2) To take care of yourself, and watch out for the autumn breezes,

 3) Don't go out walking alone,

 4) Be sure of my love and know that as I write I look at your portrait,

 5) And lastly, be cautious with your honor and with mine, and think of how things appear to others. Don't be angry with me for asking you to do this. I think you should love me more for putting such value on honor.

I eagerly await the day when we will be happily reunited. O Stru! Stri! I kiss and hug you 1095060437082 times, and am your faithful friend and husband.

W. A. Mozart

The barber entered, bowed and set up the chair and washbasin. Mozart folded the note and left it on the table.

"Do your best work, Herr Barber. I'm going to a Requiem," Mozart said as he climbed into the chair.

The barber showed no reaction to Mozart's dark humor and went about his work, shaving the composer and pulling his thick hair into a neat tail, with a black ribbon tied perfectly in the shape of a cross.

"There you are, Maestro. You look excellent."

Mozart admired himself in the mirror.

"Yes, that will do nicely."

The barber bowed again and silently packed up his belongings.

Mozart put on a clean white shirt with a slightly ruffled front and high collar, then his best black pants, black shoes with a square gold buckle, and a black frock coat. Before leaving, he looked in the floor-length mirror, studying his all-black, serious appearance, wondering if Constanze would think he looked dashing.

Smoothing his shirt and adjusting his hair once more, he stood up as straight as he could, picked up the note from the table, put it in his pocket and left the room, happily tossing his black hat back and forth from one hand to the other.

Prague's streets on this Sunday morning glistened. Families, dressed in their best clothes, strolled or rode to or from church. Mozart thought of hiring a carriage, but decided instead to go to St. Vitus on foot. He had a spring in his step as he walked through the narrow streets. Melodies filled his mind. Before he knew it, he had crossed the bridge to the other side of the Vltava River and was standing in the square before the towering spires of St. Vitus.

"Mozart."

The soft voice coming from behind him was startling.

"Who's that?"

"Giacomo."

Casanova wore a dark blue coat with matching britches; the dark color made him look younger, handsomer and more distinguished.

"You look well, Giacomo."

"Thank you. I slept soundly last night, and this morning I had a most relaxing shave. Nothing like a good shave . . . almost nothing."

"Isn't it a beautiful day?" Mozart asked, looking up at the crystal blue sky.

"A fine day for a Mass for the dead."

Mozart thought the juxtaposition was strangely amusing, but the surroundings and the occasion made him afraid to laugh out loud.

The Gothic St. Vitus Cathedral had been under construction for four centuries, stone by stone, generation after generation, and it still wasn't finished. Casanova walked next to Mozart as they approached the cathedral's ancient entrance. They paused, stepping to one side to let the mourners pass.

Casanova and Mozart quietly slipped in, passing beneath the high-arching doorways. Even the late morning sun shining through the spectacular round stained-glass window at the far end of the cathedral, its refracted beams casting colored shadows over the ornately carved statues perched on the stone pillars, couldn't cut through the musty, incense-thick air.

The polished gold pipes of the organ filled one wall. The stones of the vaulted ceiling far above reverberated with the instrument's majestic, mournful sound. Mozart recognized the stately melody as one of Bach's toccatas his father had taught him years before. Mozart shivered as he looked up at the arched ceilings and the intricate carvings covering the pillars that lined the cathedral's aisles. The organ's ponderous sound projected in his direction.

The vast cathedral was nearly empty. Casanova saw Herr Strobach, dressed in a black robe, standing to the right of the altar before a small orchestra made up primarily of string instruments. Above in the choir loft, a group of about twenty singers in white and red ceremonial robes sat silently.

Mozart and Casanova walked a few steps forward to an ornate black and gold, waist-high, wrought-iron gate. Mozart pushed it gently, but it squeaked and several of the mourners turned to look. Embarrassed, he moved quickly to an empty wood pew in the very back of the church. A lone presence, his face obscured by the collar of his worn black cloak, sat there, head bowed reverently in silent prayer.

Casanova slid into the row and sat down near the man. His breathing was steady, and it didn't take long for Casanova to realize he was asleep. Casanova gently shook the man's shoulder, waking him with a start.

"What?"

Mozart, who'd sat down on Casanova's other side, looked over.

"Lorenzo, have you no respect?"

Da Ponte wiped the sleep from his face. "I got here early. This organist plays only slow music. I must have dozed off."

Another gate near one of the small private chapels on the opposite side of the cathedral swung open. Mozart watched as the Dušeks and Constanze, all dressed in black, took seats in a pew halfway between the front and back of the vast church. From his position off to the left side, Mozart could see Constanze's soft profile, even though it was obscured by a lacy black veil attached to the front of her dainty hat.

How he yearned to sit with her, to hold her tiny hands in his. He reached into his deep coat pocket and felt for the note he'd written.

"This will bring her back," he thought.

The organ's last chord was played, echoed and faded into the massive stones. There was a profound silence, broken only by the sound of the priest's steps as he mounted the circular stairs to the pulpit. He was an old man whose severe features looked craggier still in the uneven light of the cathedral. Mozart watched the altar boys, dressed in matching red and white robes, silently perform their specific functions; from the back of the cathedral they looked like tiny marionettes, their movements controlled by invisible strings manipulated from above by unseen hands.

"*Requiem aeternam,*" the priest's deep voice boomed.

Mozart bowed his head. Casanova watched his young friend, wondering what thoughts were running through that extraordinary mind. Da Ponte stared at the prelate, silently mouthing the Latin words of the Mass for the dead, phrases he had learned while studying for the priesthood. As the prelate finished intoning the opening prayer, Strobach rose from his seat and moved to the head of the orchestra.

The first movement of the Cavalli Requiem was slow and mournful; the voices blended with the sparse orchestra. Unimpressed by the music, Mozart kept busy by looking at the artwork adorning the cathedral's walls and ceiling and taking interest in the way the antiphonal music bounced around the stone, wood and marble.

When the Dies Irae, Cavalli's musical portrayal of the day of wrath, began, the sudden, unexpected power and fervor of the music shook Mozart. The steady beats, the anguish in the vocal lines stunned him. His eyes shut; his small hands clenched into fists. The choir and orchestra stated each musical phrase with passion and feeling; their answers and echoes penetrated his very being. Mozart prayed. The Mass continued.

The Requiem ended with the final notes of the painfully sad *Lux Aeterna* echoing through the cold cathedral. Mozart's head stayed bowed as the anonymous mourners passed silently down the center aisle.

Da Ponte quickly left the pew and walked toward the altar, studying the poignant, poetic epitaphs carved into the walls, etched into the stained-glass windows or chiseled into the marble floor.

Casanova rose.

"Where are you going?" Mozart asked.

"I thought I'd congratulate Maestro Strobach."

Mozart reached into his pocket. "If you see Constanze, please give her this note."

Casanova took the folded letter. "I'll see to it."

Mozart remained in the pew, his head bowed, his eyes closed. Casanova tiptoed across the back of the church, stopping in a ray of sunlight that burned through the light blue glass of one of the stained-glass windows. Using the colorful light, he quickly read the note Mozart had given him, all the while keeping Strobach, the Dušeks and Constanze in his view so he would be able to intercept them as they neared the dark back corner of the cathedral. "Quite a love letter," he thought.

"Signor Casanova. I'm so glad you were able to come," Strobach said, muting his excitement appropriately for the surroundings and the occasion.

"It was beautiful, Maestro. Really quite moving," Casanova said as he deftly slipped the refolded note into the deep cuff of his sleeve.

"Chevalier, you honor me."

"Madame Mozart," Casanova said. "How are you today? Are you feeling well?"

"Yes, thank you. I'm quite well. And you? Are you here alone, Chevalier?"

"No. The Abbé Da Ponte joined me."

"Is he still here?" Josefa Dušek asked.

Casanova pointed toward the front of the church where Da Ponte was staring up at the crucifix.

"František, be a dear and go invite Abbé Da Ponte to the party."

"Of course, my dear. Immediately." František Dušek limped along the side aisle of the church, the uneven rhythm of his steps echoing loudly.

"Maestro Strobach, could you show me the music for the Requiem?" Josefa asked. "The soprano line was beautiful. Perhaps you could teach it to me."

"It would be my pleasure."

"Signor Casanova, I assume you'll forgive me for leaving you, but . . ."

"Absolutely. Madame Mozart will keep me company until you return," he said to Josefa. "Until we meet again, Madame. I will count the minutes." Casanova kissed her hand, lingering longer than would seem appropriate in church.

Josefa, flustered, followed Strobach toward the front of the cathedral, pretending to be interested in his excited jabbering about the Requiem. Casanova was alone with Constanze.

"Have you spoken to Wolfgang?" she asked anxiously. "Have you started your plan? Have you told him?"

"Shh. He's over there. Didn't you see him before?"

"No. I was afraid to look."

"He came with me. He claimed he wanted to hear the Requiem, but I believe he wanted to see you."

"I wish you hadn't brought him here."

"But why?"

"He has a morbid fascination with death."

"We're all fascinated by death."

"You don't understand. He often talks about how he will die young. It scares me."

"That's ridiculous."

"No, Signor. He's convinced of it. He's been asked to compose Requiems for wealthy people, but even though we need the money, he refuses. He's afraid. I should go over to him. He must be petrified."

She looked longingly in Mozart's direction. He sat in the pew, his eyes fixed on a point on the ceiling high above the altar where a painting of the Father and Son surrounded by puffy white clouds and a golden halo of light covered part of the wall.

"No. Please. I promise," Casanova insisted. "You asked for my help. Now you must let me do what I need to do. It will all work out. I promise; you have my word. Please stay away from him." His voice was soft but intense.

"But why?"

"Madame," he said in his softest whisper. "Allow me this pleasure. I'm an old man. Before too long there will be a Requiem Mass for me.

Humor me. I promise—in the end, I will bring you and your husband together."

Casanova could see Mozart walking slowly toward their hiding place. "Please. Go now. He mustn't see us together."

Constanze hesitated. Casanova reached for the letter concealed in his sleeve and gave it to her. "You can read this, but I beg you, don't act on it until I instruct you."

Constanze hid the note in the bosom of her dress and pulled the veil back over her face. She nodded farewell to Casanova and glided silently into a nearby chapel as Mozart came around the corner.

"There you are. I couldn't see you in the shadows."

"I was just coming to get you," Casanova lied. "We should find Lorenzo and leave. I think we've had enough religion for one day."

Letting Mozart go ahead of him toward the arched doorway, Casanova signaled Da Ponte to meet them outside. Mozart paused at the back of the cathedral, turned back toward the altar, bowed his head and made the sign of the cross. His lips moved in silent prayer. Casanova stopped and watched Mozart hastily leave.

Outside, the unfiltered afternoon sun made Mozart squint. He watched children dressed in bright yellows and blues playing outside in the square while their parents stood nearby talking, enjoying the sunny weather. In the far corner of the square, a young man handed a flower to a beautifully dressed girl seated on a white bench, then kissed her hand.

"Ah, the innocence of youthful love," Casanova intoned as he watched from the steps.

Da Ponte emerged from the cathedral and walked over to Casanova and Mozart. "What did you think of the music?" he asked.

"It was powerful, with more passion than I expect from music of that time," Mozart answered. "The anger of the Dies Irae was surprising, even frightening. I imagine Cavalli composed the piece for someone he loved very much."

"He wrote it for himself," Casanova said.

Mozart tensed and seemed to stumble.

"Have you ever composed a Requiem?" Casanova asked innocently.

"No. I can't seem to—"

A solemn bell tolled, interrupting him as he stopped to listen.

"Death is so final, and yet there are ways to achieve immortality. Walking around the cathedral just now, I read the memorials to the dead remembered there. Those words will live on forever. And look at the monuments in the graveyard," Da Ponte said, waving his arm in the direction of the gated graveyard behind the cathedral. Large, ornate statues and monuments of marble stood guard over the graves of long-gone nobles.

"If you're rich or powerful in life you can buy your immortal renown. Like the Commendatore in *Don Giovanni*—his statue stands for him in death."

Mozart stared at the graveyard.

"I wonder what my father's grave looks like. It's probably very plain, nothing grand or majestic. He would never want that."

"What kind of grave would you like, Mozart?" Casanova asked.

"I suppose it makes no difference. It should be a place where my wife and son can come to sit and remember, that's all. One grave's much like the next."

The three men walked in silence.

"I wonder if the graveyard scene will work," Mozart said suddenly.

"Of course it will. We can't make it look like this majestic place, but it will look all right, dramatic enough," Da Ponte replied, walking ahead of the others. He passed under the arch of the tower and onto the Charles Bridge, where carved, evenly spaced statues of historical figures and saints stood guard along the balustrade. Da Ponte led them across the bridge. At its midpoint, Mozart stopped and looked over the stone side at the rushing waters.

"Are you afraid of death, Mozart?" Casanova asked.

"I used to be. I never go to bed at night without remembering I may never see another day. Ever since my mother died, I've accustomed myself to expect death."

"How sad," Casanova said, grimacing.

"No. On the contrary. Think about this: What is death? It's actually the ultimate goal of life, and since that is an inescapable fact, I have made acquaintance with this best and truest friend of man. So, where once I feared him, his image no longer holds terrors for me, but instead is a source of consolation and peace."

"And you, Chevalier," asked Da Ponte. "I assume you've considered the question of life and death during your adventures." As the poet of the three, Da Ponte thought himself the one most able to argue philosophical points of mortality.

"Well," Casanova began, rubbing his well-groomed chin thoughtfully. "I suppose in many ways Mozart and I view death and life in the same way but from opposing sides of the problem. There are those who believe life is a series of misfortunes, and to those people, if life is unfortunate, it must be true that death—the opposite of life—is joyful. Those people are pessimists."

"I'm not a pessimist," Mozart countered. "I expect life to work out well. I only feel it's necessary to acknowledge the imminence of death, to be ready for it."

"Of course there's misfortune and worry in life," Casanova continued. "But I say as long as there's pleasure, then life itself is filled with pleasures and joy, because pleasures, physical pleasures, can be enjoyed only *during* life."

While they were talking, a little boy dressed in a somber black suit and a round black hat walked up to the side of the bridge and stood near them. Mozart looked down at the little fellow. When they made eye contact, the boy raised his arms, indicating he wanted to be lifted up so he could see the river.

Mozart knelt down and lifted him into his arms. As he did, he carefully picked up a couple of loose pebbles. When the boy could see the flowing river, Mozart dropped one of the pebbles. Together they followed its path and watched it splash into the river.

Kerplop!

The sound made them laugh. Mozart dropped another pebble. Again they laughed. Mozart gripped the child, whose tiny frame shook with excitement, and for a moment thought of his own son in Vienna.

"Jakov!"

A deep voice called out from behind them. The boy wiggled as Mozart carefully lowered him to the ground.

"Papa," the child called out as he ran to a man standing a few feet away.

Mozart watched as the father took his son's hand, then pulled him across the bridge and into the distance.

"Would you like me to show you where they've gone?" Da Ponte asked.

"Yes."

"And you, Giacomo, will you come too?"

Casanova shrugged and followed reluctantly.

Three abreast, they continued across the bridge, heading away from St. Vitus, then turned left to follow the river's bank. After a few streets, Da Ponte turned to the right, toward the center of the old town. Walking through the narrow streets, Mozart noticed that the buildings were no longer painted the cheerful colors—the pale yellows, soft blues and pinks—he had come to expect in Prague. Now they were just the natural brown and gray stone color, and most were in bad repair.

"Where are you taking us, Lorenzo?"

"To a place you've never been before."

Despite the bright sun still filling the clear blue sky, the streets and passageways seemed dark and dingy. Laundry hung from the wood-shuttered windows on the upper floors of the dwellings. Da Ponte slowed his pace, drawing Casanova and Mozart closer to him. He spoke softly.

"These streets were once filled with the same life and beauty you see in the rest of Prague. The Empress, our beloved Maria Theresa, mother of our lord and master Emperor Joseph, decided many years ago to ban all Jews from the city. Ten thousand Jews were forced to flee to a distance of at least two hours' journey."

Casanova walked slowly, looking at the buildings and the people. Da Ponte's history lesson was changing his view of this city, a place he had always cherished for its people, its buildings, its culture and its civility.

"Eventually she allowed the Jews to return, but there were severe restrictions on them. This ghetto was rebuilt as you see it now," Da Ponte continued. "But the Jews were still not treated like other citizens."

"In what way was their treatment different?" Mozart asked.

"Well, for example, Jews were forbidden to attend the theater or the opera. In 1781 Emperor Joseph finally reversed his mother's edicts, and Jews were again allowed to attend the theater, but only because the theaters were not selling out and they needed the money."

He led them past the synagogue, which was the most impressive structure in this neighborhood, but only a shadow of the majestic St. Vitus Cathedral they'd been in earlier.

Da Ponte walked through a narrow archway connecting two buildings. The sun had gone behind a slate gray cloud, and a strong breeze pushed dead leaves in a swirling pattern on the cracked cobblestone walkway. The trees were bare. Da Ponte opened an old gate and disappeared through another stone archway. Casanova and Mozart were close behind, but they stopped, struck by what they saw.

Within this broken, crumbling, forgotten courtyard was an old graveyard. Tombstones, damaged by age and lack of care, were crammed together, some leaning back, some tilting forward and the rest tipping to either side. The Hebrew lettering on most was worn away or covered with moss. Pieces had broken off the oldest stones, those nearest the center of the small square. Some markers were layered on top of other, older ones.

Mozart squeezed through the maze of askew stones, careful not to disturb anything. Da Ponte watched, hiding behind one of the taller stones.

"Mozart, you said earlier that one grave is much like another. Well, not here. This is where the Jews buried their dead," he intoned from his hiding place. "No pomp. No ceremony. No glory. No Requiems. No statues.

Twelve thousand graves; generation after generation jammed together, because this is all the land the Jews were given for their dead. There are no large monuments here."

The sound of his disembodied voice made Mozart shiver. Casanova looked up and tried to see Da Ponte, but the angles of the decrepit monuments kept the poet concealed.

"Lorenzo, come out," Casanova ordered. "Come out and explain why this is of such importance."

"Because I, in a way, am dead."

"What are you talking about?" Mozart asked.

Casanova and Mozart moved toward Da Ponte's voice. Seeing the edge of his cloak sticking out from behind the largest monument, Casanova stopped and confidently addressed the stone.

"Come out, Lorenzo. Come out and explain yourself." Da Ponte remained hidden. "Lorenzo, this isn't funny."

Mozart backed away from the stone as Casanova leaned over its top and saw Da Ponte crouching behind it. The poet stood up and forced his way around to the front of the monument. The way the light hit his face made him look pale. He leaned back against another marker as Casanova and Mozart waited.

"I was born in Italy, in Ceneda," he explained softly. "Our section of the village looked much like this part of Prague. I've changed my name since those days. When I was born, they named me Emanuel . . . Emanuel Conegliano. I was born a Jew."

"That's quite a tale, my dear Abbé. A wonderful story you've invented. Tell us the rest; explain how you made the change from Jew of Ceneda to the Court Poet of Vienna, with a brief stop to study for the priesthood," Casanova demanded.

"It's all true. My mother died when I was five. My father, rejecting our past, made us convert so he could marry a young Catholic girl. We were no longer Jews. I yearned for education, but my father was more interested in his young wife than in his children; I suppose that's why I've often envied the attention your father lavished on you, Wolfgang. In any event, the Bishop of Ceneda befriended our family, and I begged him to teach me. He accepted, and became my mentor and guide. He taught me Latin and the ways of the church. I intended to follow in his footsteps, I truly did, as God is my witness. But, the wonders of the world, the pleasures cast before us and the women distracted me, and, well . . . I suppose you know the rest."

"And this man, what was his name?"

"He was the Bishop of Ceneda, Monsignor Lorenzo Da Ponte."

"You're serious?"

Da Ponte nodded. "So you see, my friends, I was born a Jew and now I, too, am a dead Jew. But when I'm called to my maker and have to leave this world forever, I will be remembered. My words will live on; my name will live on. I won't have an aged marker covered by moss and decay in a cemetery no one visits. I will receive the last rites of the church and be honored. That's my revenge. I will never have to fear the loneliness of being forgotten; for I am the court poet even though I was not born to the position. To hell with it all! I am, and will always be, Lorenzo Da Ponte, and that can't be taken from me," he shouted as he thrust his fist toward the darkening sky.

"Let's get out of here. It's cold and it's getting late."

Casanova pulled his coat closed as he moved toward the rusted gate. When he reached the archway, he turned around and looked back. Da Ponte, wrapped in his black cloak, leaned on one of the fallen stone markers. Grinning, Mozart looked at his collaborator. A light rain began to fall. Casanova crossed himself, and hastily left the cemetery. Da Ponte laughed.

"The graveyard scene in *Don Giovanni* will be fine," he said, clasping Mozart's hand triumphantly in his. "There's nothing quite like a good graveyard scene."

Chapter Seventeen

⌓

erfectly straight lines of monuments stood guard; gravestones erected inside a black iron fence created the sense of a cemetery. But the point of focus was the overpowering stone statue of the Commendatore. It towered above the other monuments. Three wide steps led to its marble base, where an ominous inscription had been chiseled: I AWAIT HEAVEN'S REVENGE UPON THE EVIL MAN WHO SENT ME TO MY GRAVE. Above that loomed the larger-than-life statue of the Commendatore, his sword held aloft, poised to strike. Don Giovanni and Leporello, seated on the steps below, looked tiny.

"Leporello, when Don Giovanni orders you to address the statue, I want you to climb up its base and bow your head. Never look at the statue's face. You're terrified. You've just heard the Commendatore speak from the grave," Da Ponte directed, standing behind the first row of seats in the theater.

It was the final dress rehearsal. Mozart was still correcting wrong notes in the orchestra parts and was shouting instructions to the singers on phrasing and emphasis. Convinced the dramatic power of the opera was in danger of being missed, Da Ponte had taken over the job of directing. He knew what he wanted in every scene, but the singers, concerned about singing the right notes and making beautiful sounds, kept forgetting where to move and what to do. Pasquale Bondini paced the theater's narrow aisle, muttering.

The production wasn't bad, just not polished or finally shaped. Each time Da Ponte stopped the rehearsal to direct, Mozart would wait impatiently and then restart the rehearsal from a convenient place in the score. The musicians in the orchestra, though they rarely looked up from the music on their stands, knew that Mozart was conducting and correcting without ever glancing at his score.

"Don Giovanni, Signor Bassi, please," Da Ponte shouted again, stopping the action. "When you've had enough of Leporello's stammering and fumbling, show your impatience, push him out of the way. Climb onto the monument, scale the stones, end up face-to-face with the statue. Be fearless. When the Commendatore nods, accepting your invitation to dinner, you must pull away quickly so the audience sees the effect of the nodding statue. Then, and only then, show fear. Jump down off the pedestal, put your sword away and pick up your cloak. You and Leporello hurry away through the gate at the back of the stage. And Signor Commendatore, do not move a muscle until you nod. If the audience knows you're hiding in the statue they'll laugh, and this isn't one of the opera's funny moments. Understood?"

The statue nodded, slowly. The orchestra members who were watching laughed, momentarily breaking the tension.

"I'll speed up the tempo at the end of the scene to heighten the anxiety," Mozart whispered to Da Ponte. Then, turning back to the orchestra, he shouted: "We'll begin when Leporello sings: '*O statua gentilissima.*'"

This time through, the singers did as instructed, and the impact of the scene was so great that Bondini even stopped pacing to watch. As the opera moved along, he relaxed and sat down in the fourth row. Hidden by the darkness, Casanova was just three seats away. He studied the impresario, wondering if the scared little man had any idea of the miracle about to premiere on his stage, in his theater.

The final three scenes, which had been fully rehearsed the day before, went quickly. Mozart made very few corrections, evidently pleased with Don Giovanni's last meal, his deadly encounter with the statue and the opera's buoyant finale. When the final scene ended, the singers remained in place onstage as Mozart made a few more changes and suggestions. While he thanked the orchestra, the singers milled around.

"Until the opening," Mozart waved cheerfully, as if to give the singers permission to leave.

Slowly they made their way to the backstage changing areas. Packing up their instruments, the musicians bid each other good night. Mozart stood at the harpsichord looking at his score, pointing out wrong notes to the copyist. The concertmaster stood nearby, patiently waiting to speak with him.

"Maestro, I'm sorry to interrupt . . ."

"Of course. What is it?"

"Maestro, the opera opens in two days . . ."

"We're all aware of that," snapped Bondini, who had moved next to Mozart.

"Well . . . Maestro . . . if it wouldn't be impolite, may I ask when we might see the overture?"

Mozart smiled.

"I'm working on it. Let me ask you a question. Do you think the orchestra could play a work of mine at sight, without rehearsal?"

"Impossible!" Bondini blurted.

"I wasn't asking you, Signor Bondini. I was asking a musician."

"Maestro, the orchestra loves your music, and to work with you is an honor. But to ask them to sight-read an entire overture . . . I don't know."

"I'm confident, especially since I'm conducting," Mozart boasted. Then, turning to the copyist, he added: "Make the corrections I've given you. The manuscript of the overture will be done in time for you to copy the parts before the premiere. Be ready to work quickly."

Bondini threw up his hands in disgust. Mozart smirked behind Bondini's back. "I'll be ready, Maestro," the copyist affirmed with a crisp bow.

"Signor Bondini, I'm truly delighted your wife's feeling better. She sang the rehearsal without any sign of the cold she had," Mozart said. "She follows my conducting so well. She is so flexible, and her voice is so supple and delicate. Anything I ask for she gives, willingly; her soft phrases are tender, and when she gets angry . . . well . . . it's exciting. But you must know what she's like when she's angry."

Bondini's face flushed with rage, but before he could respond Casanova stepped between the two smaller men.

"The evening will be a triumph. Pasquale, your company rivals any I've heard," Casanova said.

Somewhat mollified, Bondini smiled. "Thank you, Chevalier. You're welcome in my opera house anytime. Now if you'll excuse me, I have to attend to some final details. We have many problems with the number of important people who wish to attend the premiere."

"That's good," Mozart said, genuinely pleased.

"Pasquale," Casanova whispered as the director moved away. "Have you received an invitation for a party at the Villa Bertramka tomorrow night?"

"Yes. It arrived at my home yesterday evening."

"Do you plan to attend?"

"Absolutely."

"And Madame Bondini, will she be there?"

Bondini was suspicious. "Why?"

"I've been asked to prepare a little diversion, an entertainment for the evening, and I wanted to make certain you and your wife will be there," Casanova said.

"We'll be there. I know Caterina wants to be there, although I must confess she doesn't think Madame Dušek particularly likes her. Well, we'll be there. Good evening, Giacomo. Until tomorrow, and thank you again for all your help." Bondini walked to the backstage area; as he disappeared into the wings, Casanova could hear him timidly calling his wife's name.

"Marriage," Casanova muttered.

Mozart was still correcting the score and Da Ponte was onstage giving the Donna Anna some private direction.

"I suppose that's it then," Mozart said as he closed the heavy pages of the manuscript.

"It will be wonderful, really wonderful," Casanova said.

"Thank you. It's strange, though."

"What?"

"This is the first opera I've composed that my father won't see. I never realized how much I relied on him, even when we lived in different cities."

"You were lucky to have him as long as you did. Cherish that. Having a father to guide you into manhood is a miracle I was denied. Your father would be proud, I'm certain."

"I'm never sure. He could be demanding and critical of what I did."

"But not of what you composed."

"No. That's true. When I became a father I thought I'd feel grown up as a parent should. But I didn't. After I received the letter telling me my father had died, I took my son for a walk. I realized I was now the oldest, the patriarch. It made me uncomfortable. I didn't want the position. I liked being a son." He paused.

"It's strange really . . . it struck me just the other day, when we were at St. Vitus . . . I never said good-bye to my father. I didn't go to his funeral or see him buried. I still sometimes pretend he didn't die; I imagine he's still living in Salzburg as he always did. I would have liked to say good-bye."

"The wounds are new. Give it time. You'll grow comfortable with it and find peace."

Absentmindedly Mozart picked out a sad melody on the harpsichord, stopped in mid-phrase and took his coat from a nearby seat.

"Lorenzo, are you quite done?" Casanova shouted up to the stage, where Da Ponte was still leaning against Teresa Saporiti. "We have to go, Lorenzo. I'm starving. Will you have dinner with us, Mozart?"

"I should go home and compose the overture, but since you've asked, I'd be delighted. It will be more fun than sitting alone in my room."

"Lorenzo, let Signorina Saporiti go home. She must be tired of you," Casanova needled. "Mozart and I are going to supper. Lorenzo, are you coming with us?"

Saporiti kissed Da Ponte on the cheek and glided off the stage.

"Let's go," Da Ponte said wistfully. "I'm starving."

As the stagehands swept the stage and extinguished the candles, Casanova, Da Ponte and Mozart put on their cloaks and left the theater.

It was a cold Saturday night, and Prague's streets were nearly empty. The three men walked in silence, lost in private thoughts.

They walked single file through a narrow alley surrounded by the high stone walls of the dwellings, careful not to trip down the steep steps. When they reached the Nova Hospoda Pub, they turned into the stone archway and walked through the wooden door. A fire roared in the large earthen fireplace. The room was crowded with tradesmen, merchants, their wives and some younger, unescorted women. A table was cleared, a carafe of wine was brought and glasses were filled.

"To the creative spirit," toasted Casanova.

"To returning to Vienna," said Da Ponte.

"To freedom and brotherhood," said Mozart, but as he was about to take his first sip, his arm stopped in midair.

"What's the matter?"

"Shh. Listen, Lorenzo."

Da Ponte and Casanova strained their ears. In the distance, muffled by the noise of the crowd, the soft sounds of a harp could be heard.

"The melody's familiar, but I can't remember where it's from."

"What is it?" Casanova asked, straining to hear the music.

"It's the march from the end of the first act of *Figaro*," Mozart explained proudly.

Da Ponte drank some more wine. "Is that all? I'm starving. Forget music. What are you going to eat, Giacomo?"

But Casanova wasn't thinking about food. His eyes followed Mozart, who had risen from the table and disappeared into the adjoining room. Da Ponte was considering what to eat and so was unaware of a commotion at the other end of the room, near the fireplace. Mozart, followed by the harpist and two men carrying the golden instrument, had reentered the main room.

"But Maestro, please. I didn't mean any disrespect," the harpist pleaded.

The pub's owner cleared some space around a clavier that had been pushed into a corner of the room. With élan he wiped the dust from the keys and placed a silver candelabrum with six tall candles on the clavier. The harpist nervously set up his instrument to the right of the keyboard.

"Now we'll see if you can earn your supper."

The harpist, an older man, tried to smile, but his nerves got the better of him and his hands shook as he retuned his instrument. To Da Ponte's dismay, Casanova got up from their table and went over to the instruments.

"Here's the game we're going to play," Mozart announced to the crowd. "I'll play a theme . . . a melody. My friend Signor Harpe will then improvise on my theme. When he's finished, I'll improvise on his improvisation, and we'll continue in this way until one of us runs out of ideas and has to repeat a variation that's already been played."

The crowd cheered and applauded.

"But Maestro," the harpist objected. "Who'll remember if a variation has already been played?"

Mozart's loud laugh filled the room. Da Ponte swiveled in his seat, turning his back on this impromptu musicale.

"I'll remember. Now, let's begin."

Without waiting, Mozart played a simple, cheerful melody. As he worked his way through it, any remaining conversations in the pub ended. The harpist, his eyes shut, listened intently. As a sweet chord ended the cheerful melody, Mozart looked toward the harpist.

To Mozart's surprise and delight, the harpist took the cue and launched into an intricate étude based on his theme. The old man's fingers moved nimbly around the strings; each note resounded cleanly, but he put special emphasis on the ones that had been the basis of Mozart's original melody. As the composer had done before, the harpist looked toward his collaborator. Mozart nodded his acceptance and, without missing a beat, began an even more elaborate variation.

And so it went, back and forth, up and down the scales, from major to minor and back again, each variation more virtuosic than the one before.

The crowd gathered around the instruments oohed and aahed with each variation. For those who understood music, the game was a fascinating tour de force; for the others it was delightful, free entertainment.

Casanova noticed how Mozart kept looking at the beautiful women around the clavier, winking at them through the sparkling flames of the candles. Each time, the woman who was his target would smile back.

"Ah, the power of music," Casanova noted to himself.

The harpist was working feverishly to keep up. Mozart realized victory was at hand, but he was impressed the old man had been able to continue as long as he had. The harpist finished a short variation and looked pleadingly at Mozart. With one more boyish grin aimed at the woman standing nearest to him, Mozart took his original melody, slowed it down into a melancholy dirge, then turned it upside down, syncopating the rhythm so that the original melody and several of the earlier variations blended into one unified piece. This time when he played the final chord, there was no reply from the harp.

Defeated, but pleased to have survived the battle, the harpist stood up and bowed to the victor. The crowd cheered. Mozart reached into his pocket and pulled out two gold pieces.

"This is all I have, but you've earned them," he said, tossing the coins to the old harpist.

"You do me honor, Maestro."

Casanova moved closer to Mozart, and to the two very attractive women who had positioned themselves on either side of the composer.

"Wasn't that fun, Giacomo?"

"Wonderful, but Lorenzo's annoyed. Perhaps we should get back to our table." Then, subtly pointing to the women, he added: "Do you think we should bring him a present? He looks so lonely."

The women smiled, and Mozart nodded quickly in return.

"I don't think so. It just doesn't seem right . . ."

Mozart's answer trailed off, his thoughts turning to how lonely he felt without Constanze.

"Giacomo, why don't you stay here. This is your area of expertise. I'll go sit with Lorenzo. Why waste such talent—isn't that what you would say?"

"It would be my pleasure."

Casanova moved quickly to the group of women and introduced himself as a dear friend and mentor to the composer. Mozart returned to Da Ponte, who was enjoying his meal of trout and potatoes. A new, full carafe of wine was in the middle of the table.

"You ordered more wine?"

"No. The hotelier brought it. It's payment for your concert."

Mozart refilled his glass and sat back.

"What a shame, what a pity," Casanova's voice intruded on the silence.

"What?" Da Ponte asked through a mouthful of bread.

Casanova sat down and drank a glass of wine. "They were so willing, so interested in my adventures. But I decided we three should be together tonight, so I left the ladies to the less experienced men in the crowd."

Da Ponte looked around the room, suddenly interested in what Casanova was saying.

"Who was so willing?" he asked, straining to see across the room.

"The two women who surrounded our good friend here. One wore a beautiful blue dress, the other a burgundy frock that showed her womanhood to best advantage. As Wolfgang played the clavier, they reacted to every nuance of the music. It was a pleasure to watch. After your musical duel I realized what intrigued me about them. They're sisters!"

Mozart's eyes widened.

"Sisters," Casanova repeated, excitedly drinking his wine. "Do you know what a rare treat sisters can be? They're seamstresses who live here in Prague. And to think, I gave up that incredible pleasure just to be with you."

"You've been with sisters?" Mozart asked in disbelief.

"Can we change the subject?" Da Ponte pleaded. But his request fell on deaf ears.

"You know," Mozart said, moving his chair closer to Casanova's. "Before I married Constanze, I was in love with her sister, but we never . . . um . . . never . . ."

"Then you've missed one of life's great pleasures."

"And you, Giacomo, you've been with sisters?"

"Now you've done it," Da Ponte whined.

"Done what?"

"He's going to tell us about his adventure with sisters."

"It's the least I can do to repay Mozart for his performance earlier."

Casanova settled into his chair, refilled the three wineglasses, drank his and began.

"It was in the days when France was a civilized place; when people of rank were respected and the style and élan of the royalty shone throughout the land. I was on a journey and stopped for a few days in Avignon. There was a house—a very special place—where the madam knew intimately the predilections of her clients. I had been there once before on a previous journey, and had always intended to return because, in all my travels, I'd never encountered such service."

Casanova gulped the rest of his wine and refilled the glass.

"During my first visit there I'd spent a delightful night with a young lady named Henriette. Her charms were indescribable, matched only by her imagination and her skills."

"If you'll excuse me, I've heard this before. I'll be back in a few minutes."

As Casanova drank more wine, Da Ponte got up and walked into the pub's other room.

"So what happened when you went back, Giacomo?"

"Henriette was occupied with another nobleman and couldn't be disturbed. I was disappointed, and the madam offered me a mysterious, special delight. Without saying another word, she led me to a splendid room. It was light and cheerful, with large windows facing to the south so that the afternoon sun shone through the white curtains, casting a warm glow throughout. I undressed and lay down on the large, canopied bed. It was summer, and the warm breeze felt pleasant as it tickled my naked body. Soon there was a gentle knock on the door. 'Enter,' I said from my prone, rather exposed position. In walked a beautiful young girl. '*Je suis Iréne,*' she said. Her voice, tender and sweet, sounded like a child's, but her figure told a different story. She was attractive beyond words, and I admired her perfect physique as she undressed. There was nothing wrong with her, and under normal circumstances I would have been most excited. But the madam's promise of 'something special' was locked in my mind."

Casanova paused long enough to refill his glass and wipe his cheeks.

"Iréne stood at the foot of the bed, staring at me with the most wicked leer. Our eyes locked. Slowly she backed toward the door, never taking her eyes from mine. She turned the handle and deftly swung the wooden door open. I swear, Wolfgang, if I hadn't been lying down I would have fallen to my knees in fervent prayer. There, standing in the doorway, stark naked, was Iréne's double, her perfect match in every sumptuous detail.

"'*Je suis Marcoline,*' the second young woman said. Even her voice was the same. Marcoline entered the room, closed the door behind her and took her twin sister in her arms. Watching these matching beauties embrace was more than I could stand. I was in pain from anticipation."

Casanova paused again, mostly for dramatic emphasis, but also to drink another glass of wine, and to watch Mozart shift uncomfortably in his seat.

"After a long, passionate kiss, Marcoline and Iréne climbed onto the bed. Iréne lay on top of her sister, calling her 'Wife.' Oh, Wolfgang, I swear I remained virtuous as long as possible, thrilled with my role of passive spectator. But before long they flung themselves on me with such violence, I was obligated to respond. What a memory . . ."

His voice trailed off, and Mozart noticed that Casanova's eyes had grown heavy.

"What happened?"

"Oh . . ." Casanova roused himself. "When night fell, and darkness filled the room, I reached to light the bedside candle. But the sisters implored me to keep the room dark. Then they taught me the most wonderful game. Unclothed, we walked around the room in random patterns. Whenever I would bump into one of the sisters, it was my task to figure out which one she was. If I could tell correctly simply by probing with my hands, they would perform any act my imagination could conjure. If I guessed incorrectly, the act to be performed was their choice. The next morning I ordered a splendid breakfast, the kind you can only get in Avignon, including fresh oysters, which are the best way I know to replenish the juices we expend in making love."

Casanova refilled his glass and picked at the food the waiter had brought. Da Ponte had returned just before the end of the story and was standing nearby. He slid back into his seat and refilled the glasses, urging Casanova to drink more.

"What a fantasy," Da Ponte mumbled under his breath. "You know, Wolfgang, perhaps our next opera should be about sisters. What do you think?"

"You should have de Sade write the story," Casanova suggested, his words slurring together. "I know he's used the idea of twin sisters in some novel or play."

"Have you heard from him again?" Mozart asked.

"No."

"I think about him quite often. I find myself imagining what he does in his cell all alone. I think about the violence exploding around him and wonder if he contemplates his mortality, or if he cares."

Casanova finished another glass of wine. His eyes were closed; his hands and head rested on the table.

Mozart pitied his friend, this noble relic whose mind was obsessed by faded images of his life. Casanova, who'd once seemed so invincible, appeared beaten. Mozart looked around the nearly empty pub. Da Ponte, now wearing his black cloak, stood glowering next to Casanova's slumped-over form. He leaned over so his mouth was close to Casanova's ear.

"You're a tired, drunken old man. Go home. You've wasted your night telling silly tales. You're trapped in a past that no longer exists. Let Mozart take you home, where you can dream of the past without boring anyone to death. It's all you have. Dream, old man!"

The sneer and disdain in Da Ponte's voice shocked Mozart.

"Take him home, Wolfgang. He'll sleep it off before tomorrow."

"Where are you going?"

Da Ponte raised his arms, spreading his cloak wide, like a bat's wings. From the shadows of the doorway, the two sisters, one in a blue dress, the other in burgundy, now covered by matching pelisses, appeared and walked over to the poet. He placed his arms around them.

"As promised, tonight I've won. I've taken revenge. Now you'll know what it feels like to be the one who goes home alone. I'm the winner, and, as it should be, someday this poet will tell the story."

Casanova struggled to raise his head from the table and watched through glazed-over eyes as Da Ponte, happily sandwiched between the sisters, left the pub. Confused and uncertain, Mozart placed his arm around the old man's shoulder. He didn't want this responsibility; he didn't want any responsibility.

"Oh, Father. My father in heaven," he prayed silently. "Help him. Help me."

Chapter Eighteen

louds blew across the early evening horizon. Riding in a horse-drawn carriage the Dušeks had sent for him, with the driver in front and the footman at the rear dressed in crisp dark green uniforms, Mozart looked out the small oval window. The setting sun lit the western side of the clouds, giving them a bright orange glow, while their eastern sides, remained slate gray. The air was remarkably mild for the last Sunday of October, and Mozart tried to relax.

He settled into the cushioned seat and closed his eyes. The strain of the last weeks showed on his youthful face. The difficulties of creating and preparing a new opera had seemed insurmountable during rehearsals. Though surrounded by people who were there to help him, and by people who loved him as a person and as a musician, he had felt strangely alone throughout the rehearsal period.

Rocked by the steady bounce of the carriage, the images in his head kept jumping from Da Ponte to Casanova to his dead father. The faces blended into an amalgam of the three men. He could hear Da Ponte's encouragement, Casanova's teaching and his father's boasting. They all made him uncomfortable, and every few minutes he'd wake with a start and clutch the coach's well-upholstered seat. Looking out the window helped clear his head.

"I'll think about women," he decided, wiping his eyes as if to rid his dreams of the annoying masculine images.

He closed his eyes again, now thinking of the singers who would create the roles he'd composed; Josefa, whose strength and grace he so admired; and finally, Constanze, his darling Constanze, his wife, whom he missed more than he'd have thought possible. Enjoying the daydream, he imagined himself and his wife reunited, once again like young lovers who can't bear to be apart. In this fantasy everything was as it should be; he could even hear the music to accompany this imaginary scene. The financial struggles and political problems that had dogged him were gone; he had the recognition he deserved; and at his side was Constanze, his guide. In his daydream they were a family, and he cherished the vision.

"Maestro, we've arrived."

The brusque male voice scared him. Mozart woke, his heart pounding. The footman had opened the carriage door and was standing at attention. A wood step was placed on the ground to make his descent easier. Mozart looked out the door, trying to remember where he was; he'd slept soundly as the coach had rolled across the bridge, past St. Vitus to Bertramka. Picking up his folded cloak from the seat, he got up and stepped out. The Dušeks' majordomo, splendidly dressed in a cream-colored coat with gold-braided decorations, greeted him with a deep bow and escorted him over the stones of the curved entryway. Before reaching the ornately carved wooden front door, Mozart paused to steal a look at the windows on the villa's second floor. He knew which room was Constanze's, but he couldn't tell if the shadow behind the white, billowing curtains was his wife watching him or his tired imagination playing tricks on him.

Trailing the majordomo into the grand foyer, he felt lonely and small, until the sound of the wind band in the music room rehearsing one of his serenades caught his ear. He stood at the center of the oval-shaped room, enjoying the sound of the music and absorbing the smell of the food wafting in from the kitchen.

"Wolfgang, I'm so glad you came early."

Josefa Dušek's rich voice brought him back to reality. She glided into the foyer and embraced him warmly. The scent of her perfume overwhelmed the aroma of the food. She looked stunning in her cream-colored gown, ornamented around the low-cut neck by sparkling jewels sewn into the lace.

"Is Constanze here?" he asked, knowing full well she had to be.

"Of course. She's resting."

He tried to seem uninterested.

"Who else is coming this evening?"

"Oh, everyone! It's sure to be the party of the season. I'm so excited. And then tomorrow we'll all be at the premiere of your opera. I understand it's going well." Josefa played with the oval-shaped pendant hanging from her black velvet choker.

"Who told you?"

"A friend . . . someone you know well . . . a spy . . . Why don't you go find František. I'm sure he's bumbling about somewhere." She kissed him on the cheek and walked down a corridor toward the kitchen. Left alone, Mozart looked at the staircase and thought about sneaking upstairs to find Constanze, but the music was playing again and the melody—not one of his this time—drew him to the music room.

Servants wearing starch-white gloves lit candles, arranged opulent displays of flowers, prepared glasses of champagne and filled trays with tiny pastries.

The guests were arriving. Mozart could hear the majordomo intoning names. He peered down the corridor and watched, transfixed as some of Prague's honored military leaders arrived. Their crisp uniforms—black and gold coats with black pants—fascinated him. He liked the way the men looked: bold and strong. He thought their uniforms, especially the shiny swords at their sides, gave them an air of confidence as they strolled through the house.

It wasn't long before the house was filled with splendidly clothed guests, many of whom had come from the nearby villas. With each arrival the majordomo announced the name and servants in black velvet coats led the guests into the foyer, from where they dispersed into one or another of the many adjoining rooms.

Mozart wandered around, occasionally bowing to someone he recognized or who recognized him. When he walked through the billiard room, a familiar voice called out.

"Maestro Mozart, that is you, isn't it?"

Count Thun paused between shots and waited as Mozart walked over to him and examined the lay of the balls on the table. "A difficult lay, Count."

"Would you like to try your luck, Maestro?"

"Luck has little to do with billiards. Skill, thought and a good eye are all that matters."

"Then perhaps you'll demonstrate your skills for me."

Mozart removed his coat and handed it to Count Thun. Then, taking the stick, he bent over and eyed the table, studying the position of the balls. Mozart drew the stick back, lined up his hands and shot. The balls ricocheted, the one he struck glancing off two others, leaving a perfect triangle at the center of the table.

"Bravo, Mozart," Count Thun called out. "I had no idea you were so skillful."

"Save your bravos for tomorrow night, Count. Then we'll play for real stakes."

Mozart took his coat from Count Thun and walked away, working his way through the crowd back to the music room. The musicians in the wind band nodded at him, as if to welcome one of their own. He was tempted to conduct the group, but didn't want to be busy when Constanze made her appearance, which he was certain would be soon.

"Le Chevalier de Seingalt," the majordomo intoned from the entryway.

Mozart walked toward the foyer. From a nearby corridor he watched as Casanova, dressed in a handsome gold waistcoat, entered. His outfit seemed to glow, and the jewels on the handle of his walking stick glittered. Mozart studied his every move, but he showed no signs of the drunken condition he'd been in the previous night.

Casanova's outfit had panache and style and he seemed particularly animated as he whispered with Josefa, who greeted him warmly. Mozart saw them laugh as Josefa led him up the winding staircase to the bedrooms. Mozart remained in his hiding place, shielded from sight by a heavy velvet curtain. Quietly he cursed himself for allowing Constanze to stay at Bertramka, away from him. "What strange plot are they hatching?" he wondered.

During the next half hour, Bondini and his wife, Herr Strobach, Teresa Saporiti and Da Ponte all arrived, along with about fifty other people Mozart didn't recognize. The party was loud and festive as the guests mingled, talked and ate the special patés and breads. Wine and champagne flowed freely.

"So now all the characters have assembled," Mozart mused. "I wonder when our heroine will make her appearance."

Lost in thoughts about what might develop, he wandered through the wide corridors back to the music room. There the crowd—elegantly made-up women and their escorts, the women fanning themselves as they linked arms with their companions—had grown larger. He scanned the clusters of people engaged in conversations, all of them oblivious to the music floating up to the ceiling, filling the room.

"Mozart, there you are. I knew you were here, but I couldn't find you in this crowd."

František Dušek, wearing his usual black frock coat and white chemise, limped over and embraced him.

"Come with me. I think you know these people."

František pulled him over to a cluster of men: Strobach, Casanova, Da Ponte and Bondini standing in a semicircle, drinking champagne.

"What a distinguished group. And to think, all of you together in one place. What an extraordinary coincidence," Mozart noted. He looked at the clavier that had been moved out of the way so the wind band could be at the center of the room.

"Maestro, how is your wife?" Strobach asked.

"She's quite well," Casanova interjected, much to Mozart's annoyance.

Oblivious to the mounting tension between Mozart and Casanova, Strobach rambled on.

"You know, Mozart, I haven't seen you since you were at the cathedral. What did you think of the Cavalli Requiem?"

"It was more dramatic than I'd expected," Mozart answered, pleased to have the conversation turn to music. "I must admit, I'm often surprised at how much excellent music by dead composers never gets played."

"Does that worry you?" Da Ponte asked.

"Why would that worry him?" František interrupted. "He's young, with years ahead of him."

"Never tempt the fates," Mozart said softly.

The wind band had stopped playing.

"František. Would you mind if I played the clavier?"

"Of course not."

Without wasting a second, František Dušek pointed to a servant standing like a statue near the door and ordered him to reposition the clavier so it would be in front of the wind band. Several servants lifted the instrument into place. The circle of men gathered near it. Mozart sat down and looked around, waiting for more people to notice him. Then he began playing. Of those listening, only Bondini recognized the melody as being from Mozart's opera *The Abduction from the Seraglio*. Mozart thought of the opera's heroine: Constanze. He played the tender melody, expecting it to magically call his wife to him. But she didn't appear. Frustrated and disheartened, he finished the phrase and stopped playing.

Looking around the room, he began playing one of the fugues from Bach's *The Well-Tempered Clavier*. Then, without any transition, he began to improvise on the complex phrases. Now he was comfortable, totally at ease and in control; the center of attention. When he finished, the crowd that had gathered around applauded. Mozart liked the way the women smiled as they gently tapped their fans on their wrists. Da Ponte was standing next to Bondini.

"Has he written the overture yet?" Bondini whispered.

"No."

"But he has to! We open tomorrow night."

Bondini was about to force his way closer to the clavier when a hand clamped onto his shoulder.

"Wait. It will be done. You have my word." Casanova's resonant, insistent voice froze Bondini in place.

"Mozart," Casanova said. "You must meet many interesting musicians in Vienna. After all, His Majesty does invite many people to the court to perform."

"Some are interesting," Mozart said, looking up from the keys. "But most are there to play or compose what they think the royalty wants to hear. However, I did have an interesting meeting earlier this year, just last spring. Constanze and I were about to go to the opera. Our serving girl told me a young man had been sitting in the hallway . . . waiting . . . all afternoon, to see me."

As Mozart told the story, he continued playing the clavier, which made his speech somewhat choppy. But the music flowed seamlessly as he wove together bits of melodies, some of which were known to the crowd. Mozart never took his eyes off Casanova. But Casanova wasn't paying attention to the music, because he was looking into the large mirror hanging over the fireplace. He could see most of the people in the room reflected there. After a few minutes, Mozart figured out what Casanova was doing: looking for Constanze.

"We were late for a concert," Mozart continued. "But the serving girl seemed so upset when I instructed her to tell the young man I had no time, I agreed to meet with him. She ran off . . . I waited. The door opened and she ushered him in . . . I'd say he was about seventeen, maybe eighteen . . . strangely shaped . . . slightly hunched over . . . stocky . . . wild hair. His clothes—a plain gray coat . . . very unattractive, unfashionable—nothing fit properly. But somehow I understood why she was so intent on my meeting him. There was something about him . . . compelling . . . powerful . . . well beyond his years.

"When I greeted him he grabbed my hand with incredible force . . . shook it wildly, all the while telling me what an honor it was for him. I asked what he wanted.

"'To play for you, Maestro. I've come to Vienna to perform and compose, as you did . . . I was hoping you'd take me as a student. I haven't much money, but I'll work hard.'

"He was sincere. I told him to play." Mozart paused for effect. "I walked away, across the room. He sat down and started playing . . . one of my piano concertos . . . but instead of playing just the solo line, he managed to play the orchestra part as well."

To illustrate, Mozart began the concerto, copying what this young pianist had done.

"I was impressed . . . asked him what else he could play. He reached into the pocket of his well-worn coat . . . he was so nervous, charming really . . . he pulled out some crumpled, messy, ink-stained sheets of manuscript paper. 'Perhaps I could play a piece I composed recently.'

"I sat down in the armchair and watched. I can't imitate what I saw . . . let me tell you, this fellow began to pound the keys; I almost asked him to stop . . . I've never heard anything like it. The music . . . was good . . . not yet fully formed . . . some rough transitions . . . a few shocking key changes . . . some harmonies I'd never use, but all in all, it was very good."

Mozart played on, savoring being the center of attention.

"Then, just when I thought he'd exhaust himself or break my clavier, he shifted moods . . . played a beautiful, slow, tender passage. Constanze came in . . . to remind me we had to leave for the theater. Even she was caught by his spell . . . she stared at him. When the young man finished, I went over and complimented him. His face was bright red. He muttered his thanks. 'So what do you want to do here in Vienna?' I asked."

"'To play the clavier and compose as you do, Maestro,' he repeated. Then I asked about his musical ideas. As I was leading him from the room, he grabbed my hand and stared into my eyes."

Mozart stopped playing the clavier, drawing everyone's attention to the narrative.

"'Maestro,' he whispered. 'I will compose music to shake the world, to light fires in people's hearts, to wake them from their fanciful lives and make them stand up and shout for freedom and equality. I can't compose pretty tunes. I have to compose powerful music, music fitting this troubled world we live in.'"

"And this wild-haired revolutionary," Casanova interrupted impatiently. "Do you happen to remember his name?"

"He was from Bonn. His name was Beethoven, Ludwig van Beethoven. Mark my words, he'll make a noise in this world."

To punctuate his point, Mozart pounded the clavier's keys. The power of the resounding dissonant chord silenced the disbelieving laughter of the others. Suddenly the French doors leading out to the balcony blew open. No one was there; an eerie feeling filled Mozart.

"We should leave those doors opened," Da Ponte said. "There's a lovely breeze, and this room's a little too warm for my taste."

"I agree," Casanova said. "And if you gentlemen will excuse me, I think I'll see who's in the gardens." He went over to one of the servants standing at the doorway. He glanced around the room, his gaze stopping at each woman, as he waited for the servant to return with his cloak. Quickly he threw it over his shoulders, hurried out the doors onto the stone balcony, bounded down the steps and disappeared into the gardens below.

Mozart jumped up from the clavier and followed him, calling: "Giacomo, wait. Wait, I have to ask you . . ."

But he was too late. Casanova had vanished into the garden. Inside, the musicians from the wind band, all of whom had been standing around listening to Mozart's narrative and impromptu recital, took their seats and began playing another breezy divertimento by Haydn.

Mozart came back in, but before he could blend into the crowd, Pasquale Bondini grabbed him by the shoulder.

"Maestro, I hate to be a bother, especially on such a festive night . . . I know you've been busy . . . I understand there are problems with your wife . . . I wish I could be of help . . . but there is the matter of the overture. You know the audience expects one; it clears the ears and gets them ready for the opera . . . I can't imagine an opera without—"

"Leave me alone. You'll have your overture."

Mozart pulled himself away from the director and quickly walked through a group of guests clustered around servants holding heavy silver trays. Mozart was determined to find Constanze; she had to be here. But where, and with whom?

He furtively went from room to room, stopping only when he saw a woman who, from the back, looked like she might be Constanze. But the similarity of the powdered white wigs and the formal gowns kept fooling him. Frustrated, he moved more quickly through the maze of crowded rooms until he completed the circle and found himself back in the music room. The French doors to the balcony were still open but, except for the wind band, the room was now empty. He stopped and looked around in surprise. Seeing him, the musicians quickly changed the music on their stands and started playing one of his serenades. He nodded politely toward them as he walked cautiously out to the balcony.

Standing at the white stone balustrade, he peered into the gardens. From his raised vantage point he could see glowing lanterns moving among the trees—couples, lovers meeting in secrecy. Noise from the area directly below the balcony caught his attention. Leaning over the railing, he saw three cloaked figures: a man and two women. Despite the severe angle he could see the black masks they wore to hide their eyes and noses. The three mysterious guests, seated on a bench, were embracing and kissing. The women's giggles floated up to him.

"*Viva la libertà!*" Mozart whispered, toasting the trio with an imaginary glass of champagne.

The flickering light from a passing lantern caught his attention. Through the shadows he could see a woman and a man, concealed by dark cloaks, running arm in arm toward the pavilion. As quickly as he could, he raced down the stone steps and onto the garden path, hoping to find his Constanze. But without a lantern to light his way, he had to slow down, and soon lost sight of the two fleeing figures.

Mozart stopped and stood still. The scent of Constanze's perfume filled the night air. He set off to find her. Two more intertwined, cloaked figures behind a nearby tree caught his eye. He snuck up without a sound and grabbed the man from behind.

"I've got you now, Casanova."

The man slumped, as if ashamed to be caught. Triumphantly Mozart pulled the mask from his captive's face.

"Lorenzo! But . . . I thought . . . And who's . . ."

The woman slowly lifted the hood of her cloak.

"Signorina Saporiti!" Mozart was startled. "I'm sorry. I thought you were Casanova and Constanze."

Da Ponte and Teresa Saporiti just smiled, said nothing and disappeared into the gardens. Mozart shuffled sadly toward the pavilion. The door was ajar. He could hear the muffled sounds of a woman's moan, a soft purr. He crept up the three stone steps, hiding in the shadows until he was near the door. When the moment seemed right, he burst in and grabbed the woman. It wasn't Constanze. The man held up his lantern.

"Signora Bondini . . . Pasquale . . . I'm so . . ." Embarrassed, Mozart ran from the pavilion. Another couple, in a full embrace and kissing passionately, sat on a wrought-iron bench near a fountain in the garden.

"Stand up, Casanova. That has to be you. I'll have you now, you . . . you . . . ," Mozart sputtered angrily. The kiss ended. With great difficulty the man stood and turned toward his accuser. Mozart saw at once his error.

"František . . . Josefa . . ."

"Yes, Mozart."

"Where is Constanze? Is she here? Is she with Casanova? I need to know."

His hosts said nothing, returning to their kiss; their grins angered the lost composer. Mozart walked on through the gardens, kicking loose stones, scuffing his shoes, wandering aimlessly, tempted to trap other nocturnal lovers, but afraid to embarrass himself further. Absentmindedly he made his way to a clearing about a hundred meters away from the villa. At its center stood a stone table and bench the Dušeks had had built during his first visit to Prague so he could compose outdoors. Now, in the dark, the smooth stone writing desk seemed like a safe haven. Tired, jealous, frustrated and lonely, Mozart sat down and rested his head on the cold stone. He closed his eyes.

"Wolfgang."

The sweet voice cut through the garden's darkness like the brightest church bell slicing through a cold Sunday morning. Mozart looked up.

"Wolfgang."

The sound repeated, this time coming from the opposite side of the clearing. Then, almost immediately, he hear it a third time, a fourth and a fifth, each sound emanating from a different direction, from behind a different tree. Even though the voices were disguised to sound as alike as possible, Mozart's keen ears could tell that several people were involved. Slowly a smile came to his face as he listened carefully, discerning the different timbres of the women's voices. After a few moments, he moved hesitantly toward the tree closest to the pavilion. When he reached it, he knelt down and bowed his head. The disembodied voices fell silent.

"My friends. I enjoy a game more than most people, and can usually play better than most. My colleague—the magician, the spy, the seer, the teacher, the lover: Signor Giacomo Casanova—has tricked me. He has done a splendid job and you have all played your parts to perfection. I am defeated. I surrender. Constanze, before all these hidden witnesses, friends, lovers, even foes, I tell you, Constanze, I love you and need you. You are the soul I need in order to thrive. You are the inspiration that brings forth my melodies. Come back. Constanze, forgive me; my muse and mother of my children, forgive my adolescent diversions, my fantasies."

Hidden behind the tree, Constanze felt the tears flow down her face. Casanova gave her his handkerchief.

"This is true love," he thought wistfully.

Constanze emerged from the shadows and walked around the tree to where Mozart knelt. She put her hand on Mozart's arm and slowly lifted him from his kneeling position. As they stood face-to-face, she rubbed his cheek with the back of her hand. He looked into her beautiful, dark eyes, held her chin in his hand and kissed her.

"I forgive you," she whispered. "It's a weakness, but I forgive you everything."

After a moment's pause, like a master puppeteer, Casanova clapped his hands, and all the other players stepped from behind their trees into the clearing. A circle of lanterns lit the impromptu outdoor stage, casting a warm glow through the night air. Mozart and Constanze embraced as he spun her happily around. The guests applauded and, delighted by their reaction, Casanova bowed low, adding a theatrical flourish with his hand-kerchief. Then the Dušeks' servants, each one holding aloft a bright, flaming torch, formed two facing rows, lining the winding garden path back to the villa. The archway of light was spectacular. With a beaming smile, Mozart took Constanze's hand in his and led the procession. The others, all laughing, smiling and kissing, followed.

As they approached the villa Mozart could see the wind band on the balcony, where they stood playing the wedding march from *The Marriage of Figaro*. He stepped jauntily in time to his melody. To the rhythmic applause of the guests, Mozart led Constanze up the stone stairs and onto the balcony. Standing at the balustrade, he smiled at those below. At his signal the wind band stopped playing. He pulled Constanze closer to him and kissed her passionately. Cheers filled the night air.

"Friends. This is a happy night, one of the most delightful and entertaining of my life. I'd love to stay and enjoy the rest of it with you, but my wife and I are going to retire to our room."

He kissed her again.

"And later, I'll even compose an overture! Signor Bondini, be sure to send the copyist for the manuscript at daybreak. It will be ready. I leave you now in the hands of our wonderful hosts and the master stage director, the Chevalier de Seingalt."

The guests cheered again. Pasquale Bondini, standing toward the back of the crowd, said a short prayer of thanks in Italian. The band played as Mozart and Constanze disappeared through the French doors into the villa. Sitting on opposite sides of the outdoor staircase, Casanova and Da Ponte enjoyed the scene. Suddenly Mozart, no longer wearing his frock coat, reappeared on the balcony, a concerned look on his face.

"Casanova!" he called out. "Casanova, where are you? I have one question."

"Anything, Maestro."

"Who was the masked man I saw from up here when I first came outside to look for Constanze?"

Casanova walked down the stone steps so that he was standing directly below Mozart, reached into his pocket and dramatically pulled out the black mask.

"That would have been me, Maestro."

"And what became of your masked friends?"

"They're still here."

"Then let me see them now."

"As you wish, Maestro."

Casanova raised his arms. The two women, still masked and cloaked, emerged from the shadowy archway beneath the staircase. Mozart leaned over the railing to get a better view. Da Ponte walked toward Casanova, who was flanked by the two mysterious women.

"Ladies, the time has come for you to unmask," Casanova said.

In unison, the two women removed their disguises. Da Ponte recoiled as the ladies looked up, their faces lit by the flickering torches.

"Now that's wonderful! Splendid! The sisters from the pub; what a coup. Casanova, I toast your talents," Mozart said.

"You see, Lorenzo. On the outside I may seem old, but never think of me as unable to win these games of sex and love, because the skills you need to be a great lover are found on the inside. Experience is a greater asset than the talent to write about it. You may have given Don Giovanni his words, but I've lived them."

Da Ponte slumped back onto the stone stairs as Casanova embraced the sisters.

"Lorenzo, Giacomo. You can have your conquests, your games. I gladly concede because I have my Constanze, and her love is so deep that she has joyfully given her future to share my fate, whatever it may be. *A demain mes amis, et bonsoir!*"

Mozart turned around and skipped into the house. The echo of his laugh resounded out to the flickering garden and its cast of deceitful lovers.

Chapter Nineteen

s he walked down the corridor to Constanze's bedroom, Mozart kept laughing. The image of Da Ponte staggering backward replayed in his mind. Nearing the door to the room, he reenacted Da Ponte's movements, adding a dramatic groan, which only redoubled his giddy laughter.

"What's so funny?" Constanze asked as he stumbled into the room.

"Oh . . . I was thinking about what Casanova did to poor Lorenzo."

"You should all grow up."

"Oh, Stanzi. Let them have their fun. It's a game they play, nothing more."

"How would you feel if your son played mean games like that when he grows up?"

Mozart didn't know how to answer. He'd never imagined his son growing up, preferring to think of him as a child forever. Constanze's simple blue ankle-length dress showed her growing belly. It caught Mozart's eye.

"Have you been feeling well?"

"Yes. Tired, but well. I'm getting big."

"You look lovely . . . beautiful."

"Thank you."

Mozart walked around the room, turning his feet so they fit within the herringbone pattern of the well-polished wood floors. He kept his eyes aimed at the ground, like an insecure child who's done something wrong.

"Do you love me, Stanzi?"

"Of course I do."

He kept moving, taking tiny steps, his eyes fixed on his feet.

"You have no idea how much I love you. If you only knew the things I did with your little portrait while we were apart."

Constanze snuck up behind him and put her arms around his waist. He turned and pulled her toward him. Caressing her round stomach gently with his palm, he kissed her. The tenderness made her shiver.

"Tell me what you did with my portrait."

"You'll laugh. You'll think I'm silly."

"I know you're silly. That's why I love you."

Mozart backed up, pulling Constanze with him. But before he could pull her onto the bed, she pushed him away.

"Not now. First tell me what you did with my portrait."

Sitting on the edge of the bed, Mozart kicked off his shoes and swung his feet.

"Every morning I took your portrait out and said: 'Good morrow, Stanzerl, my little Pussy-Wussy! Have a nice day, my delicate morsel.' Then every night, just before I went to bed, I looked at the portrait, kissed your sweet face and said, 'Good night, little pet. Be sure to sleep well.' I did that every day and every night."

Constanze turned away so he couldn't see the tears forming in her eyes. Clearing her throat, she tried to sound forceful.

"Wolfgang, you have to write the overture. It's after midnight. You'd better get started."

"But Stanzi, aren't we going to bed?"

"Not until you finish. I'll be your reward."

The reprimanding tone of her voice made him want her even more.

"You're unfair."

"Sit down at the table. Frantisek left manuscript paper and a quill. You compose while I get some fresh coffee and punch. We'll sit together. You compose and I'll tell stories all night to keep you awake. Then, when the overture's ready for the copyist, we'll go to bed. I promise."

Playfully she kissed his cheek and then, throwing him another kiss, danced out of the room. He looked around. The music paper and ink were on the table near the window. He removed his frock coat and sat down. As he stared at the paper, his thoughts were distracted by the sounds of the last partygoers still meandering through the gardens. Mozart got up from the table and pushed open the window. Leaning out, he could see the faint light of one or two torches flickering among the trees.

"I wonder where Casanova is and what he's doing now."

For a moment he let his thoughts wander into the gardens. He was trying to visualize the older man with the sisters, but the images his imagination produced disappointed and frustrated him. As he turned toward the writing table, he noticed a folded piece of paper on Constanze's dressing table.

"The letter I gave Casanova to give her."

Confident it would take Constanze a few minutes to get the coffee and punch, he took the letter and reread it. The ink was streaked.

"Tears," he thought happily.

"Wolfgang! What are you doing?"

Constanze's angry voice startled him, and he crammed the letter into his britches.

"You're supposed to be working."

Resigned and chastised, he returned to the writing table. Constanze was pouring a cup of coffee for him and a glass of punch for herself. She brought the coffee over to his table and set it down. With deftness and speed she pulled the letter out of his pants.

"Don't ruin this," she said, waving the letter in his face. "I save your letters. Now you have to compose your overture. I'll tell stories. What would you like to hear about?"

He smiled but didn't answer.

"Let's see," Constanze began. "The other day Josefa and I went for a walk in the gardens, and we saw the most beautiful birds."

Constanze prattled on, but as Mozart's hand sped across the pages, leaving a series of black dots in its wake, he heard less and less of what she was saying. Although he was reacting to her words with occasional grunts, his mind was lost in the phrases forming his overture.

"More coffee!"

Without pausing in her story, Constanze refilled his cup with the strong, black Turkish coffee.

". . . and Josefa and František really are dear friends. You know, Wolfgang, they think we should move here. They say you're not appreciated in Vienna. Well, how could you be when the Emperor prefers Salieri's music? Salieri's not even Austrian, and he's not nearly as talented as you. I told Josefa we'd certainly consider it as soon as the opera—"

Suddenly Mozart got up from the table.

"I need . . . I need a diversion. Let's go to bed."

"No! Not until it's finished."

Mozart put his arms around his wife.

"I've missed you so, and my mind's filled with thoughts of Casanova. If we go to bed now, I'll compose better later."

"If we go to bed now, the opera will never have an overture. I promise, as soon as you give it to the copyist, I'll do whatever you want. Now stop being so childish. Sit down and finish. The sooner you finish, the sooner we go to bed."

Mozart sulked. Resigned but filled with renewed anticipation, he sat back down and started filling in the blank lines.

"The other day," Constanze continued, "when I was alone, I was thinking about some of the stories your father told about you as a child. For some reason I remembered him telling the story about how you were afraid of trumpets. Their sound made you burst into tears, and even if you simply saw a trumpet, you'd become afraid. It seems so strange. I wonder what caused it."

"There, only because you've brought it up, I've put the trumpets right at the beginning of the overture."

"You're such a liar!" But he didn't hear her because he was again lost in the music.

Constanze wandered around the room, telling her stories, pausing only to admire the new dress Josefa had had made for her, the new dress she would wear at the opera's premiere. Walking quietly behind the writing table, she went over to the window and looked into the garden below. All was quiet; the guests had gone home, leaving the Villa Bertramka to the servants, who spent the night and the early morning hours cleaning the rooms and preparing food for the next day. It was four in the morning, and she could see the light from the large fireplace in the kitchen reflected in the downstairs windows.

"I wonder when they sleep," Constanze mused out loud.

"Who?"

"I didn't mean to disturb you. I'm sorry. Go back to the overture."

"That's all right. Who were you talking about?"

"The servants. I've been staying here nearly two weeks, and it seems they're always around doing everyone's bidding."

"It's their job."

"I know, but when do they rest and live their lives? I feel sorry for the servants, that's all."

"I was a servant to the Archbishop of Salzburg."

"That was different. You had your music, which is better than scrubbing floors or dirty garments."

"Still, I was a servant. There will come a time when a man will serve but not be a servant. There will come a time . . ."

His voice drifted off as he stared at the pages of manuscript spread out on the table.

"There will come a time, what?" Constanze wanted him to finish his thought.

"When servants will decide they've had enough of servitude, as I decided I'd had enough of being in the archbishop's service. Then they'll refuse to serve. They'll demand equality."

"Oh, Wolfgang, you're such a dreamer."

Fixing her hair in the mirror, she laughed innocently. Mozart's thoughts were far away, recalling de Sade locked in a cell in the Bastille.

"See if the copyist is here."

"Why?"

"Because the overture's finished."

"You're not serious? Even you couldn't finish an overture in so little time."

"I did."

Constanze tried to get a look at the manuscript, but Mozart had placed a blank sheet of music paper over it. She adjusted her hair one more time, kissed him on the head and left to find the copyist.

"How I wish de Sade could be here for the premiere," he thought. "It would be right—freed from a cell to attend an opera! That would be justice. *Viva la libertà!*"

How ridiculous that sounded. But as he finished writing the title page, he silently vowed to return to Paris someday to meet the man whose words from prison had moved him so deeply.

"He's coming, Wolfgang."

Constanze's cheerful voice filled the silent room.

"Who?"

Mozart was startled.

"The copyist, silly. I found him sitting downstairs alone in the entryway. Bondini sent him last night and ordered him to wait until you were finished."

Mozart gathered up the pages and put them in the right order.

"Maestro."

"Yes, yes. Come in."

The sleepy copyist, wearing a black coat and carrying a brown leather folder, pushed the door open and walked over to the writing table, bowing apologetically as he approached.

"I'm sorry, Maestro, but Signor Bondini ordered me to wait until you'd finished and to—"

"I understand. It's done now. Take the manuscript and copy out the parts. Be sure to tell the trumpets to study their parts with extra care before the performance. I've made them very important."

He winked at Constanze.

"Of course, Maestro."

The copyist pushed the pages together to make the score easier to carry. Looking at the first page, he was amazed at how neat the manuscript was: no cross-outs, no blots, no changes.

"May I read through it before I leave, Maestro . . . in case I have any questions?"

"Yes, of course."

As the copyist glanced over the pages, Mozart stood a few feet away watching for reactions. Occasionally the copyist stopped and looked more closely at a particular measure, as if about to ask a question. But each time, after he studied the questionable notes or markings, he nodded, understanding and admiring what Mozart had done. His reactions pleased Mozart.

"Maestro . . . I . . . I'm afraid I don't understand."

"What?"

"Here." The copyist pointed to the final measures of the overture.

"What? It couldn't be clearer. What don't you understand?"

"Excuse me, Maestro, perhaps there's another page still to go, but there seems to be no ending."

Mozart's raucous laugh echoed through the sleeping house.

"I know. Isn't that wonderful?"

"But Maestro, Signor Bondini ordered me to—"

"—to be sure it was finished. It is."

"Maestro, forgive me, but I can't find the ending."

"It's all there. Let me explain."

Mozart stood next to the confused copyist and reviewed the last line of the score. Pointing to the notes he'd just written, he hummed the melody and conducted with one hand. When he reached the last measure of the overture, Mozart stopped momentarily, then continued with phrases not written on the page. A look of amazement came to the copyist's face.

"Now I understand. The overture goes right into the beginning of the first act without any pause. Oh . . . Maestro . . . that's extraordinary . . . really."

"You see, the audience won't have a chance to applaud, and so the drama can begin without losing the excitement the overture has created. Now, you'd better go. It's nearly daybreak and I'm certain Signor Bondini's waiting for you."

"Of course, Maestro."

Without further delay the copyist headed for the door.

"Maestro."

"Yes, what is it?"

"It's been a great honor to have you in our theater. I'm only sorry to see it end."

"As am I, but if you don't get the overture copied, our time together may continue."

"Of course. Good night . . . I mean, good day, Maestro . . . Madame."

"I'll show you the way out," Constanze offered.

Following the copyist, she paused and peeked around the door at Wolfgang.

"I'll be back in a few minutes." She blew him a kiss.

Mozart smiled. He was comfortable and pleased. Looking out the window at the garden, his thoughts returned to Casanova. Slowly he undressed, tossing his clothes on the chair. The bed looked so inviting. Naked, he climbed into it, slid under the covers and waited. On the bedside table sat a tiny oval portrait of their son. Mozart picked it up and studied the boy's angelic face.

Within minutes, Constanze was back. She tiptoed into the bedroom, hoping to surprise her husband. But when she neared the bed, she recognized the sound of his rhythmic breathing. He was asleep; baby Karl's portrait rested on his chest. She stared for a few moments, wondering what dreams filled her husband's mind. His face was so young and peaceful; curled up on the bed, he didn't look much older than their son. Taking a blanket from the armoire, she covered him, careful not to wake him. Silently she extinguished the small stub of the candle burning on the bedside table.

She removed her dress and wrapped herself in a warm dressing gown. Walking around the room, she blew out the other candles. Filtered by the curtains, the early morning light cast a grayish calm through the room.

Constanze stared at her husband for a few more minutes, then sat down on the cushioned seat in the bay window. Looking out past the gardens and the walls surrounding the Dušeks' estate, she saw the outskirts of Prague coming to life. She rested her hand on her belly and thought of the baby girl or boy who would soon join their little family; another mouth to feed.

The sun climbed into the azure blue sky, proclaiming a new week, a new day. Constanze went over to the writing table, sat down, picked up her husband's quill pen and dipped it into the bottle of ink. Taking a sheet of paper, she wrote:

Prague
Dawn, Monday October 29, 1787

My Dearest Karl:
  Today the world will hear the premiere of your father's new opera,
Don Giovanni.

Chapter Twenty

𝒫acing outside the opera house, oblivious to the cold night air, Pasquale Bondini was muttering in Italian under his breath. As Prague's leading citizens walked past him into the theater, he interrupted his sputtering long enough to greet them, bowing when appropriate and kissing the women's hands. But with each greeting he glanced around, hoping to see the carriage he'd sent to the Villa Bertramka.

"Where is Mozart?"

"We sent the coach several hours ago, Signor Bondini. Do you want me to run toward the Villa and see if they're on the way?" asked his assistant.

"What good would that do? Stay here. No. Go. Find the carriage and tell the driver to hurry."

Without waiting for Bondini to change his mind again, the young man ran off in the direction of the river, toward the bridge. It was nearly seven o'clock, time for the opera to begin. Bondini stood alone on the steps of the opera house looking up and down the street. Finally, when he was ready to give up all hope, he heard and saw the black berlin with the gold emblem on the door, pulled by two white horses, speed around the corner. It stopped right in front of him. Grabbing the handle, he pulled the door open.

"Now that was fun! What a fine coachman you sent, Pasquale. He went so fast."

"Mozart," Bondini huffed. "You're late. All of Prague is in there waiting for you. The singers are nervous. The orchestra has just seen the parts for the overture for the first time. Everyone's waiting for you."

"And here I am," Mozart said calmly.

Bondini took Mozart by the arm and pulled him around the corner to the stage door, where a waiting line of assistants bowed respectfully. Mozart pulled one of them aside.

"Tell the orchestra to be ready. After I enter and bow to the audience, I'm going to turn around and give the downbeat without waiting. Tell them to look right at me. If they keep their eyes trained on me, everything will be fine."

Then, turning back to Bondini, he asked: "Where's Lorenzo? I need to talk to him."

"He's in Vienna."

"What?"

"A messenger arrived from Vienna early this morning with a letter from the Emperor demanding Da Ponte return immediately to complete a libretto for Salieri. Lorenzo took the next coach. He left Prague before noon."

"He left . . . with no message? No words for me?"

"He told me to wish you and the singers well."

Mozart slumped into a cane-back chair. "I'm sorry Lorenzo won't be here. It won't be the same. He's a dear friend. He's my librettist—how could he not be here? It's simply not right. He deserves to enjoy this night with me. How could you let him go?"

Bondini didn't know what to say. After a few minutes of uncomfortable silence, he cleared his throat. "Maestro . . . uh . . . Maestro, I . . . ," Bondini stammered.

"I can't believe Lorenzo went back to Vienna. He wouldn't miss a premiere unless the Emperor was very angry. This isn't good."

"Maestro . . . ," Bondini began again.

"I know. We have to start. I suppose it won't do any good to delay this any longer. It won't make Lorenzo appear."

Bondini relaxed a little and tried to look reassuring. "I'd rather not delay any longer, Maestro. The audiences here grow impatient quickly."

"Tell the singers and the orchestra we'll begin in five minutes."

Bondini suddenly and forcefully embraced Mozart. "Thank you, Maestro. Thank you."

Bondini hurried off to give the five-minute notice. Looking in a cracked mirror hung in the hallway near the entrance to the orchestra, Mozart adjusted the black ribbon that pulled the hair of his white wig into place. Then he loosened his regal-looking sky blue coat with the ornate buttons so he would be more comfortable while conducting. For a few minutes he stood by himself. The assistants had all gone off to their assigned positions, some at the sides of the stage and others under the stage, from where they could manipulate the candles to change the lighting, scene by scene.

The buzz of excited conversation in the audience slowly faded. The sounds of the musicians squeezing in last-minute practicing came to a stop. The theater was silent. Mozart waited, hidden from view at the entrance to the orchestra.

"Here we go!"

He carefully made his way through the orchestra's chairs, patting some of the musicians on the back as he passed them. When he reached his harpsichord, he bowed quickly toward the orchestra and spun around to face the audience.

The smell of melting wax from the hundreds of candles lighting the theater filled his nose as the resonant sound of three loud cheers filled his ears.

"*Eviva Mozart! Eviva! Eviva!*"

He turned and looked toward the first loge box on his right. Casanova smiled broadly and nodded to him. Bondini was next to him, busily dabbing at the beads of perspiration on his forehead. Mozart scanned the audience, slowly turning his head from right to left. When his eyes reached the first loge box on his left he saw the Dušeks with Constanze, whose dark eyes sparkled in the flickering candlelight. From where he stood he could see only the top of her new dress, but the way the rich burgundy silk and diaphanous lace rested against her creamy skin gave her a sensuous and regal look, one that was totally new for her, or that he'd never before noticed. Around her brow was a white fillet decorated by beautiful pearls, a gift from Josefa. His gaze froze on her. Mozart raised his left hand to his lips and blew her a kiss.

"For you, Stanzi," he mouthed.

Josefa saw him and turned to Constanze.

"How lucky you are," she said.

Constanze nodded slowly.

"*Avanti,*" Mozart whispered to himself.

In one swift movement, he spun around, glanced at the orchestra and gave the downbeat. The orchestra's response was instantaneous. The powerful, never-before-played initial chords surprised everyone, including Mozart, who smiled when he heard the gasp from the people seated directly behind him. And so it began.

When the overture continued directly into the first scene without pause, a theaterful of eyes shifted from Mozart's back to the stage and Leporello's complaints about being Don Giovanni's servant. This humorous beginning turns dramatic, then tragic. Defending his daughter's honor against the Don's attempted seduction, the Commendatore is stabbed to death, and his body lies motionless in the street outside his home.

The ferocious pace of the action shocked the audience. Even with his back to them, Mozart could feel the tension and surprise.

The scene in which Donna Anna discovers her slain father moved Josefa Dušek to tears; then she remembered Mozart's recently dead father, and made the sign of the cross.

Onstage the scene changes were handled smoothly. Bondini was pleased his opera company could make the complex production move so effortlessly, allowing the music and action to flow uninterrupted.

Casanova looked all around the theater, watching the audience, the musicians in the orchestra and Constanze for reactions. When Leporello sang the Catalogue Aria, Casanova laughed loudest, his laughter rising above the rest of the audience's. But when the opera focused on Don

Giovanni's attempt to seduce Zerlina, Casanova was transfixed. He anticipated and experienced every gesture, every breath, every phrase. In his
mind, Don Giovanni's conquest was his own.

František Dušek sat in the box between his wife and Constanze. This
kind of opera was new to him. During one brief scene change, he leaned
over to Constanze and whispered:

"It's very different. It's as if it's all one piece—it just keeps going. Very
new, almost revolutionary. So many different characters . . . each one with
wonderful music. I liked the tenor . . . what's the character's name . . .
Don. . . . Don . . ."

"Don Ottavio," Josefa assisted.

"Yes. Donna Anna's intended. What a nice man . . . so filled with love,
compassion and—"

"Quiet," Josefa ordered.

Constanze was silent. She too felt there was something different in this
opera, but she wasn't certain yet what it was.

Leporello and Don Giovanni were preparing for the party at Don
Giovanni's castle as the next scene began. Mozart launched the orchestra
into the introduction to Don Giovanni's Champagne Aria, his bravura toast
to feasting, drinking, dancing and seducing.

The audience loved it, and cheered its rousing end. But Constanze still
sat motionless, waiting, waiting for something else.

When the set for the shadowy garden outside Don Giovanni's palace
appeared, and Constanze saw Zerlina and her betrothed Masetto, two peasants deeply in love, she smiled. This was what she'd been waiting for. The
trials and tribulations of the characters with noble titles hadn't stirred her,
but when she heard the music her husband had composed for these people—
especially Zerlina's funny, tender aria—she was moved. It spoke to her, as
Mozart had hoped it would.

The party scene ending the first act was spectacular. Bondini's company
went beyond anything ever before done in the theater. The stage, crowded
by the chorus, was brilliantly lit. The excitement spilled across the stage

into the audience. When Don Giovanni greeted the masked trio—Donna Anna, Donna Elvira and Don Ottavio—with the phrase "*Viva la libertà!*" Mozart and Casanova both smiled, their thoughts at that moment turning to liberty and human freedom.

The music grew in intensity, an uncomfortable undercurrent overshadowing the festive party. The party guests dancing an elegant minuet brought smiles to most of the audience. It was a scene they had all experienced.

But as the music and the dancing began to spin out of control—three different rhythms were played at once by three different groups of musicians —and as Don Giovanni took Zerlina away from the party into a private part of the palace, the mounting tension made the nobles squirm in their seats. Bondini observed the nervousness spreading through the audience.

"They're not reacting well," he whispered to Casanova. "This isn't what they expected."

"It's dramatic," Casanova placated.

"They don't like it," said Bondini.

"It's because they see themselves in it. There isn't a man in this theater who hasn't at the very least contemplated taking a young woman and seducing her at his own party."

Bondini slumped in his seat. But Zerlina's offstage scream for help pulled his attention back to the opera.

Soon the pace had grown frantic. Don Giovanni accuses Leporello of attacking Zerlina. But his lie fools no one. Suddenly, in his own palace, Don Giovanni's accusers—Donna Anna, Donna Elvira and Don Ottavio— surround him. Drawing his sword and using Leporello as a human shield, Don Giovanni climbs over the dining table, escaping to the balcony and out into the garden.

The first act's ending left the audience in shock. At first the applause was scattered. But then cheers of approval rang out. Mozart smiled and made his way through the orchestra to the backstage area. Liveried guards were busily relighting the candles for intermission.

"Well, that certainly was different," František announced as he stood up, carefully stretching his weak leg.

"You sound like you didn't like it," Josefa noted with annoyance.

"No, no . . . that's not at all the case. It's just so different. I suppose we'll get used to this style. It will take time. Time will tell . . . only time will tell."

"What didn't you like?"

"Well," František said. "The arias are beautiful . . . flowing, the way Wolfgang always writes. But the ensembles are so complex I had difficulty understanding them. Also, the way the opera moves from one scene to the next without pause is hard to grasp. I mean . . . the key changes happen so fast . . . I just can't imagine how it all fits together . . . happy to sad in a matter of measures . . . I've never heard anything like it before. I can't imagine what others are thinking. What about you, Constanze?"

There was no answer. Constanze's gaze was fixed on the loge box directly opposite theirs. It was empty. "Bondini's probably gone backstage to talk to the singers," she thought. "But where is Casanova?"

As she stared absentmindedly, she noticed that the velvet curtain at the rear of his box was moving back and forth. She leaned forward, as if being a few inches closer would give her a better view.

"Constanze, what did you think?"

František's insistent voice broke her concentration.

"I'm sorry, were you talking to me?"

"I asked how you liked the first act."

"Oh . . . I'm sorry . . . I was distracted. It was . . . it was nice. I thought it went quickly. The singers were good, don't you agree, Josefa?"

Josefa, standing behind Constanze, had also noticed the moving curtain in the box opposite theirs.

"Yes, the singers were good, if you like the Italian style," she critiqued. "František, why don't you go see if you can find Herr Strobach. I know he's here. Ask him if he's coming to our house after the performance."

"Very well."

Josefa sat down next to Constanze. The two women looked across the theater, straining to uncover what was going on behind the bouncing, drawn velvet curtain. The minutes dragged by. Below them in the parterre, the elegantly dressed men and the extravagantly made-up women, all in newly tailored clothes, talked excitedly about the opera. The drama touched each and every one of them: those who wanted to be tender and kind like Zerlina, and those who fantasized about being Don Giovanni; those who loved, and those who wanted to seduce or be seduced. And the music, a rapidly changing series of emotions, with phrases spread throughout the orchestra, captured the personality of each character, all seemed to agree.

The musicians returned to their seats and retuned. The instruments then fell silent as the audience awaited the start of the second act. The curtains in the loge box on the far right side of the auditorium were suddenly pulled open. Constanze and Josefa leaned forward in their chairs. Casanova, adjusting his gold brocade coat, emerged from the shadows across the theater. Realizing he was being watched, he moved forward into the light, placed his hands on the railing and with a big grin bowed toward the stunned ladies.

"Bravo, Mozart!" a voice from the back of the theater yelled as the youthful-looking composer made his way through the orchestra.

The musicians tapped their bows on the music stands, clapped or stamped their feet as he entered. When he reached his position at the harpsichord, Mozart turned toward the musicians and accepted their warm greeting with a low bow. Their acknowledgment was the one which, in his heart, he most respected and craved. As he straightened up from his bow, Mozart looked around at the orchestra members, smiled and clasped his hands together to let them know how much he appreciated the way they were playing his music.

The audience continued applauding and cheering. But Mozart stood still, facing the orchestra, refusing to turn around, his eyes firmly closed. After a few moments, as the applause began to die down, he opened his eyes. The concertmaster noticed the tears. But before he could point it out to the violinist next to him, Mozart had begun the second act.

"I'm tired of almost getting killed!" the audience heard Leporello complain as he and Don Giovanni walk through the streets of Seville. "At least you could stop chasing women."

The audience laughed, which seemed to buoy Mozart, who was now bouncing as he kept the music and action moving. As the scene progressed, Casanova pulled his chair forward, leaning over the railing to get a better view of the stage.

"Why are you so nervous?" Bondini asked.

"This is the scene when Don Giovanni and Leporello exchange cloaks. It was hard to rehearse."

"Yes, I remember," Bondini said.

Onstage the actors moved into the shadows as Donna Elvira appeared in the window of the house on the right side of the stage. Casanova grinned. The cloak exchange went unnoticed; the audience couldn't tell master from servant.

"Don Giovanni's voice has changed," František noted to his wife.

But she was transfixed by the action on the stage, in which Don Giovanni—still disguised as his servant—pummels Masetto. Lying there hurt, the peasant is discovered by his fiancée, Zerlina, who tends to his injuries. The love and caring imbued in the aria spoke directly to Constanze. This music was for her, and no one else.

The second act was even better than the first; the singers were more at ease with their characters, allowing the drama and the humor to project all the way to the last row of the auditorium. Every member of the orchestra sat on the edge of his seat, watching Mozart's gestures as he shaped the music, following his lead and trying to fill every phrase with the nuances communicated by his gentle hands and soft eyes.

A whisper ran through the audience as the graveyard scene began. There, at the center of the stage, obscured only by the mysterious, theatrical darkness of midnight, was the massive statue of the murdered Commendatore. And on its stone base lounged Don Giovanni, while Leporello paced nearby. They bantered about their recent adventures, but when Giovanni laughed uproariously, the distant sound of the dead Commendatore's voice booming from the statue brought a sharp intake of breath from the surprised audience.

Every member of the orchestra saw a grin light Mozart's face. He was directing the performance while standing on his toes, craning to get a clear look at the stage as Don Giovanni ordered Leporello to invite the statue to dinner. When the statue, in a deep, solemn voice, accepted the invitation, another gasp resounded in the auditorium.

"Now that's drama," Casanova proclaimed, leaning back in his chair.

Bondini wiped the perspiration from his brow, glad the scene was over but concerned about the statue's next appearance.

Josefa Dušek held Constanze's hand. The composer's wife showed no sign of concern. Onstage Don Ottavio was assuring Donna Anna that the villain who killed her father would be brought to justice. The audience then heard him ask her to marry him, and heard Donna Anna counsel him to be patient with her.

"Don Ottavio seems so weak and unexciting next to Don Giovanni," Josefa whispered to Constanze, who nodded her agreement.

František, perpetually uncertain, overheard his wife's observation and was ready to disagree, but the comment he was about to make was cut off by the explosive beginning of the next scene. The stage was brilliantly lit; torches burned on every wall, and the long banquet table at the center of Don Giovanni's grand dining room had eight silver candelabra, all fully lit, spread out from one end to the other. The excitement and fast pace of the music brought smiles to the faces of Prague's elite, who were expecting a happy ending.

The food on the table, a veritable feast of breads, capon and grapes, made Casanova's mouth water. As Don Giovanni ate and drank with gusto, and a touch of decadence, Casanova rocked in his chair, silently savoring every bite and every sip. The onstage band played delightful music to accompany the supper.

"That's a nice touch," František whispered to Constanze. "I like the sound of a wind band. We had one at our party just the other evening."

Constanze nodded.

"That tune's so familiar. What is it?"

"*Figaro*," Constanze said.

Those who recognized *Figaro* whispered Mozart's little joke into the ears of those who didn't know the melody, until eventually the whole audience was grinning, along with the orchestra members and the composer. But the smiles vanished when Donna Elvira burst in, begging Don Giovanni to give up his wanton life, and he chased her away with the brash taunt, "Long live fine wine, long live women!" As she raced through the large doors at the back of the stage, her bloodcurdling scream shook the theater.

In the opera's next moments, an undaunted Don Giovanni, swigging wine from his large pewter goblet, orders Leporello to investigate, and the terrified servant soon returns breathlessly to report that the statue is outside, banging repeatedly on the door, demanding to be admitted.

"TA! TA! TA! TA!"

And again:

"TA! TA! TA! TA!"

Bondini didn't know whether to watch the stage or the audience. He kept looking back and forth, excited by the action, concerned by the reactions.

And then the moment Mozart had anticipated all evening arrived. With a ferocious downbeat, he cued the brass instruments and the timpani. The force of their entrance, a repeat of the dark chords he'd composed for the opening measures of the overture, but now more meaningful and powerful, pinned the audience back in their seats. In a matter of seconds, all remaining traces of comedy disappeared. The audience raptly watched as Leporello cowered, leaving only Don Giovanni, defiant to the end, to face the avenging statue of the Commendatore.

The orchestra kept pace with Mozart, whose hand movements begged them for more sound, more intensity, more anger. He wanted darkness, fear and rage to explode. The audience held their collective breath, afraid of what might happen if they disturbed the scene in any way. As Don Giovanni struggled with the statue—screaming, passionately refusing to repent—Casanova writhed in his seat. The Don's final anguish, his visceral refusals, coursed through Casanova's body.

Despite having to pull all the musical forces together, Mozart couldn't help thinking about de Sade's observation that a man like Don Giovanni would rather go to hell than give up his freedom. Thinking of de Sade locked in his tiny, dark, dirty cell, Mozart seemed to become possessed, and conducted with even more energy, pulling dramatic, thrilling sounds from the orchestra and the singers.

When the puff of smoke into which the condemned Don Giovanni disappeared had cleared from the stage, the statue was gone. Cheers filled the auditorium. Bondini smiled, relieved. It was only after complimenting himself silently that he noticed Casanova slumped over in his seat, his face covered in perspiration. "Are you ill?"

Casanova didn't respond.

"Giacomo . . . are you all right? Should I get help?"

"I'll be fine . . . I thought . . . I saw . . . I thought it was . . ." he stammered as his voice drifted off.

Bondini pulled away and looked at the stage, where the final scene was being played. In it, a befuddled Leporello, crawling out from under the tablecloth, explains what he has seen, muttering how the whole episode couldn't possibly have actually occurred. Donna Anna makes Don Ottavio agree to wait a year for her heart to heal, even though the Commendatore's death has been avenged.

"I wonder if she misses her father or Don Giovanni," Josefa whispered to Constanze. But Mozart's wife was smiling, because Zerlina and Masetto were at last together and happy.

In a joyful final ensemble, the singers stepped to the edge of the stage and moralized: all sinners get their just rewards. The cheerful music brought smiles to the faces of the audience. When the final notes had sounded and the last reverberations had faded into the farthest corners of the opera house, all that remained was an eerie silence.

∞

Then.

"Bravo, Mozart!"

That yell set free all the excitement that had built over the last three hours. As each singer stepped forward the cheers remained constant, never relenting or softening.

Leaning on the harpsichord, Mozart wiped the perspiration from his face. After all of the singers had taken their solo bows, he slowly turned to face the audience. The wave of shouts, more wild and intense than any which had come before, pushed his small frame back against the harpsichord.

"They liked it. But did they understand?" he wondered.

Turning to his left, he saw Constanze and the Dušeks, standing together in their box, clapping. As he did at the performance's outset, he blew a kiss to his wife. Then, turning his head from left to right, he looked toward the first loge box. There, all alone, sat Casanova, his head bent forward, cradled in his hands. From the steady movements, Mozart could tell the old man was sobbing. Mozart, oblivious to the shouting crowd, watched his friend.

The cheering went on for more than half an hour. Every time he tried to leave, cries of "Eviva Mozart" echoed. Some members of the orchestra lifted the spent conductor onto their shoulders and raised him onto the stage, where he stood in the center of the applauding, appreciative cast.

It was past midnight when the cheering finally stopped. The audience made their way out the doors and into the cold Prague night. Onstage

Mozart thanked the singers and the stage staff, who stood around, not wanting the night, this event, to end. When Mozart finally got offstage, Bondini was standing there, beaming and waiting. He kissed the composer once on each cheek, held him by the shoulders, looked into his eyes and declared:

"Tonight will change opera forever. A triumph, Mozart. *Don Giovanni* is a triumph."

Chapter Twenty-One

◯◯

After spending more than an hour accepting the congratulations of the singers, their friends and Prague's musical elite, Mozart and Constanze were finally alone in his dressing room. *Don Giovanni*'s success was assured, and Bondini was already scheduling additional performances.

"And you, Stanzi. What did you like most?"

"Zerlina and Masetto. I liked them most."

"I knew you would."

Mozart stared at the *Don Giovanni* score lying on the large table near the door. By the distracted, faraway look in his eyes, Constanze could tell he was reliving some moment in the performance. He didn't hear the soft knocking at his dressing room door. Constanze, her long gown rustling on the floor, glided across the small room and pulled the door open.

"Signor Casanova," she said with surprise as she curtsied.

Mozart looked up from the score. Quickly he stepped between Constanze and Casanova.

"Giacomo. I'm so glad—"

But before he could say another word, Casanova raised his index finger and placed it in front of his mouth. Mozart stopped talking. Staring at the bewildered composer, Casanova grabbed the younger man's shoulders and pulled him into an intense, silent embrace.

Constanze backed away, positioning herself to get a better view. She was filled with pride. Casanova gradually eased his powerful grasp. Mozart stepped backward.

"Then . . . then you liked it?"

"It was magnificent. I've spent the last hour sitting in my seat trying to find the right words, a way to fully express what's in my heart."

"And?" Mozart asked hopefully.

Casanova shook his head sadly and looked at the floor.

"I've concluded that there are no words."

Mozart beamed. Constanze clasped her hands together and smiled.

"I don't think the opera would be as good if you hadn't been here, Giacomo. I wish Lorenzo had been here tonight. He should share the excitement, the praise, our triumph . . ."

"Your triumph," Constanze corrected.

"He'll hear about it soon enough," Casanova added. "Word will spread to Vienna and then throughout Europe: to Italy, to France, to England. *Don Giovanni* will revolutionize opera."

"But will it make us rich?" Constanze questioned.

Casanova looked directly at her, pointing like a schoolteacher chastising a misbehaving child.

"You have a property greater in value than anything owned by any emperor."

"And what is that?" Mozart asked.

"Creative genius," Casanova replied, turning to face him.

Mozart looked away, dejected.

"No. Don't be angry. Don't you understand? You have a fabulous power—the power to bring forth new creations, works of art to last through the ages, to make people laugh and cry for centuries to come. You create works of permanence."

Constanze's wry, almost disbelieving laugh returned Casanova's glare to her.

"And you, Constanze, most beautiful and wondrous of women, you, who showed me the great value of what I have missed in my life, and made me want to live it again in an entirely different manner." Casanova took her hands in his. "You must always be with your husband—a muse. Grow old with him, inspire him, comfort him. It's your duty so that the world will have the joy of his gifts. His music will become civilized man's harbor, a port to find safety in, forever and ever."

Mozart looked awkwardly at the wood floor.

"And you, Giacomo. What about you?"

"Me? I've already overstayed my welcome. My time here in Prague must end. I return tomorrow to Dux and the library I'm supposed to be caring for."

"Why not come to Vienna with us?"

"My memoirs await. When I came here I vowed that, regardless of what happened, I would return to Dux."

Casanova sat down in the chair and looked up at the young couple standing hand in hand before him.

"I must stay true to my vow," he explained. "I've always believed in the words of some ancient author—I can't remember which one—who taught that if you've done nothing worthy of being recorded, then, at the very least, you should write something worth reading. For better or worse, my life is my story, and the story I have to tell is just my life."

A strange sadness filled Mozart. Casanova looked old and tired; the vibrant sparkle so evident during the rehearsals had vanished from his sensitive eyes.

"Will you include the story of the last four weeks in your memoirs?" Constanze asked. "It would be a wonderful history to have remembered, especially by you."

"No."

"Why not?" Mozart asked, sounding almost insulted.

"I learned something tonight, during the performance. A man who's lived life as I have is interesting only as long as his experiences can excite others. Once we become old, the best stories must be in the past tense. These weeks have been rewarding . . . an experience I'll never forget because, through Don Giovanni, I was able to relive some of my most thrilling moments. But I was *re*living . . . not living. No. I want to be remembered as a younger man—dashing, debonair. So, I've decided my memoirs will end at age fifty."

"But you are still exciting."

"Dear lovely lady, you flatter me. I assure you, you wouldn't want to see Don Giovanni as an old man. It would diminish his stature, make him less legendary. I will relive my youthful adventures by writing them down. If sometime in the future, long after I've moved on to my ultimate adventure, some composer with half your husband's talent chooses to use my life as the basis for an opera, then my writings would not have been in vain. Since we can't stay here forever, the history of my life is simply my poor attempt to secure my tenuous place on this earth."

Mozart had turned away, so that his back was to Casanova.

"Don't talk of mortality. It frightens me."

Casanova stood up, walked over to Mozart and put his hand on the shorter man's shoulders.

"You've nothing to fear, my son. You're young. Your greatest years, your greatest triumphs lie before you. Your place in history is assured. Mankind will honor the name of Wolfgang Amadeus Mozart. I guarantee it."

"His father always said that," Constanze remarked.

"Come now," Casanova said, forcing a smile into his voice. "Enough of this. It's time to enjoy this . . . *your* triumph."

"*Our* triumph," Mozart corrected.

Casanova picked up Mozart's coat, brushed it off and held it for him.

"Your servant," Casanova intoned, trying to sound like Leporello.

"Your servant," Mozart echoed, sliding his arms into the sleeves.

"Will you come with us to the Dušeks'?" Constanze asked.

"No. I'd love to, but I must pack my belongings."

"That won't take all night," Mozart pressed. "Please come."

"I also have a few farewells here in Prague, and those sometimes take longer than I plan for. The coach leaves early tomorrow."

Mozart pulled his black cloak over his shoulders.

"So . . . then . . . this is farewell."

"Don't make it sound so final," said Casanova. "I have no intention of dying anytime soon."

Casanova slid one arm into Mozart's and gently slipped his other arm around Constanze's waist. Silently they left the dressing room.

When they reached the stage door, Casanova embraced Constanze and kissed her gently on the cheek. He rested his hands on the waist of her elegant gown.

"Perhaps in a different life, at a different time . . . ," he mused with a touch of lasciviousness. "Take care of our little man."

Constanze nodded. "I will, Signor Casanova. I . . . we are indebted to you."

"I was prompted by true love: Wolfgang's love for you. It's in his music; you can hear it. Listen."

Constanze kissed Casanova once on each cheek. Mozart's small physique was framed by the doorway. It had begun to rain, and the drops bounced off the cobblestone streets.

"I'll miss you, Giacomo," Mozart said.

"And I you. But we have our memories, and no one can ever take that away. Whenever a happy melody fills my ears, I'll think of this time; I'll think of you."

Impulsively Mozart lunged at Casanova and hugged him with all his might. Casanova patted him repeatedly on the back.

"At least I get to say good-bye to you," Mozart whispered.

"You'd think that after the long life I've had, I could say farewell more easily." Casanova said.

Mozart broke the embrace, grinned and looked directly into Casanova's eyes.

"I had a great grandmother," Mozart said, "who told her daughter, who told her husband, who told me this advice: to talk well and eloquently is a very great art, but an equally great one is to know the right moment to stop."

Without another word, Mozart turned away from Casanova, put his arm around his pregnant wife, covered her head with his cloak and pulled her out into the rainy night. Casanova could hear their voices as they skipped happily across the cobblestones and into the waiting carriage. The coachman closed the door, lifted the wood step and jumped into his seat. The crack of his whip startled Casanova, who watched the carriage hurry toward the bridge spanning the Vltava River. He remained alone in the doorway until the sight and sound of the Mozarts' coach disappeared into Prague's rainy night.

Slowly Casanova walked back into the theater, then tiptoed onto the stage. In the shadows a man dressed all in black diligently swept the dirt and dust into a neat pile.

"I'm a friend of Signor Bondini's. He asked me to look at the stage," Casanova lied, shouting at the man.

The sweeper didn't react. Casanova watched him push the dirt from the side of the stage.

"Why don't you stop sweeping. Come, sit here with me," Casanova invited, pointing to the chairs from Don Giovanni's dining hall. "You can sit with me."

The stagehand leaned his broom against a pillar, adjusted his collar and walked slowly and humbly toward the center of the stage, his face obscured by the shadows cast by a single torch glowing nearby. Casanova righted Don Giovanni's chair, which had been thrown back during his deadly confrontation with the Commendatore, and moved it near the table. The remains of the final meal were scattered across the white tablecloth. The silver candelabrum was extinguished. Casanova carried it over to the still-burning torch, where he carefully relit the six candle stubs. The stage seemed to spark back to life.

With a dramatic flourish, Casanova sat down in Don Giovanni's chair. A half-filled glass of wine rested near his hand. He raised it. The sweeper stood still, his back to Casanova, looking out into the empty theater.

"To beautiful women and fine wine," the sweeper toasted.

The echoing voice surprised Casanova, who quickly swallowed the wine. He stood up and approached the stagehand, who stared, motionless, into the dark empty theater.

"I know you," Casanova began. "I know your voice. Turn so I can see your face. Let me see who you are."

"I'm not your servant," the man answered, refusing to turn. "I serve only one master."

Casanova stared, silently measuring the man's height and size in his mind.

"I believe I'm in the presence of the most honorable Abbé Lorenzo Da Ponte!"

"I am that man," the figure replied, turning around.

Casanova embraced him.

"I thought you'd gone back to Vienna."

Da Ponte smiled mysteriously, moved over to the table and sat down. Casanova joined him, then filled two silver goblets.

He was amused by Da Ponte's sudden reappearance. Feeling at home on the stage, in Don Giovanni's palace, at his dining table, Casanova took a piece of the leftover bread, leaned back in the chair and put his feet on the edge of the table.

"No word from de Sade?" Da Ponte asked.

"None."

"I've read reports that the situation in France worsens every day. De Sade may have died in prison or been killed. Anything's possible."

"Tell me, Lorenzo, what kind of death do you want?"

"I haven't thought about it."

Casanova stood up and walked over to the Commendatore's statue.

"I'd like a grand exit from this world. One with fire and drama, with witnesses who'll tell the world I died as I lived. I want the kind of death legends are given."

Da Ponte held his goblet up.

"To you, Casanova. May you get what you desire and not what you deserve."

"What about Mozart?" Casanova asked. "What kind of death do you think he wants?"

"I have no idea. He's young; he'll outlive us both. He's a strange little man with a God-given talent greater than any I've ever known. God will give him whatever he wants. Listen to Mozart's music—it's perfect."

Casanova walked back to the dining table, where the candles were nearly burned out. Seeing Casanova's cloak draped over a nearby piece of scenery in the backstage area, Da Ponte went over and picked it up. Beneath it rested Casanova's sturdy walking stick, its worn leather handle held in place by tiny brass nails.

"Here's your cloak and walking stick, Giacomo. We'd better go. The last candle's about to expire."

Casanova took one more look around the stage, sighed and walked slowly over to Da Ponte, who helped him put on his cloak.

"Promise me one thing," Casanova whispered.

"What?"

"Should you ever write another libretto for Mozart, include a part for an older man, a worldly man, a man who teaches other men about women, their ways, and about love."

"I promise. Good-bye, Giacomo. God be with you."

Casanova took the torch from its holder on the wall and looked at Da Ponte.

"Adieu, *mon frère*."

Casanova walked into the backstage area. Within seconds the trail of light and smoke was gone and Casanova had disappeared.

After a moment or two, Da Ponte removed the last burning candle from the candelabrum on the table and glanced around the remains of Don Giovanni's dining hall. A contented smile came to his face. His gaze rested on the harpsichord.

"Thank you, Mozart."

Lorenzo Da Ponte walked into the wings of the stage, and vanished into the shadows.

The opera house was dark and empty. All that remained was the silent echo of the music.

Chapter Twenty-Two

Postlude

re you happy, Constanze?"

"I'll be happier when we get back to Vienna and can be with Karl, like a real family."

As the carriage rolled through Prague's dark streets, Mozart held Constanze in his arms, slowly rubbing the back of her slender neck. She rested her head on his chest. A contented calm flowed between them, expressed by small movements, deep breaths and occasional soft kisses.

"I wonder if Lorenzo will have a new libretto for me."

"When do you think you'll return to Vienna?"

"Bondini's scheduled four more performances of *Don Giovanni*. If he doesn't add any more, I'll return after those."

"Don't let him get away without paying you."

"Oh, Stanzi! Do you think I'm an idiot?"

"No. Only a bad businessman." She gave him a peck on the cheek.

"I'll get paid and then I'll come back to Vienna and we'll see about taking care of this 'family' of yours."

"Don't kid me, Wolfgang."

"I'm not kidding. You'll see. I promise. We'll have a big family," he announced. Then, pointing to her belly, he added: "First we'll have a little Mozartina."

Constanze gazed into his eyes.

"Then we'll have another Mozartino," she played along.

"Then we'll have another Mozartina."

"And then, another Mozartino."

Their laughter shook the carriage. They kissed, passionately.

"Tell me a story. Tell me what it will be like; tell me what our family will be like," she whispered.

Mozart gently stroked her cheek, moving his hand in time to the rhythm set by the *clippity-clop* of the horses.

"You're a silly dreamer."

"Tell me," she ordered firmly but tenderly.

Mozart looked out the window.

"I see a big house in Vienna," he began quietly. "With lots of children. The girls are all beautiful and the boys handsome, just like their father. There are servants everywhere. Our home is filled with the most beautiful furnishings money can buy; there's a garden with elegant pathways and rare flowers and birds. All the children play instruments and every night after supper we gather in the salon for a musicale, like my sister and I used to do in Salzburg."

Mozart paused, noticing that the carriage was nearing the river.

"We, the parents of these extraordinary musicians, are the toast of Vienna. You, my most beautiful Pussy-Wussy, are Madame Constanze Mozart, whose home is the center of Vienna's social life. Every day, people from all over come to call, all bringing expensive gifts. And you're beautiful and have the most fabulous clothes in Vienna, with more jewels than the Empress herself. Maids and seamstresses wait on you, but you're nice to them."

"And what about you? Tell me about you." The carriage turned, rolling across the Charles Bridge.

"I, Wolfgang Amadeus Mozart, am court composer to the Emperor. Every day and every night there are concerts of my music. I have an endless stream of commissions for operas. Every opera house in the world wants an opera by Wolfgang Amadeus Mozart. My music is so popular I can afford to stay in bed all day and do nothing if I choose, because we are rich . . . rich beyond our wildest dreams."

"And when we get old, younger musicians will journey to Vienna to meet me. My opinion will matter more than anyone else's. Our children will bring their children to our home. I'll play the clavier for our grandchildren and we can tell them about the time when we were poor—and best of all, they won't believe us. . . . So, Stanzi, what do you think of my dream?"

Constanze had fallen asleep, her head resting snugly on Mozart's chest. He kissed her forehead.

"It's a dream," he whispered. "A happy dream we'll make come true."

The carriage had crossed the bridge. Mozart stared absentmindedly out the window; his fantasy filled his thoughts. Through the shadows cast by the moon, he could tell they were passing in front of St. Vitus Cathedral. Silhouetted against the night sky, its spires looked threatening. Suddenly Mozart's fantasy was interrupted by the music of the Dies Irae from Cavalli's Requiem. Those ominous chords in the minor key infiltrated his thoughts, shattering his dreams.

"*Dies Irae; dies illa,*" he heard in his head.

Mozart's hands trembled; beads of perspiration appeared on his furrowed brow. He stroked Constanze's soft cheek, trying to calm himself. He closed his eyes, hoping to return to his pleasant dream of the future. But now the only thought running unceasingly through his mind was: "What if? . . . What if? . . . What if something happens . . ."

The carriage rolled toward Bertramka.

∞

Vienna, October 1791

Dearest Most Beloved Little Wife,

How I long for a letter from you!

I saw the Dušeks today. They are well and send their love. They came to the opera tonight. It was a good performance. The audience loved it and applauded so much at the Papageno-Papagena duet it had to be repeated.

The Dušeks commented on how different Magic Flute *is from* Don Giovanni. *Talking with them reminded me of the time we spent in*

Prague. How I long to hold you as I did then. It was only four years ago,
but it seems forever.

I only wish now to settle my affairs so I can be with you. You can't
imagine how I ache for you. I can't describe the feelings . . . an emptiness
which hurts dreadfully . . . an insatiable longing which never ends, and
which persists . . . no, rather increases every day. I think of how happy we
once were . . . like children. My hours now are weary and sad. Even my
work gives me no pleasure, because I miss being able to stop and talk with
you. This simple pleasure is no longer possible. If I go to the clavier to
sing something from Magic Flute, I must stop, because I become too
emotional to continue.

I will do everything possible to avoid further financial difficulties; for I
have discovered the most pleasant thing imaginable is to have peace of
mind. To achieve this one must work hard, and thank God, I like hard
work. I have even accepted a commission for a Requiem and am working
on it. It is not yet finished.

Kiss Karl for me, and enjoy Baden. Take care of yourself.

Adieu, dear little wife! May the coach bring you this letter with all my
love. I hope I have a letter from you today, and with this sweetest of
hopes, I kiss you a thousand times. Someday soon I'll talk to you and hold
you in my arms with all my heart.

Farewell.

Ever your loving husband,
Mozart

Author's Note

W hile the story of the premiere of *Don Giovanni* has been fictionalized here, the characters, the dates, and the delays are based in history.

Mozart, Da Ponte and Casanova were all in Prague during the weeks leading up to the premiere of *Don Giovanni*. However, only Mozart was there for the entire period.

Casanova did offer his assistance with the production, and among the papers found in his library at Dux when he died were several pages of a libretto for the sextet in the second act.

The letters, writings and memoirs of the central characters were used as a source of ideas.

Acknowledgments

N o book is written in total isolation; at the very least the characters are there to keep you company. But, in this case, there are several very important people who helped in many ways. To these, and to many others, I owe my deepest gratitude.

To my wife, Kristy, who has to tolerate the anxiety that appears when my characters refuse to do what I want and expect.

To my father, Julius Rudel, who showed me at a very early age what drama in music is all about, and who let me sit at his side in the orchestra pit during some incredible performances of *Don Giovanni*.

There comes a time in the process when encouragement turns into belief. It was Eric Simonoff, friend and guide, who provided both, along with invaluable advice. Thank you.

To my publisher, Morgan Entrekin, for getting excited about characters who have been dead for two hundred years!

To Elisabeth Schmitz, a fabulous editor, who brought perspective and love to the endeavor; to Molly Boren for her patience and help; and to everyone at Grove/Atlantic, my deepest thanks.

To Linda Biagi for listening patiently, and advising when asked.

To David Reuben, an early reader who understood and helped in many ways, and to James Arnold for the time and understanding.

Finally, I owe a huge debt to the characters themselves. We are fortunate they lived in an era when creativity and the written word were cherished.